Praise

"*Check Six!* is the best flying story to come along in years. . . . Norris took me back to the carriers—I could almost smell the jet exhaust and salty trade winds."

—Stephen Coonts

"*Check Six!* is a gripping, authentic, suspenseful thriller from a newcomer that is sure to leave his mark on readers all over the world. Bob Norris not only takes you inside the dangerous world of nuclear aircraft carrier flight ops, but masterfully takes you inside the hearts and minds of the men and women at the forefront of today's military. It's a first-rate mystery and military techno-thriller combined."

—Dale Norris

"A great first novel. Afterburner or ejection seat, Norris takes you on a wild ride. The flight ops are authentic, the story too real, and the enemy is at your six."

—Richard Herman, Jr., author of *Power Curve* and *Against All Enemies*

"*Check Six!* is a helluva good read! Norris's plotting is crisp and dynamic. . . . He makes the reader live, breathe, and taste carrier aviation in a way that few writers in my experience have ever come close to."

—James H. Cobb, author of *Choosers of the Slain*

FLY-OFF

FLY-OFF

Bob Norris

HarperPaperbacks
A Division of HarperCollinsPublishers

HarperPaperbacks
A Division of HarperCollins*Publishers*
10 East 53rd Street, New York, NY 10022–5299

This is a work of fiction. The characters, incidents, and
dialogues are products of the author's imagination
and are not to be construed as real. Any resemblance to actual
events or persons, living or dead, is entirely coincidental.

ISBN 0-06-101354-4

HarperCollins®, ⛰®, and HarperPaperbacks™ are trademarks of
HarperCollins Publishers Inc.

Cover illustration © 1999 by John Berkey

First HarperPaperbacks printing: August 1999

Printed in the United States of America

Visit HarperPaperbacks on the World Wide Web at
http://www.harpercollins.com

❖ 10 9 8 7 6 5 4 3 2 1

To Mom and Dad,
who always ran a tight ship,
but (bless their hearts),
knew when to look the other way.

CHAPTER 1

The arrogance of his employers brought a smile to Achmed's weathered lips, as it did every time he paused to consider the folly of building this idiotic highway into the heart of Saudi Arabia's great desert, the Rub Al-Khali. Surely Allah—*His Name Be Praised*—was amused by the absurdity of the city dwellers' attempts to pave a path through the dunes, some as high as one hundred meters, which dominated the vast expanse known as the Empty Quarter to generations of disappointed and humbled explorers. It could only be a divine sense of humor that kept the 250-kilometer roadbed covered in windswept sand and virtually unusable.

Achmed, an uncomplicated man, wasn't complaining. As long as his employers persisted in this folly, he was guaranteed a high-paying job driving the air-conditioned street sweeper. Well suited to the task, he actually enjoyed patrolling the road in an endless loop, nudging the sand off the concrete only to watch it reappear in his rearview mirror. For this he was paid one hundred thousand riyals a year—more money than his father and his father's father had made in their lifetimes as craftsmen and traders. A generous provider, Achmed used his salary to support twenty family members, all of whom were camped near the sweeper's garage.

He'd just finished his midday cigarette when he spied the headlights in the sweeper's side mirror. Since this task represented his only driving experience, the sight of cars and trucks was still novel. In fact, in nearly five months of sweeping, Achmed had encountered only a handful of vehicles. A couple had been from ARAMCO, the Saudi oil and gas conglomerate, while the others had been military. He'd never seen more than one at a time, and, in each case, the vehicle would stop—right on the roadway so as not to risk getting stuck in the sand—and he would share figs and goat's milk with his visitors, as was the Bedouin custom.

Achmed looked forward to these interruptions; he'd come to feel a sense of stewardship for the desert and sensed that his guests respected his wisdom since they asked many questions about his life. And of course there was the chance they might exchange gifts. He'd developed a particular fondness for American tobacco.

The flashing lights puzzled him as he stepped out of his machine. Shielding his eyes against the afternoon sun, he could tell only that the vehicle was enormous, and judging from the amount of sand being kicked up, that it was moving much faster than anything he'd yet encountered. He quickly stepped back onto the running board, waving vigorously to encourage the behemoth to slow down.

The driver of the lead truck couldn't understand why this idiot refused to clear the highway despite his signals. Told the road to the airfield would be empty and having been offered a bonus for good time, he'd steadily pushed up the speed since leaving the outskirts of Riyadh. With his onboard navigation system projecting the centerline of the roadbed onto the windshield-mounted Head's Up Display, the obscuring sand was no problem, at least for him. The rest of the drivers in the hundred-truck convoy were faithfully glued to the taillights of the truck they were following. At this speed, all he could do was shift the gaggle into the far lane. Using the radio, he passed the warning to the other drivers. That done, he said a quick prayer for this desert madman.

The windblast from the lead trucks nearly swept Achmed off the running board and under their wheels. Blinded from the stinging sand, he scrambled to the far side of his sweeper and huddled on the floorboard as the onslaught continued. Terrified, he prayed fervently to the Prophet—*Peace Be Upon Him*—to deliver him from this nightmare. But the hellish experience seemed to last forever . . . the little cocoon rocked precariously and slid sideways with each passing truck.

When, at last, the final truck passed by—offering a blast on its air horn in mocking salute—Achmed crawled from the sweeper, fell in supplication, and offered tearful prayers of thanks.

Leaving the sweeper where it sat—all the riyals in the kingdom would not be enough to get him behind the wheel again—he began the trek toward his family's camp. Without a backward glance he left behind the devil's highway for the solace and refuge of the ancient dunes.

CHAPTER 2

Whiskey—72 Op-Area, Virginia Coast— USS *Independence*/1500

For the first time in her career, Lieutenant Randi Cole was not excited by the prospect of a catapult launch. Parked on the number two cat, she had already waited an interminable forty-five minutes as the deck crew prepared for the most dangerous event in the F/A–18E Super Hornet's carrier suitability flight test.

Despite its innocuous designation on her knee-board checklist as the final trial in the "minimum end-speed launch sequence," there was no denying that the mission was fit only for a raving lunatic. Randi would soon be launched by the weakest of a long series of ever-slower catapult shots. This speed, assuming she survived, would be published to all future aviators as the minimum speed they could accept for flying. Anything less and immediate ejection was mandated.

As the lead test pilot for the carrier-suit phase, it was Randi's call when to wave the white flag to stop the sequence. She'd almost done it after the last one. The jet had wallowed off the cat, actually settling below the flight deck as the automatic flight controls fought to arrest the sink rate. And, of course, she had longed to grab the stick, but the F/A–18 required the pilot to ride a hands-off launch. Competing with the flight-control computers after a catapult launch was a mistake few pilots lived to regret.

Randi surprised herself, along with the witnesses—especially those who wore gold pilot wings—when she responded affirmatively to the lead engineer's request for one more shot. It was doubly surprising to those in the know, because Lieutenant Cole was being reassigned the very next day to fly a special project. Nevertheless, the ground team was thrilled; this speed would exceed the specification. As was their custom, the old-timers had a pool going, each trying to pick what would be the test pilot's final end speed. No one had put money on the young woman's busting the spec.

The ship's CO, also an aviator, was dubious. "Sierra-zero-two, confirm you have sufficient margin of safety to proceed. That last one, at least from where I sit, looked like Mr. Toad's Wild Ride."

"Affirmative, sir. It looked uglier than it was. As long as the winds are steady and the deck is up, we have room to take it down a notch."

"Roger that, zero-two . . ." The long pause did nothing to inspire her confidence. "It's your call."

*   *   *

At last the launch team signaled its readiness to continue. After confirming her launch weight and repeating the familiar sequence of the takeoff checklist, Randi brought the power up just enough to taxi the final few inches needed to engage the catapult holdback mechanism. As the jet-blast deflector rose from the deckplates behind her, the catapult officer—an aviator himself—took a deep breath and gave her the signal to run the throttles up. Randi, busily monitoring her instruments, did not notice his quick genuflection and whispered prayer.

The Hornet's powerful engines pushed the aircraft against the restraint mechanism, while Randi completed a full wipeout of the control surfaces under the watchful eyes of the final checkers. When she was satisfied that her engines, hydraulics, and electrical systems were on-line and functioning, she saluted the catapult officer and grabbed the windshield-mounted handgrip with her right hand, while her left held the throttles firmly in place.

After receiving a thumbs-up from each of the final checkers, the cat officer returned the pilot's salute and turned his attention to the flight deck. It was his task to launch the Hornet with the deck up, or at least on the way up, as the big ship rode the ocean swells. To send her off with the flight deck going down would be catastrophic since the Hornet's vector, much like a BB in a slingshot, would be toward the water not the sky. The process was not as simple as it sounded, since the catapult officer on the Forrestal-class carrier did not actually fire the cat. He would signal to a trusted crewman positioned on the deck-edge catwalk, who, after confirming that the launch area was clear and that the final checkers were still in agreement, would hit the fire-control button to begin the launch sequence. These procedures had evolved over dozens of years and hundreds of thousands of launches.

A good launch team was like a well-oiled machine. The third member was the ship's captain. His job was to keep the wind coming down the deck, usually accomplished with small rudder commands. Normally, he would not be concerned if the wind speed was higher than expected—extra wind meant a cushion of safety for the aviators—but today his task was to keep the wind steady, and he found himself making both steering and speed adjustments. At the moment, he was concerned that his last speed reduction had been a tad premature. As the wind readout dipped precariously below the eighteen-knot threshold, he called for a touch of power and a half degree of right rudder.

This is the one, thought the cat officer. The deck was plowing through a trough, but coming up. It was time. He risked one more glance at the aircraft. *Can't be too careful with this one*, he thought. With a little prayer, *Please God, let this work*, he stepped forward with his right foot, knelt on his left knee, touched the deck with his gloved right hand, and pointed to the bow with a practiced flourish.

The last speed change took effect even as the cat officer was kneeling. The ship's pace quickened as it plowed through the swell. Along with the speed increase, the slight heading change reduced the angle of the hull to the wave crest. Imperceptible to most, these changes were sufficient to reduce the time it would take for the deck to reach its maximum height and begin the next downward cycle.

Witnessing the cat officer's signal, the young sailor on the catwalk—understanding only too well how important and dangerous this shot was—checked and double-checked the flight deck.

With dawning realization, the cat officer recognized the impact of the cumulative effects of the extra care and caution contributed by each member of the team. A nanosecond too late, he stood to suspend the launch, but the sailor had mashed the fire-control button.

Randi's eyes widened as she felt the initial jolt of the catapult launch sequence even as the horizon began to fill with blue-gray ocean. Unbelievably, the launch team's best intentions had contributed to the worst possible scenario: a minimum launch speed, light winds, and a downward launch angle, all of which combined to put the Super Hornet and its pilot into a massive hurt locker.

The shot felt horribly soft. To the uninitiated, any cat shot would appear so violent as to preclude human reaction, but to Randi Cole, veteran of hundreds of carrier flights, the delay in accelerating through one hundred knots was agonizing. During the first third of the stroke, Randi's finely tuned survival instincts implored her to grasp the yellow-and-black-striped handle and pull, ejecting her from the fifty-million-dollar test aircraft.

"Deck's down—bad shot!" transmitted the cat officer on the FM launch-control circuit.

"Prepare for a William's turn," the captain advised his helmsmen. He already had the microphone to his lips to call for the ejection.

Inside the cockpit, Randi's hands outpaced conscious thought. Halfway down the stroke she pushed the throttles into afterburner while simultaneously grabbing the stick just beneath the handgrip to squeeze the paddle switch and disengage the automatic flight-control computers. Recognizing that the aircraft would run out of altitude and settle into the sea if the automatic flight controls tried to minimize sink rate as they were programmed to do, she chose to risk manual control. Randi needed airspeed to buy time for the engines to spool up, and the only thing she had in the bank was the sixty feet between her and the water.

"What the hell?" asked the captain, shocked by the sight of the Hornet's horizontal stabilators shifting from their normal attitude of trailing edge up— the climb position—to trailing edge down. The command to eject froze in his throat.

Before the nosewheel even cleared the deck edge, Randi selected emergency jettison to clear off the fuel tank. And as the main gear broke free and the Super Hornet began its flight, she snapped the gear handle up. With the trim set for takeoff climb, it took both hands to push the stick forward. Taking the aircraft toward the water was the only way she could gain a couple knots.

Nobody on the flight deck, least of all the cat officer, was prepared to see the aircraft plunge off the deck. Most of the crew were seasoned veterans—having witnessed other mishaps—who expected to see the aircraft try to claw its way into the sky. To watch a jet simply dive for the water was almost surreal.

The cat officer realized that Randi's bold move put her out of the ejection envelope. Simple physics decreed that the seat could not compensate for her rate of descent. When she pulled the handle—if she pulled the handle—it was doubtful that the seat would propel her to sufficient height to allow the chute to blossom.

The book said that the afterburners would fully stage in a shade less than seven seconds; given her dilemma, it might as well have been seven hours. With the gear still retracting, there was no benefit from reduced drag, and the weight loss, though helpful, wasn't enough to offset the other factors. The bottom line was that, even with the weight loss and the dive, the jet wasn't accelerating fast enough to avoid a stall if Randi tried to pick the nose up. Something more was needed. To the witnesses, it looked as if the test pilot had run out of airspeed, altitude, and ideas.

But Lieutenant Randi Cole had one more trick up her sleeve. If she could place the aircraft extremely low—close enough to the wave tops to enter ground effect—she could take advantage of the lift that would be generated by the compressed air trapped between the wings and the water. The phenomenon was the same that let coastal birds glide effortlessly along the waves at the beach. With luck, the effect would keep her airborne long enough for the burners to kick in.

Ground effect began at a height equal to two-thirds of the wingspan. But that was over flat terrain. It was anybody's guess what was needed over the rolling sea. Ignoring the thousand and one distractions clamoring for her attention, Randi kept her eyes glued to the vertical speed indicator, knowing that her only chance was to keep from climbing. Fighting the instinct to pull up, she allowed the aircraft to settle ever closer to the water.

From the flight deck, the ocean spray kicked up by the jet's engines and the splash made by the fuel tank coincided to convince the observers that Sierra-zero-two had pancaked in. There'd been no ejection. Dozens of crewmen, convinced that the big ship would run over the wreckage, ran to the deck edge, some hollering beseechingly at the pilot to, "Get out!"

But the captain's bird's-eye perspective from the bridge revealed a different story.

"Sir?" asked the helmsman, hoping to shake his captain from frozen silence, eager to execute the series of maneuvers necessary to allow the big ship to avoid the wreckage.

The captain nodded. He could understand how his crew might think he had choked at the prospect of losing this valuable test aircraft and its pilot. "Belay that order, son. Damned if she doesn't have it under control."

As if in response to the captain's declaration, the Hornet's afterburners began kicking up twin rooster tails, and the Super Hornet accelerated. Seconds later, unable to hold the nose down with the speed rapidly building and the trim still set for takeoff, Randi released pressure on the stick and let the aircraft climb steeply, happy to gain some altitude. The effect was inspiring to the incredulous crewmen, all of whom would add another sea story to their arsenal about the woman pilot who, after cheating death, actually hotdogged it.

Even the flight-deck bosun, a salty veteran of twenty-nine years, was impressed. "God damn if that young lady doesn't have a pair of brass balls," he transmitted.

Everyone tied into the radio circuit understood that something remarkable had happened. It was, after all, the highest compliment any master chief could bestow.

CHAPTER 3

"Lights, please." As the lights dimmed, Jack Warner stepped away from the comfort of the podium, purposely abandoning his notes. It was a risk worth taking; he'd have only one chance to capture the imaginations of this group.

Seated around the scimitar-shaped table in the palace boardroom, grim-faced to the point of hostility, were all thirteen provincial governors. At the center sat the elder, who happened to be the king's half brother and political rival. It was as tough a crowd as Jack had faced in a twenty-five-year career as a reporter and writer. That he must now brief the status of the highly controversial Fly-Off Project—due to begin in just three days—made the challenge all the more daunting.

Jack was acutely aware that his selection as the director of public affairs had generated heated arguments within the royal family. Not only was he a member of the notorious American press; there were other, more fundamental complications. Though the gentlemen he was facing were savvy, world-class businessmen, Saudi Arabia remained, at its core, the conservative nexus of the Muslim religion. Jack Warner, for all his talents, would forever be an infidel. As such, his mere presence in the inner sanctum of the king's palace was an affront to several of the men seated before him.

With a surreptitious flick of the remote control, Jack filled the room with the sound of jet engines. A half dozen wall-mounted plasma displays brightened, then pulsed with a whirling collage of vivid photographs of the six unique aircraft in the competition. The exotic, high-tech fighters were visually striking. Using his high-profile job as leverage, Jack had coerced and cajoled the manufacturers to hand over dozens of stunning photos and short video clips depicting their jets in action. Most of the shots were making their debut today.

This opening sequence alone cost Jack a month of sleepless nights. Into the mix, he blended team logos depicting a veritable Who's Who of the international military-industrial complex along with landmarks, symbols, and flags of the sponsoring countries. On cue, the high-fidelity sound system delivered a room-shaking crescendo of jet engines going into full afterburner. As the imaginary jet took flight, and the engine noise faded, the screens dimmed until all that remained were aircraft silhouettes.

Approaching the table, Jack covertly adjusted the lighting. Small spotlights positioned over the chairs softly illuminated each of the decision-makers. He quickly took stock.

Though great effort was being made to keep

expressions neutral, Jack's reporter's vision noted, in widened eyes, pursed lips, and flared nostrils, that he'd achieved his primary objective—he had their attention. It was now or never.

"Gentlemen, under the guidance of His Royal Highness, Prince Salman Ibn Abdul Aziz, our public affairs team has prepared today's briefing." Jack bowed in deference to the young prince seated against the wall, who, despite the objections of many of the men in this room, had been the king's choice to manage the project. It didn't help that the twenty-nine-year-old hotshot frequently eschewed Arab tradition. Preferring Versace to the traditional garb of robe and headdress worn by the others, he had developed a reputation as the least devout member of the royal family.

In the year since their first meeting, Jack found the young man to have a brilliant, if unconventional business mind. He also had a penchant for taking risk, as evidenced by hiring an American to handle the PR, especially since Jack was a reporter, not a marketing maven. Jack said as much when a Saudi official first put the offer on the table. Not to be dissuaded, Prince Salman flew to San Diego personally to request Jack's services. Jack found the Wharton grad to be a relentless negotiator.

"Jack," he said, "I need someone with a reputation for integrity, with an understanding of the media and military aviation, and who can earn the respect of my family. I can't bring a Madison Avenue snake-oil salesman into Riyadh. They'd post his head on a

stake . . . and mine, too. We're going to get precisely
one chance to do this right. With your background,
contacts, and, of course, that Pulitzer, you're my
man."

The prince politely refrained from mentioning
that Jack, weary of his second book tour on the rubber-
chicken circuit, was adrift between projects and rela-
tionships. A clean break and a chance to sink his teeth
into something new and different were compelling
incentives. And the money was good . . . very good.

Jack was hooked, reeled in, and landed without a
struggle. But the reporter in him was difficult to bury.
In the forty-eight hours before he departed for the
Middle East, Jack ran a full background check on
his new boss. Despite the man's high profile, there
wasn't much to go on. Athletic, bright, opportunistic,
the prince had done the private school bit in England,
had a solid run through Oxford, and then entered the
Saudi military. Given Prince Salman's confident,
almost cocky approach to life, Jack was not surprised
to find that his new boss had himself been a fighter
pilot in the Saudi Royal Air Force before being
tapped by the family to enter the political arena. The
kid was on the fast track, no doubt about it.

The prince nodded for the briefing to continue.

"As you know, in seventy-two hours six teams
will arrive at the Shaybah airfield. Each will be vying
to win the competition and capture the production
contract. Add in the opportunity to stake claim as the

world's best fighter aircraft—and pilot, for that matter—and we're expecting these consortiums to go to extraordinary measures. As you know, we've charged each a premium to defray costs of the competition, and they've all signed releases that acknowledge acceptance of the risks and rules.

"In four days, our VIPs, nearly five hundred of them, will arrive via Riyadh and Jeddah. For the first time ever, the most powerful decision-makers and trendsetters in the world of high finance will congregate for a holiday. No detail of their comfort has been omitted. And, as we will demonstrate this morning, for a five-day period Saudi Arabia will host an event that will capture the world's attention."

One of the governors motioned Jack to stop.

"Sir?"

"Mr. Warner," the man said in impeccable English, "we are well aware that this . . . this event, as you call it, begins in a mere four days. After all, we have committed a significant amount of funding to this venture. Funding, by the way, that most certainly will not be defrayed by the fees charged to the competitors. And that is precisely why we cannot understand why there is no evidence of advertising." There were vigorous nods around the table. "Perhaps you can enlighten us about a marketing strategy that seems determined to keep this event a secret?"

"Of course, Governor." Jack dimmed the lights and initiated the next phase of the presentation. Photos of six of the world's richest and most powerful individuals appeared. While most of the faces would not be recognized as celebrities by the public, to the men seated around the table, they represented the absolute pinnacle of international influence. These were followed by six more images, then another set. Dozens more followed.

Jack spoke matter-of-factly as the photo sequence continued behind him. "Conventional marketing strategy would have us spend our advertising budget on space and time in the various media. We've all seen that type of effort. The Olympics comes to mind. We found that approach to be expensive, but more importantly, its effectiveness is difficult to measure.

"Allow me to say that I think Prince Salman made an enlightened decision when he directed me to target each of the individuals you have seen on-screen as a market-of-one. It was really quite elegant in concept. One by one, we concentrated on what it would take to entice these individuals to attend. We discovered that we had to convey that this event was both unique and exclusive."

Jack faced the questioner. "You are absolutely correct, Governor. There hasn't been a single riyal of our budget spent on mainstream advertising."

After a glance at the prince, who signaled his approval with a nod, Jack was emboldened. "For six months we concentrated our efforts on key individuals by carefully stoking a rumor mill about a secret competition held in the remotest corner of the earth. Once we knew we had their curiosity piqued, we pulled back. How to get invited became a tantalizing mystery and the topic of conversation at socials and power lunches all over the world. In that manner the marketing campaign was executed on our behalf by the whispers of our guests. We succeeded in establishing an invitation to attend as a make-or-break commodity among the world's rich and powerful."

A voice from the darkness asked, "I grant you that it will be to our advantage to socialize with these people. But tell me, Mr. Warner, are we not missing an even bigger opportunity to exploit the appeal of this event if it remains a secret?"

Jack's presentation had been geared to elicit this one question. With a showman's sense of timing, he paused to let it linger. Then, with another tap on the remote, the screens displayed the front pages of the world's most widely read newspapers. Following these were splash screens of the largest television news organizations.

"Even as we speak, each of these organizations is tracking the movement of selected members of our guest list." Close-ups of famous news anchors appeared. "Where necessary, we've provided sufficient leads so they may make the connection with our event."

Jack turned to face the table once more. "Gentlemen, we aren't chasing the market, it's coming to us."

"Just a minute," interrupted one of the governors. "Are you saying we're about to be inundated with foreign media? I have seen no such plan. If that is the case, Mr. Warner . . ."

"Please, Cousin," interjected Prince Salman, his calm voice conveying bemusement. "You must give us some credit. And let us remember our manners. We should let Mr. Warner finish answering one question before we pounce with another."

The rebuke hit strongly. The offended governor angrily started to rise, but was restrained by the hand of the elder, who spoke for the first time. "My young nephew, Prince Salman, is absolutely correct. We must all remember our manners . . . which includes demonstrating proper respect for one's elders." All heads turned to the prince. "There will be no more of this."

Prince Salman respectfully nodded his understanding, though the smile never quite left his face.

The elder turned to Jack. "Please, Mr. Warner, go on. As you can see, you certainly have captured our interest."

"Thank you, Governor." Jack carefully kept his expression neutral. "Governor Jalawi's question is most perceptive. Please forgive me for not briefing this important point earlier. There have been absolutely no visas granted to non-Arab media."

The revelation sparked a murmur among the panel.

The elder gestured for silence, and spoke again. "I must admit, Mr. Warner, I have been unable to anticipate a single element of your strategy. It appears that my nephew has chosen well. You have the spirit of a desert tradesman." Turning to his fellow governors, he said, "I suspect, my brothers, that if we were to research this man's genealogy, we might well find Bedouin blood in his veins."

The mood around the table lightened perceptibly. "Please continue, Mr. Warner."

The center panel displayed an overhead picture of the Shaybah airfield, desolate by any standards. "We control all communications out of the complex." A graphic map of the Middle East followed. "Picture the news media poised on our borders, roasting in Yemen and Oman, eager for any news, but unable to deliver more than a few snippets and conjecture." Jack paused when one of the governors cleared his throat as if to speak. But after a glance from the elder, the man kept silent.

"I realize that I have not yet answered the fundamental question of how we intend to engage a worldwide audience without relying on the paper and television news media." The screens again displayed silhouettes of each aircraft. "It was Prince Salman's idea to exploit this opportunity as a catalyst for creating the first, and we believe most exciting, twenty-first-century news organization."

The sound system suddenly reverberated with the cacophony of a dozen jet engines as the animated silhouettes took flight, then muted as the jets disappeared.

"Gentlemen, may I introduce you to the next generation global news and learning network . . . ArabNet!"

The screens switched to Internet browsers that, in turn, displayed the event's interactive website, a different language on each one. The demonstration automatically stepped through page after page of rich graphics, animations, audio, and video streaming. Pilot photos and biographies replaced schematics of their respective aircraft and were followed by animations that depicted each of the competition's key events. An interactive calendar and scorecard were shown that enabled the viewer to track a favorite team. The virtual newsroom contained up-to-the-minute status reports. The briefing room allowed net surfers to sit in on the pilot briefs and debriefs. Fans could sign up for automatic updates on their favorite teams.

There were product giveaways and contests, along with chat rooms and archives of technical material. Merchandise with team logos, including hats, T-shirts, patches, photos, and model airplanes were available for order and rush shipment. Of course, Jack explained, the site encrypted credit-card information with state-of-the-art security.

The men seated at the table exchanged glances, nodding their approval. The elder spoke again. "Mr. Warner, this is excellent. Do you, by chance, have projections about revenue?"

At Prince Salman's signal, an assistant distributed leather-bound briefers. The prince spoke quietly, without a trace of nervousness. "We have included sections on total cost, income from the tariffs, and projected revenues from the sale of merchandise and other Internet-based services. Given anticipated buying patterns, our analysis indicates that the break-even point occurs at fifty million visitors through the website."

Governor Jalawi spoke for the first time since the flare-up. "So many? Don't get me wrong, my cousin, I'm very impressed with your strategy, it's just that I wonder if there are that many people out there who have the time and capability to do this sort of thing."

"Governor Jalawi has raised a good point," said the prince. "Many of the site's visitors will not spend a single riyal, no matter how enticing we make it. That is why we have built a special site for those visitors inclined to pay for a more . . . shall we say, *engaging* experience. Jack?"

The displays shifted once more, this time picking up live camera feeds. Jack toggled through each of a dozen views of workmen and spacious rooms. "These cameras are mounted inside the complex. Imagine when these venues are filled with our guests. Subscribers will have the ability to virtually join in the party so to speak. We've set up kiosks where our guests, when they are so inclined, can actually engage in on-line banter with the electronic visitors." Jack paused, then casually dropped the bombshell. "Then, of course, there is the casino."

The elder smiled. "I was wondering when you would get around to it, Mr. Warner. It seems that this event was made for wagering."

"All of our guests, including the subscribers, will be encouraged to bet on their favorite teams. Prince Salman had the foresight to hire a gaming consultant from Las Vegas. With his help, we have put together a very exciting gambler's package that, while certainly being fair, will provide a source of revenue since the odds favor the house."

The elder spoke again. "Very impressive, Mr. Warner. You are to be commended." The tone of his voice indicated that the briefing was complete.

"Thank you, Governor, for the compliment. But please be aware that this project reflects the vision of your nephew, Prince Salman. And what you see is the product of many months of work by some of your most talented citizens. It has been my privilege to work with this team."

"Yes, of course." The elder included the others seated at the table in a sweeping gesture. "I'm confident that I speak for my fellow governors when I say that we are gratified that you have found the experience of working with our bright young citizens to be a positive one, Mr. Warner. For much too long, we have looked elsewhere for talent. You have reminded us that our heritage is one of creativity. It appears that we've found new skills to replace those of rug and jewelry making. As for my nephew, he has again demonstrated that though he may be a bit unconventional, he has been blessed with a brilliant mind. But, Mr. Warner, we also recognize and appreciate your contributions. I believe all of us have read your books and realize that we are lucky to have such an exceptional man working with us. That being said, I want to ask you an important question. Is there anything that you need that you haven't been provided?"

"No, Governor, not yet. However, I am departing

for the airfield in the morning and will provide a status report that may include specific requests."

"Good. Good. Now, I am afraid that I must ask you to excuse us for a few minutes so that we might discuss some routine family business before prayers. I'm sure you understand."

CHAPTER 4

"Everyone but the principals please leave." All eyes at the table were on the elder. When the door closed, he said, "General?"

General Majeed emerged from his listening post behind a tapestry.

The prince stiffened out of habit, then purposely relaxed his posture. Until recently, he had been under the general's command.

The general positioned himself in front of the table and spoke with authority. "All defensive measures are in place. We are on full alert and prepared to respond to a threat from any sector. Known dissidents have been quietly rounded up and will be held until the competition has been completed."

"Is there any evidence of buildup along our borders?" asked the elder.

"No, Governor. Nevertheless, we are vigilant and are prepared to respond forcefully should there be any provocative activity."

"Excellent. Keep me advised."

"Yes, Governor."

"Continue with your brief, Nephew."

"We, too, are fully prepared and have established the highest possible level of security. Each bag and person entering the compound is passed through a series of scanners. All food is tested. We have virtually every inch of the compound under full surveillance twenty-four hours a day. And your agents are in place in every support organization, including housekeeping, food service, airfield operations, communications, and the casino. Major Khalim is in charge. There will be no problems with security."

"And the competition itself?"

"As you directed, Governor, I personally designed each flying event to favor our partner."

"Might the other teams protest?"

Try as he might, the prince could not keep the smirk from creeping onto his face. Pretending to ponder the question, he hid his chin and mouth with his hand. *These old men are as nervous as women*, he thought. One day, perhaps sooner than even he expected, he would take his rightful place as the leader of this group. Regaining his composure, he said, "Since the same rules apply to everyone, there is no basis for complaint. Any team that protests will appear weak. None of them will risk it."

"Do not take offense, but how can we be sure that your arrangements will be sufficient?" asked the governor of the Jizan Province. "Surely the other teams have the technology to overcome a slight disadvantage in the rules. Given the publicity that this American has orchestrated . . ." The governor's pause left no doubt that the implications of failure were unspeakable.

"I understand your concerns, Governor," said the prince. "If their pilot is as good as we've been told, none of this will be necessary. However, for added insurance, I built in a special event I call *the Gauntlet*. The teams will be opposed on a low-level mission by F–15s from the Saudi Royal Air Force. General Majeed"—he bowed slightly in deference to his former commander—"has assured me that he will personally ensure that the other teams face our very best pilots."

The elder nodded his approval and addressed the governors on either side of him. "I am satisfied that Prince Salman and General Majeed have this matter in hand. I ask each of you to continue to provide your full support. It is vital that we take advantage of every opportunity this competition presents. However, despite the assurances we have heard here, we must be alert to the extreme risks of assuming so high a profile. Many of our misguided neighbors will be tempted to exploit this opportunity to strike a blow against the infidels. We cannot allow this to happen on our soil. Even as our country is on the verge of garnering great wealth, and even more importantly, the respect of the world, we must understand that failure to protect our guests will result in complete ignominy."

Turning to the prince, he said, "Collectively, every province has made strategic commitments, including investments in resources and infrastructure, based on the assumption that we know who will win the contract. There must be no uncertainty about this, and, of course, it must be kept absolutely secret. Which brings me to this point, Nephew. You cannot forget for an instant that Warner is both a reporter and a nonbeliever. The man is not to be trusted."

"Yes, I know that, Uncle." The prince let a tinge of exasperation creep into his voice. "I am, after all, the one who hired him." There were audible gasps at his audacity.

The elder shot up from his seat and slammed the tabletop with an open palm, his rings making a sharp *crack!* that jolted everyone. His voice was a growl of barely contained fury. "Listen to me, you insolent pup! The future of our family is at stake. Warner is a reporter; it is in his blood to look for conspiracy. Do not be deceived by his manners or how well he's learned our customs. The man is a viper that you've seen fit to invite into our tent! Understand this, my nephew, if Warner poisons this project, the responsibility will be on your head."

Head bowed, apparently contrite at last, the prince said, "Yes, Uncle. Please forgive my arrogance. I will not let the family down."

"Very well." The elder seemed mollified. "Gentlemen, the key to controlling the world economy lies at our feet. If we succeed in our quest, our next step will be to bring every man, woman, and child to their knees before the power of Allah.

"It is nearly time for prayer. Let each of us reflect upon his role in the task before us. Glory to God, my brothers."

"Glory to God!"

PART 1

ARRIVAL

Jack closed his eyes in appreciation; never had a beer tasted so good. Since he had abstained for nearly six months, any brand would have been fine. That he was sipping a premium lager, specially crafted for the Fly-Off by one of the finest brewmeisters on the Continent, made the experience exquisite. He longed to drain the glass, but there was work to be done.

"Mr. Warner?"

Jack's reverie was broken by the operations officer, Major Mustafe Khalim, a man whose judgment Jack had come to respect despite his formal, even aloof manner. Jack took for granted that Khalim's duties included monitoring and reporting on his actions. Khalim wore the same world-weary look of disbelief Jack found common to police the world over. "Yes, Major?"

"The American Raptor team has just checked in. They'll be overhead in ten minutes."

With a tinge of regret, Jack returned the glass, saying, "That is the finest beer I've ever tasted, Herr Schmidt. *Es ist wunderbar!*"

"*Danke schön*, Herr Warner. Please come back when you have time to enjoy a full stein."

"You can count on it."

Jack didn't need to glance up to confirm there was a look of disapproval on his companion's face. And he couldn't resist pulling his chain a little. "You better get used to it, Major. In a couple days, this place is going to be awash in alcohol and exotic women. Are you going to be able to cope?"

The sarcasm was lost on the major. "We have been assured that the sewage from this site will be processed and trucked out so as not to defile our land. Those of us who have duty within the compound have been given prayers and special dispensation from our religious leaders. We are prepared, but thank you for your concern, Mr. Warner."

As Khalim led them quickly across the floor of the converted underground hangar, Jack marveled at the transformation. The designers had crafted a resplendent desert oasis. The ceiling beams were hidden by flowing layers of translucent fabric above which was mounted computer-driven lighting programmed to display a choreographed light show that included a convincing simulation of the night sky. There were dozens of palm trees of all shapes and sizes. Even a pond had been constructed, around which authentic tents were grouped in clusters according to purpose. Guests could eat, drink, get a massage, take a whirlpool, catch a workout, make a phone call, check e-mail, or avail themselves of a host of distractions. Professional entertainers from all over the world had been carefully scheduled to fill in the gaps between flying events.

Using one of the underground corridors that

joined all ten buildings in the compound, guests
would be invited to walk or ride in electric carts to
the adjacent hangar, which hosted an amphitheater.
Each of the plush leather seats had an unobstructed
view of a monstrous, one-of-a-kind multimedia system. Augmented by a phenomenal sound system, the
sky-shaped dome encased the audience in real-time
digital imagery of the Fly-Off events.

Live video and telemetry data captured from
each aircraft in the competition would be beamed via
a wing-mounted pod to the airborne mission-control
aircraft, which in turn would relay the synthesized
data to the cluster of communications vans parked
nearby. Observers would see graphic depictions of
the aircraft as each maneuvered overhead, while on
plasma screens along the perimeter they could view
live-feed video of what the pilot was seeing over the
nose of the jet. Radio communications would be
piped in as well.

Meanwhile, in the third hangar, one hundred of
the world's most successful vendors of high technology would demonstrate their wares. Though the price
tag for the privilege had been steep—one-half million dollars per bay—and each vendor had been
forced to sign an ironclad nondisclosure agreement,
the demonstration area was filled to capacity. Guests
would be enticed to test-drive the latest technologies
with all manner of virtual-reality simulations. There
was even a list suggesting suitable giveaway articles,
including fine apparel, tasteful jewelry, electronic
goodies, designer sunglasses, and, of course, gam-

bling chits. The vendors were pulling out all the stops to attract and impress the VIPs, most of whom were decision-makers for more than one corporation. Virtually anyone on the guest list would be capable of inking a billion-dollar contract on the spot.

Major Khalim led Jack past one of the discreet but ubiquitous security stations and through the double-door air lock. They snagged an electric cart for the drive up the ramp and rolled out, past open blast doors, into the brilliant sunshine. Once again, Jack was pleasantly surprised to find that the dry desert heat was not uncomfortable despite afternoon temperatures that hovered at the century mark.

While the major huddled with a couple assistants, Jack surveyed the airfield facilities. Two ten-thousand-foot runways paralleled each other, but were offset, so that they barely overlapped. One extended west from the center compound and the other east. It was an efficient design for a combat base. After popping out from an underground hangar, fighters had only a short distance to taxi to the takeoff runway. Upon landing on the other, the return taxi would be just as quick, thus minimizing the time a jet would be exposed and vulnerable to a strafing attack or the prying eyes of a satellite.

Jack had been comforted to learn that an attacker would face many tough obstacles. With the exception of the air-control tower, only the rooftops of the sand-colored buildings extended above ground. The fuel- and munitions-storage areas were widely dispersed and buried, impossible to detect with the unaided eye. Even the runway concrete had been colored to blend into the desert. Pilots relied on satellite navigation systems and special lighting to land. Were an enemy to locate the field and identify a target, the airfield's perimeter was ringed with carefully concealed surface-to-air missile sites and antiaircraft-gun emplacements. From any perspective above ground, the Shaybah base wasn't much to look at, but then that was the point.

Though all facilities were accessible through the maze of underground corridors, several would remain off-limits for the duration of the competition. Guests would stay in small, but nicely appointed suites in the honeycombed residential structure. To request services or ask directions, a guest could access interactive computer panels that were mounted in every suite and at key intersections. To ensure comfort, the facility's support functions, including concierge, bellman, laundry, maid service, and janitorial, had been contracted to an international executive hotel corporation with an impeccable reputation for elegant and discreet, albeit costly, service.

To preclude any embarrassing incidents, soldiers garbed in traditional Arab costume would patrol the corridors with instructions tactfully to help inebriated guests to their accommodations. Given a one-to-one ratio of support staff to guests, the planners had guaranteed that every whim, even those that struck at 2 A.M., would be immediately addressed. And it was all gratis. Tips would be graciously, but firmly declined. Literally, the only opportunity a guest would have to spend money would be in the casino. There, guests could wager as much as they wanted.

The blast of an air horn, part of the airfield's alert system, heralded the arrival of the first team. Seconds later, a spec appeared on the western horizon. Shielding his eyes, Jack was mesmerized as the dark, sinister-looking shape of the Raptor rapidly took form.

The F–22 pilot, Captain Steven Whitefoot, dropped his altitude to precisely five hundred feet as he followed the script he'd prepared for the simulated attack. Using a combination of onboard infrared and global-positioning satellite (GPS) data, Whitefoot located and designated the camouflaged command and control center, made a small adjustment to correct for wind, then scanned his warning gear. The Raptor's signal-processing computers cataloged no fewer than seven target-tracking radars and one laser range finder. If the attack were real, Whitefoot would engage the Raptor's suite of countermeasures, including active and passive jamming. And, of course, the flight would have taken place at night to preclude visually guided antiaircraft fire.

For that day's mission, Whitefoot was intent on testing the Raptor's navigation, target-acquisition, and threat-classification systems. It never occurred to him that his hosts might expect to see more than a simple flyover.

United States Air Force Captain Steven, No-Middle-Initial, Whitefoot, rarely concerned himself with the expectations of others. An undersized, but respected quarterback at the Air Force Academy, the five-foot-ten pilot was a loner driven to excel on his own merit. Most observers attributed his reticence to his Native American heritage. In any case, White-foot's economy of words and flat emotions were legendary though often perplexing.

After personally advising the young captain that he had been selected to join the Raptor's flight-test team—over several senior and more experienced test pilots—the commanding general was heard to remark, "I wasn't sure he even heard me. You'd have thought I'd dropped a turd in his corn flakes instead of giving him the keys to the hottest bird in the world."

Even to those who worked with him daily, Captain Whitefoot was an enigma. His officer efficiency reports, though universally laudatory, were bereft of the flowery language that crept into the records of his peers. An astute observer would note what wasn't said. Though his performance was consistently flawless and unquestionably impressive, Whitefoot was never singled out for providing inspirational leadership or contributing to more effective teamwork. The narrative of his record depicted a man whose personality was as gray as the plane he flew.

After simulating the release of air-to-surface munitions and toggling off the attack display, White-foot gracefully pitched the Raptor into the overhead pattern, configured it for landing, and executed a flawless approach. Only he knew that his timing—after flying nonstop across the Mediterranean from Spain—was off by nearly four seconds. Though within the mission's target parameters of plus-or-minus five seconds, Whitefoot noted the discrepancy and would pore over the mission-reconstruction data to identify the error.

CHAPTER 6

"Captain Whitefoot? I'm Jack Warner, public affairs, and this is Major Khalim." Noting the pilot's stern expression and appraising stare, Jack quickly shifted gears to keep his enthusiasm in check. "Welcome aboard. You're the first arrival. I'm told that all arrangements have been made to the satisfaction of your team's operations coordinator. Is there anything I can do to help?"

"No." The response wasn't so much curt as factual, delivered without embellishment.

"Excellent." Jack handed over a custom-made leather valise, artfully inscribed with the pilot's name and a depiction of the aircraft. "This contains updated briefing material on the rules, ranges, and event schedule. For last-minute changes and weather briefs, check the mission channel on any television. Your team is housed in Hangar One. Major Khalim has seen to it that your equipment has been prestaged. You should contact him if there are any logistic problems. There will be a pilot's briefing tonight at twenty-hundred in the ready room. Last chance: Any questions for me?"

A slight shake of the pilot's head was all Jack got in return.

"Then I'll see you there."

Just as Jack turned to leave, the major's cell phone rang. After answering with a gruff, "Khalim," he stiffened noticeably. Whitefoot remained impassive, but Jack's curiosity was piqued. After a brief one-way conversation, punctuated only by the major's, "Yes, Your Highness," Khalim held the phone out for Jack.

"The Super Hornet team has checked in," he said. "Prince Salman wishes to speak to you in private." Khalim escorted Whitefoot out of earshot. Jack figured the two men, who each spoke as if paying by the word, would get along fine.

"Jack?"

"Yes, Your Highness." Jack was careful to convey respect in public, though in private the two shared an informal friendship.

"Knock it off, sport. This is a secure line. Look, we've got a nasty problem with the second American team. It's going to require some delicate work, and we don't have much time." His voice dropped a notch. "Frankly, Jack . . ."

Listening between the lines, Jack pictured the prince pacing his office, running his hand through his hair, completely agitated. Whatever was coming had to be very bad to cause His Coolness such distress.

"I'm not sure that we can recover. The truth is that it's jeopardizing the whole program."

Despite the desert heat, Jack felt a chill run down his spine. Not once, in all the time he'd worked with the prince, had the man's confidence wavered. "You've certainly got my attention."

"The king has ordered me to take Lieutenant Cole out of the competition. He's decreed that no women will be allowed to fly."

The enormity of the problem hit Jack with the force of a sucker punch.

"Jack, are you still there?"

"You've got to be shitting me! Why now?"

"His Majesty doesn't often confide his reasoning to me."

"Look, we never hid the fact that she was on the team. We didn't make a big deal out of it, either, but this . . . this is just plain stupid. Trust me, Cole is more than qualified to compete. Isn't that enough?"

"Jack, listen to me. I know it sounds screwed up to an outsider, but in our culture it doesn't matter if she's the best thing since Lindbergh. All that matters is that there is a pair of breasts in that flight suit. And, believe me, that's a deal-breaker. The shit hit the fan when she checked in; apparently, the military brass weren't clued in. I should have seen this coming. The captain called the colonel. The colonel called the general, who called the chief of staff, who called the king. It was over before I had a chance to intervene."

"So there's absolutely no chance she can compete?"

"None."

"Then the Super Hornet is out. I don't see any other options. You know this is going to blow up in our faces don't you? And it's huge. We're talking a backlash against your country that will take years . . ."

"No, Jack. That scenario is unacceptable. We have to unscrew this."

"But how?"

"Jack, we fix it or lose our heads. And I do mean that literally. You understand?" The prince paused but didn't receive an answer. "Failure is not an option. That's another thing about our culture you must accept. Now look, I'll be down there in a couple hours. In the meantime, you break the news to the Hornet team, get them to identify a backup pilot, and we'll fly him out here tonight. I've already got a charter being prepped in New York. It's crunch time, Jack. Are you with me?"

Not seeing any other alternative, Jack acquiesced. "I don't see that I have a choice."

"You haven't answered my question."

"Yes."

"Excellent."

The airfield, what there was of it, was a sight for sore eyes. After being stuck in the penalty box and forced to fly circles on the border for an hour—she had been five minutes from having to abort the mission and divert to another field—Lieutenant Miranda "Randi" Cole, United States Navy, was relieved to have arrived. She'd debrief the issue of airspace coordination later; right now she just wanted to land the machine. The sooner the better; she had to pee. It had been a helluva long flight from Naples.

Jack watched the Super Hornet execute a crisp overhead break in preparation for landing. Tormented by a bevy of emotions, he struggled to come to terms with the conflict between friendship and duty. Randi was a close friend, and he had been eagerly anticipating their reunion. Jack had made quite a splash in the literary world chronicling the events leading up to her MiG–29 kill over Libya. He'd bagged the Pulitzer for it. And she credited him with saving her life when he exposed a plot by a handful of men determined to rid the Hornet community of women pilots at all costs. How the hell could he possibly be expected to tell her she was grounded? It was insane.

Randi unstrapped and climbed out of the jet before the engines wound down. After a brief discussion with her crew chief, whereupon he pointed toward the ramp leading to Hangar Two, she ducked under the long nose of the jet and walked purposefully toward it. Jack jumped in his cart and hustled to catch up.

"Hey, lady, don't you have a minute for your fan club?" he asked from behind.

Hearing his voice, she turned without stopping and nailed him with a dazzling smile that tore at his heart. "Hi, Jack! Wow, it's good to see you. Forgive me, I've been strapped in that jet forever and I need to hit the head."

"Climb aboard, my dear. Your chariot awaits."

Despite the bulky flight gear, Randi nimbly

stepped into the moving cart, sat down, and gave Jack a kiss on the cheek. She spoke softly, her lips brushing his ear. "So you come to my rescue again, Jack Warner." She laughed as he blushed.

"Here we are."

Randi was out of the cart and in the rest room before the cart came to a complete stop.

Jack's stomach churned as he parked and waited; he couldn't believe what he was about to do. When Randi emerged, looking much relieved and eager for action, Jack decided he needed to break the news as soon as possible.

But she beat him to the punch. "Hey, I've got a surprise for you. Guess what," she said, as they walked toward the Super Hornet team's locker room, where she would stow her gear.

"You're pregnant."

She slugged him in the arm. "Bite your tongue.

His biceps stung like hell. Randi, among other things, was a terrific athlete.

"Give up?"

"Well I'm not guessing anymore," he said, rubbing his shoulder.

"Don't be a baby."

Jack followed her into the locker room and took a seat on a nearby bench as she peeled off the flight gear. The engine whine from a large aircraft filtered down from outside.

"That's him."

"Who?"

With one foot up on a bench as she unzipped her

G suit, Randi peered at Jack, who was struggling unsuccessfully not to gawk at her figure in the tight-fitting flight suit. It felt good to be appreciated. "Hoser's here," she said matter-of-factly.

Jack popped to his feet. "You're kidding, right? I haven't seen that old bastard for over a year. How'd you get him out here?"

"He joined our team a couple months ago as a technical advisor. And you know Hoser. It only took a week before he'd wormed his way into the flight-test program. He's been testing the two-seater. It's been great having him around, Jack. Just like old times."

Memories flooded back. Hoser, aka Joe Santana, was Randi Cole's mentor, a role he'd assumed after her father—Santana's best friend and wingman in Vietnam—died in an air-show mishap a dozen years earlier. Santana was nearly killed himself in a flight-deck mishap on the USS *Ranger* on the same cruise during which Randi had bagged her MiG. Jack, who had enjoyed the time of his life flying aboard in Hoser's backseat as a pool reporter, witnessed the horrific crash from the bridge. The shared experience of waiting for Hoser to emerge from his coma had bonded Jack and Randi.

"The military is letting him fly again?"

"Not the military, Jack. The team." She arched her eyebrows at the significance of the distinction. "You have no idea what you've unleashed back home, my friend. It's crazy. All of a sudden, we've got the State Department, the FAA, and the Navy bending over backwards to help. We've got new gear coming out our ears. And upgrades from the manufacturers are coming so fast I can't keep up with the testing. Jack, in less than a week the budget for my test program *doubled*!" She smiled. "So I told them I needed help. I thought they'd laugh me out of there when I asked to bring the old codger onboard. But they jumped at it."

Jack couldn't believe his luck. As good as Randi was, Hoser's cunning and skill in a dogfight were legendary. The Super Hornet team would still have a chance with him in the cockpit. "Well, let's go see the man."

CHAPTER 7

The C–17 transport disgorged support crew for both American teams. It was clear from the spirited banter as they unloaded baggage and equipment that the competition had its first rivalry.

At six-foot-four and clad in a sand-colored flight suit, Captain Joe "Hoser" Santana, United States Navy (retired), was easy to spot. Jack and Randi tried to sneak up on him as he surveyed the airfield, but he turned as they closed to within earshot.

"Would you look at what the cat dragged in?" Jack said, determined to get in the first insult.

"Nice place you got here, Jack," Hoser said. "I've seen better-looking prisons."

"Why doesn't that surprise me?"

"Hey, you two . . ." Randi cautioned.

Jack couldn't keep a straight face. "Damn, it's good to see you, big guy."

Hoser stepped forward and put one big arm each around Jack and Randi and pulled them into a tight hug. "Same here, Jack. Same here. Now . . . where's the brewskis?"

*   *   *

Hoser drained the stein in one long pull and returned it to the bar with a resounding *thunk*. "That's the best damn beer I ever drank," he exclaimed to the delight of the brewmeister. "You'd better set aside a keg with my name on it, my friend. I have a feeling I'm going to be awful thirsty out here."

"*Ja*, you are my first customer, Herr Santana." From beneath the bar, the old man pulled out an intricately detailed, ancient pewter stein. "This has been in my family for generations. For our time here, it will be yours. A man who appreciates beer must have the proper tool."

Hoser, looking like a kid who'd been given the keys to the candy factory, thanked his host profusely and promised to return the favor. But Randi dragged him away before he could begin another round. "There's time for that later. Jack has to attend to the other teams, and he says he has something important to tell us."

Jack led them to an office tucked in the corner of the hangar. After his two friends took seats, he closed the door and turned to face them.

"What's wrong, Jack?" Randi asked. "You look like somebody died."

"Yeah, Warner, what's eating you?" asked Hoser.

Jack swallowed hard. "There's a problem, and I don't know how to fix it." Forcing himself to maintain eye contact, he added, "It's bad."

Randi and Hoser exchanged glances. Hoser

spoke first, "Spill it. There's nothing we can't work through."

"All right then. Randi?"

"Yes?"

"The king of Saudi Arabia decreed less than two hours ago that you cannot fly in the competition because you are a woman."

She was out of the chair in a flash. "What? What did you just say?" she demanded, advancing on Jack. "Tell me I heard wrong, mister."

Jack unconsciously retreated until his back hit the wall. "No. You heard correctly. You're grounded, and there's nothing you, me, or anybody else, can do about it."

"That's bullshit!"

"No. It's their game, their rules, their country."

Randi's anger was palpable, her effort to control it tenuous. She spoke through clenched teeth, emphasizing each point with a finger jab to Jack's chest. "Unacceptable answer. This contract is worth billions, and there are thousands of jobs on the line. What did the State Department say?"

"They're being notified through the consulate. Don't expect anything. From the outset they haven't officially sanctioned this event. State is taking a hand's-off position."

"And . . . and the consortium?" Randi's voice wavered slightly.

"That's another story. They were notified by the Saudis less than an hour ago. I'm awaiting a call from their lead agent."

"Jesus Christ, Jack! What the hell are you waiting for? This is dead wrong, and you know it. I would have thought you would have straightened these chauvinist bastards out. Why are you dragging us around to drink beer when you should be on the phone?"

"That's a good question, Jack," said Hoser. "Is there something you're not telling us?"

Jack took a deep breath and stepped away from Randi. He sat down and closed his eyes for several seconds. When he opened them, he spoke in a monotone. "I work for these people. Have been for nearly a year. I answer to Prince Salman, who answers to the council of provincial governors and, ultimately, the king."

He looked up and found Randi glaring. Jack tried to explain how the momentum had grown. "This event is going to be huge. You have no idea how big. Believe me, for every dime you've spent, they've spent a thousand. In twenty-four hours this place will be crawling with five hundred of the world's most influential people. And we have worldwide, twenty-four-hour, and seven-media coverage."

Randi was impatient. "So what? That's all well and good, Jack, but . . ."

"We should let the man finish," said Hoser.

Randi's jaw snapped shut.

Jack glanced at Hoser with gratitude, but found himself the target of a deep scowl.

Jack tried again. "I'm sorry. Look, I don't have all the answers, but you've got to know that there's

much more to this competition than selling airplanes."

"Like what?" asked Randi, her voice a tight
monotone.

"Just take a second to look at the players. We've
got multinational corporations, in many cases aided
by sovereign governments, in cutthroat competition.
You said yourself that the Navy is in it up to its ears.
You can bet the Raptor team has total Air Force back-
ing. That means the Department of Defense has been
told to toe the line. And don't forget about the
EuroFighter. The entire French government is pushing that program. On top of that the Israelis are coming. Can you imagine? That alone ought to tell you
that the stakes are much higher than a twenty-five-
billion-dollar contract."

"That's all the more reason that the competition
has to be above reproach. We can't let them get away
with torpedoing our chances before we even get clear
of the chocks."

"It's not that simple. There's so much overlap, it's
hard to tell who's who. The EuroFighter is a mix of
French, German, and Brit with some Asian money
thrown in. The Lancer is a Brit-only dark horse. Then
there are the two American teams, and the Israelis,
who, many think, might as well be American. The
wild card is the Russians. They're on their own . . . I
think. It gets muddy when you factor in the engine,
radar, and avionics manufacturers since most of
them support more than one team. There's just no
way of knowing what's going on behind closed

doors. It's a crapshoot. You can bet that your team will howl, but in the end, they will acquiesce because they have to. The Super Hornet team cannot afford to cut its nose off to spite its face. And on top of that, I'm on the hook for this thing going off as planned. If it doesn't, I'm toast."

"I don't follow," said Randi.

"I think I know where he's going. Press on, Jack," said Hoser.

"Okay. But you need to understand my situation first. These guys play for keeps. I don't want to be melodramatic, but the prince as much as told me that if we fail to pull this off, we could be taken out."

"Give me a break," said Randi, clearly incredulous. "That's absurd. Your prince sounds like he's seen too many American movies."

"Trust me. They're capable of it. There's a religious undercurrent to everything they do. And we've all seen how ruthless a religious zealot can be. You have to understand that we're infidels on sacred ground. Don't be fooled by the smiles; some of our hosts would just as soon slit our throats as speak to us. You have a copy of the Koran in your rooms. Check it out, it's interesting reading."

"Okay, so we're despised. So is every other team, none more than the Israelis. How does this relate to these bastards deciding at the last possible second that I cannot fly?"

"Again, I have no proof, but we didn't hide the fact that you were a woman. Hell, you're famous in this part of the world since the Libyan shootdown.

There's no way the king was ignorant of it. I don't know what their motivation is. I don't have enough information yet. With these guys it could be anything. Who knows? I just know that it sucks. You have earned the right to fly."

Randi's heart felt like it was being squeezed in a vise. The too-familiar weight of prejudice—absent from her life since she became a test pilot—settled on her shoulders. But she had responsibilities to handle, and the solution was clear. "Jack, tell our hosts that there's been a change in pilots. From now on, Hoser will be flying the Super Hornet. I have to go notify the team." She spoke quietly, relieved that her voice was steady. Then she spun on her heel, snatched open the door, and left. Hot tears of frustration and rage stung her eyes.

Jack rose from his seat and started to follow her.

"Let her go," Hoser commanded.

Jack stopped at the door, helpless, as he watched Randi walk away. Once more, he found himself humbled by her strength when confronting an enemy. Not that long ago, he'd been privileged to help, but this time, he was on the wrong side.

CHAPTER 8

Lieutenant Colonel Moshe Kohl's flight was certainly one for the record book. Though he had the shortest distance to travel of the six teams, his could be described as the longest journey. Within the Israeli Parliament, the project's supporters had gone so far as to claim that this mission was another step in a pilgrimage begun in biblical times. Even their opponents agreed, but then cautioned that the chosen path was much too perilous and needlessly threatened the security of the Israeli people. Regardless, thirty-eight-year-old Moshe Kohl would soon become the first Israeli fighter pilot to fly across the sands of Saudi Arabia's great deserts.

Kohl, respected by his peers for his lack of ego and a smooth—some would say, elegant—style, was an ace with half a dozen MiG kills to his credit, each of which had caused him consternation instead of elation. An artist and pacifist by temperament, Kohl nevertheless felt obligated to serve in the Israeli Air Force, unable to justify leaving until someone with better skills arrived. He'd been waiting twenty years.

As a schoolboy—identified as a pilot candidate through a routine government screening process—nobody was more surprised than he to learn of his innate ability to think conceptually in three dimensions. Even in flight school, his skill was such that, in a dogfight, his graceful maneuvers appeared effortless. While his opponents staggered under the G forces, Moshe Kohl used exquisite timing deftly to orchestrate the fight to his advantage. Few pilots held their own against him. It had been nearly a decade since anyone had put him on the defensive.

Kohl learned long ago to leave the political ramifications of his missions to others. This wasn't the first time he'd been ordered to cross the border of an Arab neighbor. But it was the only time he'd done it unarmed. Even as he threaded his way down the Gulf of Aqaba—a sliver of water bisecting Egypt and Saudi Arabia and capped at its apex by Jordan and Israel—Kohl couldn't shake the feeling that this mission was a mistake his country could ill afford.

When apprised of the assignment, Moshe sought the counsel of his rabbi, a man of indeterminate age and possessed of uncanny wisdom. Moshe shared his concerns. "They will not let us win. And in the meantime, we reveal our capabilities. It seems to me to be a mistake."

"You are a soldier, no? And you have been given an order, correct? So you obey. What happens, happens."

"But I do not want to lose."

"Ah . . . that is another matter. This is something

personal for you, then? Let me ask this of you: Is there another pilot in the Israeli Air Force who would have a better chance of succeeding?"

"No, I suppose not."

"Then this mission is like any other except that there should be no one trying to kill you." The rabbi's eyes twinkled. "That's a small cockpit on your fighter, is it not?"

"Yes."

"Then leave your ego at home, my son. You'll need the room."

A new warning from the KFIR II's electronic-warfare suite blared in Moshe's headset as a pair of air-intercept radars joined the array of weapons systems painting the Israeli aircraft. Within milliseconds, a bank of sophisticated signal processors categorized the threat as Saudi F–15s. Moshe left his radar in its passive sniff-mode, content to follow the course of the Eagles by tracking their emissions. Israeli engineers had built a system that, if this had been combat, allowed Moshe to launch a specially modified missile designed to guide passively on the Eagle's own radar. Again, not today.

Moshe rechecked the green light that signified that the high-density magnetic-tape unit installed hours earlier by Israeli intelligence agents was operating. He smiled beneath his oxygen mask. If nothing else, at least he could appreciate the irony. The

maiden mission of the KFIR II—a state-of-the-art
aircraft cunningly designed to evade and destroy—
had the deadliest pilot in the Israeli Air Force droning
unarmed through the world's most heavily defended
airspace.

CHAPTER 9

Jack felt drained, and the day wasn't yet half-over. He'd handled a thousand and one details in the past ten hours, everything from the pilot change on the American Super Hornet team to an international crisis when the EuroFighter blew a tire on landing and came within inches of cartwheeling in the sand. The Saudi crash-and-salvage team had clashed with the Euro-Fighter's multiethnic maintenance crew over who would be in charge of towing the aircraft to the hangar. By the time Jack was summoned by Major Khalim to mediate the dispute, tempers had flared in five languages, none of them English. After listening to a spirited if unintelligible litany of complaints, Jack blotted his forehead with a handkerchief, calmly pointed out that it was only going to get hotter on the runway, and reminded the combatants that cold drinks and air-conditioning awaited in their hangar.

The Saudi crew began preparations to tow the aircraft, and Jack moved on to the next crisis. The Brits were inbound.

*　　*　　*

Simon Buckingham waited patiently until his escort
had closed to three hundred meters before he put on
the brakes. He laughed merrily as the Eagle skittered
by, badly overshooting the much smaller, vector-
thrust-equipped Lancer.

The Saudi pilot floundered while trying to bleed
off airspeed, first by deploying his enormous speedbrake and then by ham-fisting the stick.

Buckingham deftly maneuvered into guns range
and, with the precision of a surgeon, placed the sight-
reticle on the F–15's cockpit, the pipper settling omi-
nously on his opponent's helmet.

"You should be driving camels for a living, my
friend," Buckingham said for the benefit of his mission recorder. His ground crew would get a kick out
of it. Over the air he transmitted, "I say . . . If you'll
straighten out, I shall join on you. I do believe our
heading should be one-zero-zero."

The Saudi pilot, educated at Oxford and attuned
to Brit sarcasm, seethed but grudgingly complied.
There would be other opportunities to take this arrogant Brit down a notch.

Simon Buckingham had made his first enemy at
the contest; it wouldn't be his last. People were never
neutral about Buckingham. His supporters cited his
quick wit, good looks, and charm. To the rest of the
world he was a boorish egomaniac. But everyone
agreed, however begrudgingly, that he could fly the
hell out of an airplane. And in the Lancer, an obscure
little jet built as a follow-on to the Harrier jump jet,
he'd found a nontraditional machine that suited his

style perfectly. In secret tests against Brit Tornados and German MiG–29s, Buckingham and his Lancer had scored an impressive string of victories. He was eager for better competition.

The Iranian minister of defense was being stubborn. The Saudi Royal Air Force chief of staff had called, as had the prince, but the man was unmoved. Overflight rights for the Russian team—negotiated over a month ago—had been rescinded without warning, leaving the SU–34 Strike Flanker stuck in a holding pattern over the Caspian Sea.

It required a discussion between the respective ministers of state to break the logjam. The Iranian minister cited the government's concern for the sovereignty of Iranian airspace and safety of its citizens. After all, there was the potential for disaster should the aircraft crash into a populated area. His Saudi counterpart sincerely echoed the king's empathy. Both understood that this was a simple matter of custom between Arab neighbors where one side exploited a position of temporary advantage. Certainly nothing to get upset about. A two-million-dollar tariff was agreed upon, paid in U.S. dollars to a numbered Swiss account, and the go-ahead was issued. As the gentlemen discussed children and summer plans, the Russian fighter crossed the coast inbound for Tehran.

*   *   *

"Sergei, have you been practicing your English?"
Mikhail Zhukov asked his older, taciturn weapon-
systems operator.

"Da."

"In *English*, please," said Mikhail, sounding
exasperated but silently amused by his partner's distrust of anything not Russian, even words. The two
had been flying together for only two months.
Though they were polar opposites in personality, as
aviators, they complemented each other's strengths
and had developed into a formidable combination.
And with this particular Strike Flanker, they had a jet
of unmatched performance.

"Yes, Mikhail. I can speak the language. I was
speaking English while you were soiling your dia-
pers."

"Very good! We shall dazzle these bumpkins
with our charm and sophistication, my friend."

"I think you intend to dazzle the women, do you
not?"

"Da!"

With the highway in sight, Simon Buckingham
saluted his escort pilot, lit the burner on the Rolls
Royce Advanced Pegasus engine, and peeled off.
Though the Lancer's top speed was no match for the
mach-2 Eagle, nothing in the air could outpace his
machine in a sprint to five hundred knots. His acceleration was so swift, the Eagle pilot thumbed his speedbrake toggle, convinced it had inadvertently deployed.

After three years of flying in Oman, Buckingham was as comfortable racing flat out across the desert as driving his Austin-Healey to the corner pub. The nimble Lancer was a joy to fly. Incredibly responsive in roll—a mere flick of the wrist could spin it around its longitudinal axis—it was also comfortably stable at low altitude, a rare combination. In it, Buckingham reveled in his role as a long shot in the competition.

The Eagle pilot couldn't believe his eyes. The crazy Brit was streaking down the sand-covered highway, flying so low that he kicked up a rooster tail of sand. With its camouflage paint job obscuring the jet itself, it looked for all the world as if the aircraft was tunneling its way toward the airfield. "That bastard's not going to live through the week," he said to himself.

Leaving the highway to hedgehop amid the giant dunes, Buckingham used his satellite navigation system carefully to align his heading with the taxiway in hopes of surprising an unsuspecting foe. His diligence was rewarded when he spied a crew towing an aircraft toward the center of the field. A target of opportunity. Buckingham wriggled in the hard-backed ejection seat in anticipation. As he closed on the unsuspecting ensemble, he was delighted to discover that it was the EuroFighter.

"Frogs!" he exclaimed for the benefit of the tape. "Stupid bastards already pranged their jet, and the festivities have yet to begin." Buckingham nudged the Lancer just slightly off the taxiway, grinning under his mask in anticipation of the havoc he was about to wreak.

"What the hell is that?" Jack heard one of the American ground crew ask of another. Jack turned in time to see a small, brownish fighter approach at alarming speed. In a flash, the aircraft streaked by with a thunderous roar, trailing a billowing tail of sand that enveloped the EuroFighter. He'd never seen an aircraft so low with its wheels up. There didn't appear to be an inch of daylight between the jet's belly and the sand.

"Abandon ship!" hollered another member of the ground crew, laughingly pointing to the victims who, after bailing off the tow tractor, emerged from the sand cloud, blind and stumbling as if escaping a smoke-filled building.

Jack had to admit that the scene was fairly comical in a Keystone Kops way, and, truth be told, he wasn't terribly unhappy to see the obnoxious crew leader get his comeuppance.

Meanwhile, Simon ripped the Lancer into a hard bank while simultaneously commanding the variable-exhaust nozzle to redirect the engine thrust away from the jet's underbelly. To observers, the effect produced an uncanny skidding stop, not unlike that of a snowboarder. Harrier pilots had developed the technique and dubbed it, vif-fing, short for, vectoring in flight.

"That guy's nuts!" Randi Cole said to Hoser, as they watched the Brit jet settle delicately onto the concrete pad.

Hoser nodded. "I'll grant you that he might be a brick or two short of a full load, but that move is going to fool people. And he does it better than anyone I've ever seen. You definitely wouldn't want to get into a knife fight with that little beast."

"That's a good camouflage job, too," she said.

"Yup. He's got the tools to be a giant-killer. Want to meet the pilot?"

"You know him?"

"We've crossed paths a few times."

"Sure. Why not?"

Hoser turned the cart around and drove off the flight line.

"Where are we going?" she asked. "I thought you said we were going to meet the guy."

"We are, my dear. That Brit is a desert rat. He can smell the pub from his cockpit."

"Yeah, right. Any excuse you old reprobate."

"Now . . . now."

The sun was setting as Mikhail slipped the throttle behind the cutoff and Sergei raised the canopy on the Strike Flanker. It had been a long day for the Russian crew. Right after the trouble with the Iranians, the oil pressure on the number two engine had begun fluctuating, forcing Mikhail to shut it down and risk flying several hundred kilometers over uninhabitable desert on one motor. Likewise, the Sukoi's unique rearward-facing radar was giving Sergei fits. Technicians and a spare motor waited in the underground hangar. There was much work to do to prepare the jet for tomorrow's flight.

"Mikhail, you go to the pilots' meeting; I'm going to stay with the jet," said Sergei when the two had climbed down from the cockpits.

"We have a maintenance team for that, Sergei. Join me for something to drink, my friend, and let these men do their jobs."

"*Nyet.* These are the same idiots who prepared the jet for today's flight," Sergei said loud enough for the crew to hear him. Several turned their heads at the rebuke. "Obviously they need adult supervision."

"You worry too much, Sergei," whispered Mikhail.

"And you worry not enough. Do not forget why we are here, comrade. It is not to drink vodka and chase women."

"No? Damn, Sergei, I wish you had told me that earlier . . . I would have stayed home."

CHAPTER 10

"Well there goes the neighborhood," Hoser said while peering over his stein into the bar mirror.

Buckingham stopped in his tracks, clearly surprised, but he recovered quickly. "What's that I hear?" he asked, theatrically cupping his hand to one ear, his eyes closed in rapt concentration. "A voice from my distant past, I should say. Hold on there . . . it's coming to me. Why . . . why it's none other than Joe Santana, fighter pilot extraordinaire!" As he stepped forward, Buckingham—in perfect parody of an incorrigible womanizer—abruptly turned to Randi, leaving Hoser's outstretched hand grasping air. "And . . . hello? Who might this incredibly lovely woman be?" he asked with a raised eyebrow and very British accent.

It was the first time anyone had kissed Randi's hand. Despite the overacting and Hoser's laughter, she found it charming. And there was no denying that the man was definitely handsome. Drawn to his wicked smile, she mentally slipped him out of his flight suit before she caught herself.

"Randi, meet Squadron Leader Buckingham, a

legend in his own mind. Simon, this is Randi." Hoser decided to let her fill in the details.

Fully aware of his effect on American women, Buckingham cocked his head and gave Randi a wink before relinquishing her hand. He'd have her in bed inside forty-eight hours, he was sure of it. "Barman," he announced, "a round for my friends, if you please."

"The beer's free, you cheap bastard," Hoser said.

"Well then, a round for the house!" he announced with a flourish.

Randi laughed and excused herself. "Good meeting you, Simon. Here . . . take my chair. Gentlemen, and I use that term loosely, you'll have to excuse me."

"But you mustn't go, my dear," Buckingham said. "Otherwise, I'll be forced to endure this man's interminably boring sea stories."

"Better you than me." Turning to Hoser, she said, "See you in twenty minutes." She cut her eyes at his beer, the message clear.

Hoser smiled, picked up the stein, and took a long pull, his eyes daring her to say something.

As she walked away, Randi was acutely aware of the stares she attracted.

"That's a tidy package you've got there, Hoser," Buckingham said as he accepted a lager from the brewmeister.

"At ease, you limey prick. I'm surprised you didn't recognize her. That's Randi Cole, MiG killer, and until this morning, your competition."

"Well, yes . . . of course! I remember now." He took has first drink, paused, and took another. "Oh, this is quite nice. I was afraid we'd be drinking one of those dreadful American imports. By the way, are you two an item?"

"Let's just say that I take my role as godfather very seriously."

"Ah . . . so that's how it is. Very good, my friend. I shall endeavor to remain a gentlemen in her presence." Shifting gears, he asked, "So how'd they drag you here? I'd heard that you retired and were flying vintage machines as a firefighter."

"You've got good intel."

"Certainly. But you have not answered my question then, have you?"

"I was the backup. Randi was the lead pilot. She's still the officer-in-charge, but she was grounded today when the king decided at the last minute to ban women from the competition."

"Tough break for her . . . but, bully for you. Their excuse sounds like rubbish, though."

"It is. It looks like a cheap shot to disrupt the Hornet team. I checked the manifest. They had me listed as an engineer, not a backup pilot. By the way, I caught your arrival show. That's the first Lancer I've seen. Looks like a sweet-handling little thing."

"You have no idea. You strap it on like a second skin. But then, you'll soon find out for yourself how well it maneuvers."

As their eyes locked, both men grinned at the prospect of crossing swords again.

Buckingham was the first to speak. "Let's have us a toast, then."

"I don't see why not."

They stood; each continuing to take the measure of the other.

"To fast machines, fast women, and leaving a good-looking corpse."

"Cheers. And may the best man win," said Hoser.

"Indeed."

"So that's it, then? You've chosen to do nothing?" Randi stared pointedly at the monitor, more precisely at the four-inch inset picture of the rodent-faced representative from the State Department. The tele-videoconference had been set up by one of Jack's minions, a Saudi teenage wunderkind, wearing the requisite techie garb, complete with backwards ball cap and baggy jeans, who was clearly infatuated with Randi. He'd introduced himself as Pharaoh, and led her to a room crammed to the ceiling with racks of computers and other high-tech equipment.

"Lieutenant Cole . . ."

Randi considered it a bad sign that the ferret from State used her rank.

"As I've explained, it is not that we've chosen to do nothing. It is that we have carefully balanced the potential ramifications and decided that it is in the best interest of the United States not to pursue a formal objection due to the stigma and embarrassment it would no doubt cause our hosts. They are, after all, quite proud of their newfound technical prowess. We must understand that not all societies are as socially advanced as we are. To make a federal case out of one of their most deep-seated cultural prejudices would offset the positive leverage realized to date." He stared out from the monitor with an expression of parental patience. "I hope you understand. I simply cannot state it any plainer."

"No, I can see that."

The sarcasm flew over his head. Relieved to have broken through, his concerned look was replaced by a wide smile worthy of a toddler's first steps. "Excellent! I will pass on to my superiors that you are . . . on board." The jerk actually accompanied his nautical reference with a wink. "Rest assured that we are empathetic to your personal sense of injustice. But I can see that you're a team player. Believe me, that fact will not be ignored."

Randi felt a tap on her shoulder. Pharaoh slid her a clipboard, on which he'd written: "What an asshole! *Please* let me give him the flush."

Randi had no idea what the "flush" was, but she was fed up with the talking head from state. Beneath the camera's line of sight she gave Pharaoh a thumbs-up.

As his fingers danced across the keyboard, a computer animation began.

A scantily clad, buxom character wiggled its way across the screen, peeled a snapshot of the man's face off the little screen they used for the videoconference, and placed it on top of a toilet that suddenly appeared.

"What the . . ."

Pharaoh had engineered it so that the man from State saw the same thing on his computer.

With a lascivious wink, the character depressed the handle. The photo of the man began to spin slowly at first, then with increasing speed as it descended into the bowl. Realistic sound effects accompanied the animation.

"Miss Cole! Miss Cole!" The sophisticated program added an echo effect, making it sound for all the world as if the guy were calling for help from the bottom of the toilet bowl.

Randi collapsed in a fit of laughter.

Pharaoh beamed.

CHAPTER 11

Ready Room/1930 hours

"Gentlemen, welcome to Saudi Arabia and the world's first Fly-Off competition. I've met each of you, but for the record, my name is Jack Warner. I'm the director of PR for this shindig. I believe you have also met our operations officer, Major Khalim." There was no sign of recognition or interest from the aircrew. "Feel free to contact either of us if you have questions or problems. Speaking of which, are there any questions I can answer at this time?"

Another tough crowd. He knew it would be. Fighter pilots, as a breed, were notoriously independent. In his twenty-plus years covering military flying, Jack had learned that, unlike other aviators, fighter pilots mistrusted any form of organized activity. Their behavior that evening was textbook. Though the ready room was relatively small, holding only thirty large upholstered chairs, the pilots were dispersed from one end to the other. Whitefoot, Kohl, Antoskin, and the six-man EuroFighter team sat stone-faced, while Zukov, Buckingham, and Santana shared what could best be described as smirks. As Jack made eye contact with each, only Randi reacted with an expression of interest.

Jack knew better than to let them get under his skin. Sitting in this room were arguably the best fighter pilots in the world, men who would soon be engaged in combat. That they would not be using live weapons on one another did not lessen the stakes. In addition to the danger of the extended competition, every team in the room save one would carry home the stigma of losing. And, with Jack's help, their failure would be shared with the entire world.

"Before you hear from Major Khalim, allow me to take a few moments to outline what you can expect over the course of the next five days." Jack elected not to go high-tech with this brief, relying instead on his ability to communicate the essence of the competition in what he called his Joe Friday—just the facts Ma'am—style, after the old *Dragnet* television character.

"Even as we sit here, a carefully orchestrated media blitz has begun to focus global attention on our activities. Tomorrow morning, the guests will arrive. The king has invited five hundred of the world's most influential people to be your on-site audience. And though you may recognize many of them, it is you who are the celebrities. This compound, with all of its splendor, was built to bring the two groups together. When you're not flying or briefing, we invite you to join the festivities."

Still no response. It was time to shake them up a

little. "As you know, the competition has five events, one for each day. Each will be scored independently. Major Khalim will go over the criteria with you in a moment. But you may want to know that, as each day progresses, your scores will be posted worldwide—on the Internet, television, and in every major newspaper."

That got to them. There was a flurry of shuffling amid surreptitious glances.

"But reporting scores alone wouldn't be all that interesting, would it?" Answering his own question, Jack said, "We didn't think so either. Not when you have the top six teams from around the world competing head-to-head. We needed something special to showcase your talents. So we have equipped each aircraft with a data-link pod to transmit your flight data to our command center. You've all flown on instrumented ranges where your maneuvers are recorded and animated for review. This will be similar, but wait until you see what our state-of-the-art system can do. We use 3-D modeling to generate extremely realistic graphics. To those we'll add shots from the special high-speed cameras we've mounted on the range. And our production team will blend in snippets of cockpit audio and live pictures from your HUD cameras.

"Our guests will observe a full-blown three-dimensional depiction of your flights projected on our one-of-a-kind dome theater. It is truly extraordinary. And our Internet audience will have access to as much data as they can download. Even those with the slowest connections will hear your fights live and track your performance via the website."

Jack paused for a sip of water and to take stock. The EuroFighter team huddled up and began talking earnestly. The rest, especially Kohl and Antoskin, looked shell-shocked.

"Some of you may have concerns about the level of publicity and how it will affect your privacy. I can't speak for when you leave here, but while you are at the compound, you can rest assured that the press will not hound you. The reason is simple: I am the press. There are no television crews or foreign reporters here. And I'm certain that you'll find our guests extremely sympathetic and understanding about the fishbowl syndrome. Many of them live with it every day.

"Whether you do on-line or remote interviews is left up to you and your sponsors. We have the communications facilities to handle just about anything. I can tell you that the world's major news organizations are hungry for anything you have to say. You should consider this opportunity carefully."

One of the EuroFighter crew stood and bowed.

"Yes, Captain Matsasuta?"

"Mr. Warner, my colleagues have asked me to speak on their behalf."

"Please, go ahead." Jack considered it a breakthrough to have them select a spokesman. Dealing with the six individually had been a struggle. And Hiro Matsasuta, having been educated in the U.S., was a good choice.

"We are impressed by your accomplishments and mean no disrespect to our hosts, but we are concerned that the primary focus of the competition seems to have shifted to the pilots. The mission we came here to accomplish, and we suspect that of the other teams, is to demonstrate the superiority of our aircraft. That is why our sponsors have elected to use a team of pilots selected to fly specific events. Frankly, it is not fair to pit the pilots in competition with each other. After all, we do not fly the same aircraft. And, of course, the EuroFighter team has a distinct advantage since we have specialists trained for each event." He bowed again and sat.

"I understand your concerns . . ."

"Hold on there, sport," said Simon Buckingham. All heads turned to the Brit. "If my ears do not deceive me, gentlemen, we are having smoke blown up our arses by the *spokesman* for the EuroFighter team." He pronounced "spokesman" with disdain.

Jack tried to intervene. "I'm sure that Captain . . ."

"Jack, mate, this is a pilot's meeting, correct? Let's have the pilots talk, shall we?" Though it was said with a smile, the message was clear. Jack sat down and exchanged glances with Major Khalim, who, for once, seemed intrigued by the proceedings.

"So what's on your mind, Buckingham?" Hoser asked. "That is if you can see through the smoke." Several pilots chuckled at the insult.

Buckingham stood and leaned against the back of a chair. He had everyone's attention. "Touché, *Messieurs*. Allow me to cut to the chase. This competition is most certainly about us." Pointing to Khalim, he said, "Make no mistake, we are here to entertain and amuse them. And I, for one, plan to take full advantage of the situation."

Kohl spoke for the first time. "What does that mean—'full advantage'?"

"Perhaps he means the rest of us should—how you say, 'pack our kits,' and fly home?" said Mikhail.

The two adversaries matched stares for several seconds. Buckingham spoke with casual disdain. "Suit yourself, mate." With a nod toward the EuroFighter team, he said, "Of course we're here to win the competition. And while I do not begin to understand the 'fly by committee' approach, I really do not care who is strapped into a cockpit. But I do resent hypocrisy. For better or worse, all of us are in this goldfish bowl Jack has built. To ignore that fact is absurd. And to miss out on the opportunity for publicity is sheer stupidity.

"If you want to come off like a statue"—he glanced at Whitefoot, whose scowl deepened in response—"by all means proceed, but you are missing the chance of a lifetime. I simply want to state for the record that you can expect me to be devastatingly charming with guests, available for interviews, and the life of the pub. If you think it is all an act, you are absolutely correct. We have the world by the bollocks, gentlemen. Why not squeeze them a trifle?"

"Unlike you, we are not here for personal gain," one of the EuroFighter pilots said, clearly angry with his British opponent.

"That's too bad, sport, I would think you'd need funds to buy training wheels to keep that kite of yours on the runway."

Several EuroFighter pilots angrily responded at once. Captain Matsasuta silenced them by standing and addressing Jack, pointedly ignoring Buckingham and the others. "Perhaps we should continue with the meeting, Mr. Warner. Some of us have work to do."

"What I don't understand is why Buckingham said those things tonight. What was he trying to accomplish?" Randi asked Hoser, as they walked to his room after the briefing.

"That's easy, sweetheart. He was trying to get under everyone's skin. Piss us off. Make us think more about him than about flying our own jet. From the looks of it, it may have worked. Matsasuta was playing a version of the same game, trying to crawl in our heads with all that 'specialists' crap. Buckingham's got a point about cooperating with Jack, though. Hell, I had no idea this was going to be done under such a big spotlight. Did you?"

"Nope. I thought it was out in the boonies to keep it secret. You know, in a way, I guess I'm glad that it's you not me. Can you imagine the attention I'd get as the only woman?"

"Right now, that's an advantage I wouldn't mind," Hoser said.

Randi burst out laughing, slumping against the door.

"What's so funny, young lady?"

"That's the first time anyone has claimed that being a woman fighter pilot was an advantage. Trust me, big guy, none of you boys could handle it."

"I think you're peeking through the wrong end of the scope, babe. You were born with an edge Buckingham would kill for. Fighting a woman gets into a guy's head. They're more concerned about not losing to you than winning."

"Well, as much as I'd love to stay here and debate that point, I have to go see the man."

Hoser raised his eyebrows but didn't ask.

The figure stood stock-still, silhouetted against the moonlit horizon, arms folded against the crisp night air.

Minutes earlier Jack had been summoned to the security center by Major Khalim when the perimeter low-light cameras picked up the American woman wandering unescorted toward the dunes. "Given the circumstances, I thought it best to call you, Mr. Warner. Obviously Lieutenant Cole is unhappy about the grounding, but as you know, we have strict security procedures . . ."

"Thank you, Major. I just need a moment with her."

"Hey, stranger, you okay?" Jack spoke softly so as not to startle his friend as he approached.

Randi glanced briefly over her shoulder at Jack as he trudged through the sand, but made no effort to speak.

Jack climbed to the top of the small rise and, unsure what to say, chose to examine the expanse of stars and sweeping vista of moon-shadowed dunes. As his vision adjusted to the darkness he glanced surreptitiously at Randi to gauge her mood.

She caught him and cut her eyes scornfully. "You look guilty, Warner."

"I feel guilty. Listen, I'm sorry about what happened. I swear I had no idea they would pull this stunt. Are you going to be okay with this?"

She responded with a mirthless chuckle. "You're concerned that little Miss Cole has her feelings hurt. Is that it?"

Jack wasn't sure where the conversation was headed. "I know you were counting on flying in the competition, and to have this happen . . . well, it's so unfair." He put his hand on her shoulder. "Can't you look at me, Randi? You understand that our friendship is more important to me than this stupid job, don't you?"

Instead of responding, she slipped out of his grasp and headed down the face of the dune away from the compound.

He followed her down the slope into a small depression. "Randi, we really should be getting back. Let me buy you a drink, and we can talk this out."

"Cut the crap, Jack."

"Pardon?"

"You heard me. Sit down." She turned and, with a quick jab to his chest, pushed him backward into the dune. "We only have a few minutes until the goons come looking for us."

"I'm not following you."

"Were you or were you not told to come out here and bring the American woman back inside?"

"Yes, that's true. But Major Khalim was simply doing me a favor. He didn't want to embarrass you."

"You really don't get it, do you? They're watching, bright guy, because they don't trust either of us. And right now, Khalim is having a cow because we're out of sight, and unless you're wearing a wire, out of listening range as well."

"A wire? Get off it! There's no way I'd do that. Besides, why the hell would they care what we're talking about? I think your imagination is working overtime."

"Jack, I know you don't buy that I was grounded because I'm a woman. And I know you don't want to hear this, but this competition you're running is a sham."

The words stung. "I don't think this is getting us anywhere."

"Jack, I was bumped at the eleventh hour to torpedo the Super Hornet team. What other reason could there be? And don't even try to tell me that you think for one second the Israeli team has a snowball's chance in this desert."

His face flushed with anger, Jack didn't trust himself to speak.

"You've always said that you deal in facts. Here's a fact for you: These guys are supposed to be evaluating our jet as a contender for a multibillion-dollar acquisition, right?"

Jack nodded.

"Then why don't we have Saudi engineers crawling all over us? Where are their maintenance technicians? How come we couldn't find anybody who wants to examine our technical documents and training materials? I'll tell you why, buddy." She leaned forward until their faces were inches apart. "They have no intention of buying our machine. And unless I miss my guess, they already know precisely which one they *will* buy."

"Do you have any proof?"

"I know that the State Department caved in without a fight and muzzled my team in the process. But to answer your question, no, I don't have any proof. But I can feel it here, Jack." She patted her stomach.

"And this elaborate conspiracy accomplishes what, exactly?" Jack instantly regretted his sarcasm.

"I don't know yet. But then, I'm not the Pulitzer-winning journalist, am I?" She stood up, hands on hips, putting the challenge between them. "I'm just a pilot without a ride."

The sound of an approaching vehicle brought Jack to his feet. "Okay. You have my word. If there's something going on here, I'm going to find out about it. But you've got to stay out of it. Promise me you'll leave this to me."

"I can't promise that, Jack. But I will be careful."

"Mr. Warner? Lieutenant Cole?" It was Khalim calling from the other side of the dune. He did not sound pleased.

Randi nodded as if to say, "See?"

"We're down here, Major," Jack answered. "It's a good thing you came to get us; I'm freezing out here." He'd heard enough. Pulling her head to his shoulder, he whispered, "Squeeze your eyes hard; pretend you've been crying."

PART 2

EVENT ONE

INDIVIDUAL AIR SHOW

CHAPTER 12

Shaybah Airfield/1250

Nearly all the guests chose to brave the heat to observe the first event in person. Dressed in loose-fitting cotton and silks, they mingled under a huge Bedouin tent that shaded their gourmet lunch and refreshments. Most were sporting the pocket-sized German binoculars they'd found in their welcome package. Discreetly placed racks held designer sunglasses and team ball caps available for the taking. As they waited for the F–22 to kick off the competition, conversation centered on the first-class accommodations. The consensus held that the king was a generous and elegant host.

Each aircraft would have a maximum of ten minutes to showcase its strengths. Show center, a mere kilometer from the tent, was marked for the pilots by one of the luxury buses that brought the guests from Riyadh. At 1300 precisely, an announcement invited the attention of the guests to Hangar Number One. On cue, the large, black, almost sinister shape of the Raptor dramatically taxied up the ramp, emerging from the desert sand as if conjured by magic.

Captain Steve Whitefoot squinted in the bright sunlight, but his optical-gradient visor quickly adapted. He cross-checked his taxi speed and GPS position against the mission pacesetter displayed on his HUD.

"Alice: systems check," he said, invoking the Raptor's onboard intelligent agent through her programmed persona.

"All systems go, Steve," she replied.

"Roger that. Begin cues." It had taken Whitefoot, a man renowned for his quiet nature, months before he became comfortable with the Alice interface. But Alice had an adaptive personality. Truth be told, he had come to enjoy their exchanges and found himself relying on her honest critique. With Whitefoot, she affected a cool yet reassuring manner that complemented his own. After nearly five hundred flight hours and three times as many in the simulator, Alice knew when he needed prompting and could interpret his subtlest responses with the accuracy of a lifelong spouse.

A glance at the wind sock confirmed tower's report that the winds were less than three knots.

Whitefoot ran the engines up to military power.

"As you know, Steve, our first maneuver is a half–Cuban eight followed by a right-hand three-sixty at two hundred feet," Alice said.

"Copy."

"Brake release in three . . . two . . . one . . . now."

*   *   *

"Look at their faces. They love it."

Jack turned to find Prince Salman at his side. He followed the prince's gaze and saw that, indeed, the guests were enthralled by the spectacle of watching the teams try to outdo one another. Moreover, from what he'd overheard in snippets of conversations, it seemed that each team had developed a loyal following. The aloof elegance of the Raptor attracted some, while the little Lancer jump jet captivated those inclined to root for the underdog. The EuroFighter had its backers, mostly Europeans and Asians, and the KFIR II had earned the crowd's respect with a show so tightly choreographed that the aircraft seemed like it never left show center.

The Super Hornet was up next. Having just gotten the ride, Hoser knew he was at a distinct disadvantage in the choreographed events where practice would add polish. Rather than try to mimic Randi's carefully scripted show, he elected to dust off his old shipboard VIP routine with the added twist of a spectacular opening move.

Unlike his predecessors, he chose not to load the maneuver parameters into the mission computer, relying instead on a neatly composed briefing card held in place on a battle-scarred knee-board strapped to his right thigh. When Randi offered to input the data for him, he responded by tapping the knee-board, and saying, "You can't automate responsibility, missy."

Randi thought he was out of his mind and told him so.

Except for the Lancer, each of his predecessors

had elected to begin his takeoff rolls from the end of the runway and keep low after liftoff to build speed for the first maneuver. In sharp contrast, the Super Hornet was positioned only one thousand feet from the bus, nearly halfway down the runway. To compensate, Hoser had light-loaded the aircraft so that he was only carrying two-thirds the normal internal fuel load. During tests on the team's portable desktop simulator he found that it was the only way to offset the power-robbing effect of the heat.

Randi overheard one guest observe, "Look at him. Is he going to do a vertical takeoff like that little Lancer job?" She found herself wondering the same thing.

"C'mon, sweetheart . . ." Hoser beseeched the jet as he shoved the throttles into afterburner and released the brakes. "We can do this."

The rate of acceleration was eye-popping. Hoser allowed the stick to come aft of its own volition as the airspeed indicator passed through 100 knots. The wheels were off the deck before 120 knots—in a mere 800 feet—well below takeoff speed. Hoser had programmed an additional three degrees of takeoff trim since he had a completely slick jet. As the nose climbed steeply on twin tails of flame belching from the afterburners, he snapped the gear handle up but left the flaps down. In the ascent, the airspeed barely topped out at 150 knots; there were no crushing G forces at that speed.

Conditioned to see the fighters scream down the runway, leap off the deck at the bus, and rocket into the azure sky, the crowd did not fail to notice the dramatic effect of this gravity-defying maneuver. Few breathed, as the Hornet clawed its way upward, moving so slowly as to appear a trick of the imagination.

Randi watched, at first impressed, then concerned, as the Hornet's nose continued to rotate through vertical. She knew very well that at the Hornet's present speed and configuration, it had a dead zone. If Hoser tried to eke out more altitude and thereby allowed the rate of nose movement to slow—even a fraction—the aircraft would quickly lose pitch authority. Trapped on his back this close to the ground, Hoser would find himself in a world of hurt. Even if he were to eject, surviving the attempt would be doubtful.

Hoser planned a cutoff at the top—an educated guess as a no-go criterion—of 1800 feet and 150 knots. Too little speed, and he wouldn't get the nose down; too little altitude, and he wouldn't have sufficient clearance on the back side. The key, he knew, was patience. He had to allow the jet to fly as cleanly as possible and avoid the almost overwhelming temptation to overcontrol it at that top. Finessing the stick, while hanging in the straps, he craned his neck back to look through the top of the canopy and found the runway centerline. He was gratified to discover that a lack of wind had kept him on course, but the proximity of the ground was startling.

"It's now or never," he said, coaxing the machine through the delicate transition.

"My God, Hoser, what the hell are you doing?" Jack was one of the first nonflyers to become alarmed.

"That crazy bastard is going to loop it!" Prince Salman said, before keying his radio handset and speaking urgently. "Khalim? Prepare for a crash; he's never going to make it."

Ironically, while most of the audience assumed that the pilot in front of them was executing a maneuver he'd practiced a thousand times, every aviator watching was stunned. Most concluded they were watching a dead man if the Hornet didn't roll upright into an Immelmann or drop into a half–Cuban eight. None could conceive of a way the fighter could complete a loop from where it topped out.

For Hoser the most difficult part was just beginning. Simple physics dictated that he had to keep the airspeed under control, and that meant he actually had to throttle back as the nose dropped. He had to battle the instinct to keep the power up and pull harder, since the increase in drag would result in a lethal sink rate.

"Warning! Altitude . . . Altitude." Bitching Betty, Hoser's not-so-friendly companion in the cockpit, announced her displeasure. The Hornet's bank of computers—diligently cross-checking all flight parameters—concluded that the pilot did not have a sufficient margin of safety. Unlike Whitefoot and Alice, Hoser and Betty did not get along. She was a nag, plain and simple, and not a very bright one at that.

"Warning! Gear Up!" Another useless interruption, pointing out that the Hornet was low and slow enough to land, but the gear was not down. Betty didn't have a clue that they were in an air show.

"Tell me something I don't know, you bimbo."

The nose passed through the horizon at 1800 feet, with the airspeed pegged precisely on 150 knots. The pull of gravity beckoned the aircraft. Hoser took a deep breath, wiggled the fingers of his right hand, consciously loosened his grip on the stick, and started sliding the throttles aft.

Once committed to the maneuver, all trepidation faded. After all, it made no sense to worry about the outcome. There was nothing to do but hit the numbers and see where it put them.

"He'll make it, dear. Not to worry." Simon Buckingham, who had been hobnobbing with the guests after his own flight in the Lancer, had purposefully made his way toward the good-looking woman pilot. Fascinated with the drama, he assumed she must be terrified and offered words of encouragement. He misjudged.

Randi Cole was furious and in no mood to be patronized. "Worry? About that jackass? I'm not worried . . ." she said without bothering to look at the startled pilot. "I'm pissed! Now, roll it out, you stubborn sonuvabitch!"

Several heads turned at her outburst. She snagged a pair of binoculars from the nearest guest. "Excuse me. I need these." Randi zoomed in on the horizontal tails and was relieved to find them steady at the takeoff attitude. At least he was giving himself a slim chance. "I hope you make this, you old bastard, because if you do, I'm going to kill you."

The engine roar faded to a whisper, halting the buzzing murmur of the crowd. An eerie quiet enveloped the scene as the Hornet approached vertical, its nose pointed directly at the ground at an absurd height. Even the least experienced observer—after mentally projecting the flight path of the aircraft—could see that it was too close to call.

A siren's wail pierced the silence. The lead truck from Khalim's crash crew responded as ordered. Despite the desert heat, the foreshadowing of catastrophe sent a shiver through the crowd. Gasps from startled guests rippled down the flight line. A few covered their eyes. Most stood transfixed.

As the nose of the Hornet tracked through vertical, Hoser smoothly advanced the throttles, once again needing the power to battle gravity. To manage the delicate pull, he focused on the oversize angle-of-attack indicator—an add-on for the flight-test program—which displayed the measure of the angle between the wing's chord and the relative wind. By pegging the needle at the optimum angle, where the difference between lift and drag was at a maximum, Hoser allowed the aircraft to fly as efficiently as possible.

With forty-five degrees to go, Hoser's mind, calibrated by three decades of flying high-performance jets, precisely calculated the descent and pitch rates and concluded that he was two, maybe three feet shy.

He wondered if it was going to hurt much.

* * *

While some witnesses described the last couple of seconds of Hoser's takeoff loop as slow motion, most recalled a blur as the aircraft and ground merged in a flurry of sand and jet exhaust. Others, particularly those with a religious orientation, claimed a divine power intervened.

Even the most objective scientist would say that Hoser was damn lucky. While baking in heat that sapped his engines from delivering maximum thrust, the concrete runway generated a steady column of rising air. As the Hornet entered ground effect—still descending to certain impact—the updraft increased the cushion beneath the Super Hornet's wings. The F/A–18 stopped descending mere inches from the runway, as if reaching the end of a perfectly designed bungee cord.

During the engineers' debrief, it was noted that the digital altitude readout bottomed out at minus two feet. A good-natured complaint about system accuracy was raised, but squelched when the lead avionics technician pointed out that the aircraft was indeed flying that much lower than its parking height.

CHAPTER 13

Strike Flanker/1543

"Ladies and gentlemen, please direct your attention to the end of the runway. Our next competitor is the SU–34 Strike Flanker. The weapons-systems officer is Major Sergei Antoskin, while in the front sits the pilot, Lieutenant Mikhail Zhukov."

The Strike Flanker was dressed in an eye-catching sky-blue camouflage. Massive twin tails offset a sleek, arched-back cockpit. Like the EuroFighter, it sported forward canards, small winglets used for slow-speed maneuvering. Most notable was a two-meter rearward extension that looked for all the world like the stinger on an enormous insect. Though the Russians were closed-mouthed about its function, rumor had it that the pod held the world's first rearward-facing fighter radar.

"Ready, Sergei?" asked Mikhail, as the second hand approached the hour.

"Da."

"Let's rock and roll!"

The instant the brawny motors staged into afterburner, the crowd was forewarned that this was a different breed of aircraft. The engine roar eclipsed anything they'd heard, literally shaking the ground beneath their feet.

Youngest of the pilot cadre, Mikhail—the somewhat pampered son of moneyed parents—had grown up among the Moscow elite on a steady diet of sports, girls, and black-market video games. Single, attractive, and relentlessly happy, he was also fearless, much to the consternation of his copilot, Sergei Antoskin. In contrast, Sergei was married and intent on ending his flying career in one piece. It was his job to keep the hotshot Mikhail from stepping over the edge.

"One-four-zero," said Sergei, calling out the airspeed.

Mikhail kept the aircraft on deck an extra count to compensate for the thrust-robbing heat and lack of wind. Even so, at 150 knots the Strike Flanker fairly leapt into the air. Mikhail raised the gear immediately. When the wheels indicated up and locked, he allowed the nose to rotate until they were pointed straight up, rocketing into the sky.

"Good Lord!" The guests surrounding Jack were drop-jawed at the brute power displayed by the Russian aircraft.

Still pointed upward, Mikhail gracefully pirouetted the fighter 180 degrees. Passing twenty-five hundred feet, he pulled over the top and dropped into a half loop that resulted in the Flanker charging down the runway opposite the takeoff direction.

"Hold on, Sergei."

"*Da*. Two-fifty."

Approaching show center, Mikhail executed the first Cobra maneuver, or "skyhook." Reefing the fighter in a maximum-G pitch that carried the nose up and well past vertical, he held the unusual attitude long enough for the crowd to realize that the jet was actually traveling backward on its tails without losing or gaining altitude. Swirling exhaust smoke contributed to the illusion that the jet was kicking up debris like a skidding ice-skater. When it seemed that the big fighter was certain to tumble out of the sky, Mikhail demonstrated the effectiveness of the canards by pitching the nose back to level. From nearly a dead stop, the jet quickly scooted forward as the afterburners reverberated across the dunes.

A twisting reversal was followed by a slice turn that brought the aircraft perilously close to the ground, drawing shudders and gasps from the audience and a scathing rebuke from Sergei.

An Immelmann—a half-loop climb with a roll-out on top—led to a second Cobra, which Mikhail modified with a ninety-degree pirouette at the top that presented the aircraft's back to the audience as the Flanker skittered across center stage. Another pirouette rolled into a split-S—the bottom half of a loop—to put the Flanker low, headed straight toward the crowd. Mikhail waited until he was directly over the bus before again pulling into the vertical. Once more the aircraft rocketed upward on sheer power, but instead of pulling over the top as the crowd expected, Mikhail held the attitude as the airspeed gradually decayed and the climb stalled. Poised at the top, standing motionless on the big twin tails, the Strike Flanker began to settle, sliding backward, its nose pointed stubbornly to the sky. Few present had observed a high-performance tactical jet perform a hammerhead stall; none had seen the sustained tail slide that preceded it.

The canards twitched, like cat's whiskers, reflecting Mikhail's precise control inputs as he fought to maintain the delicate balance. Pilots marveled at Mikhail's skill, and technicians pondered how the engines kept running without overtemping. At last, to the relief of everyone, Mikhail kicked in a full boot of rudder, slicing the nose toward the ground. Again, he swept dangerously close to the runway before rising once more, but by now, the audience was conditioned to trust the man's infallibility. The spiral transition to landing was gracefully executed, and the feather-light touchdown placed the stinger no more than a centimeter from the runway—a position Mikhail stubbornly held without wavering—as the Strike Flanker slowly drifted past the stunned audience.

There was no need to inquire who won the competition's first event.

CHAPTER 14

Pub/1900

"I really am sorry," Hoser apologized for the umpteenth time. "I shouldn't have put you through that."

After reaming Hoser in the locker room for risking the jet, Randi had given her mentor the silent treatment for hours. It took Jack's intervention to bring them together. Seated at the corner table in the crowded pub, Hoser's beer sat untouched between the two pilots, a testament to his sincerity. Both knew this had more to do with her father's fatal accident—Bill Cole hit the water during an air show a dozen years earlier—than it did with today's competition.

"Damn it, Hoser," she said while angrily brushing aside a stray tear, determined not to let her eyes betray her. "First they ground me, then you nearly splatter yourself and my number one test bird all over the countryside in front of the whole damn world. Besides killing yourself, you would have scuttled the Super Hornet project. Don't you see that you had no right to risk all of that? And don't give me that smartass 'I know you love me, this is all going to blow over' look. We've got some serious problems to straighten out."

Randi leaned over the table, her eyes boring into his. "Unless you can explain to me what would possess you to pull that stunt, in front of all those people, *and* it makes some kind of sense, I'm going to recommend pulling the plug on the whole thing." She was no longer angry; it was the officer in charge speaking.

Joe Santana hadn't received an ass-chewing since his days as a fire-breathing rookie pilot. And to take one from the shavetail daughter of his long-dead best friend and combat wingman was almost too much to bear. He shoved his chair back, intending to get up, pack up, and blow this desert Popsicle stand. Hell, if anyone else spoke like that to him, they would be swallowing their teeth.

But, as suddenly as it flared, his temper cooled. The range of emotions her outburst stimulated in him was completely alien. Amid swirling thoughts, one fact was inescapable: She had a point; he'd almost screwed the pooch.

After a time, he became aware that he was staring at his hands. Suddenly they looked ancient, the mottled skin nearly translucent in places, but worse yet, they seemed disturbingly unfamiliar, as if they belonged on someone else. For the first time, Joe Santana tasted the relentless weight of age. He'd carried the burden effortlessly for so long—each year merely another brick tossed into the pack—that he was stupefied by the accumulation. Now it totaled fifty years; too damn old to cut it so close. Truth be told, he hadn't even admitted to himself why he pushed it so hard right out of the chocks, but it had nothing to do with the fact that millions were watching. In point of fact, he hadn't given the audience a second thought.

"Hoser?"

Her voice, tinged with uncertainty, bubbled up from the depths, eventually penetrating his consciousness. He wasn't even sure she had spoken aloud. A light touch on his bare forearm snapped him alert.

"Uncle Hoser?" A term she hadn't used in years. He recognized the look in her eyes as maternal concern.

He grunted a response, not trusting his voice.

"You've been quiet so long, I thought maybe . . . is everything okay? I didn't mean to . . ."

He'd rather chew broken glass than absorb that look from Randi. Sucking it up, he said, "Look, doll, I apologize. It was stupid, plain and simple. I knew I was rusty and thought I needed an edge. It won't happen again. You have my word. Fair enough?" He held out an enormous hand to shake.

Hoser's plea for forgiveness melted her resolve. Against her better judgment, she took his hand and squeezed it hard. "I love you, you big oaf. But next time I'm just going to shoot you dead."

"Roger that." Relieved, he snagged the beer stein

and washed down the bile in his throat. When he spoke again, the uncertainties were buried, tucked away in a compartment he'd not needed for a long time. "Now let's figure out how we're going to win this damn thing. Even with that showstopper, we're only tied for third."

SECRET DESERT COMPETITION
PITS WORLD'S BEST
PILOTS IN EXOTIC JETS—
WINNER TAKE ALL—
EXCLUSIVE!

Variations of the headline were echoed in dozens of papers. Nearly every publication had it on page one. Some had been printed from the Internet, as for the others, Jack couldn't begin to guess what it cost the kingdom to have freshly printed copies flown into Riyadh and shuttled to the compound. Nevertheless, it was impressive to have proof of the effectiveness of their media blitz in hand. The coverage on the networks was just as effusive. After an hour in the communications center spent trolling through the broadcast media, Jack left instructions to piece together a promo tape for the council, one that showcased the highlights.

The tactic of providing the home country with detailed information about its favorite son had worked beautifully. Even the staid BBC had breathlessly recounted the exploits of Squadron Leader Buckingham. The article hinted, albeit with a stiff upper lip, that his score—which tied him for third with the F/A–18 behind the Russian and the Israeli, but ahead of the Raptor and the dreaded French— was significantly less than it should have been.

Not surprisingly, the scent of jingoism was present in much of what was being reported. Jack was disappointed in his peers since no one had commented on the fact that an Israeli was ranked near the top in an Arab competition. And though he'd been alert—after watching the day's event firsthand—Jack had not discovered any basis for questioning the fairness of the judging. As for the press, with tomorrow's event being a live-fire demo against real aircraft, the hooks were set to keep this story on the front burner.

"Mr. Warner?"

"Yes, Major?"

"Everything is on track for tomorrow's event. We have six drones and four spares. All the teams have been issued their ammo."

"Anyone having maintenance problems?"

"Everyone has minor problems." At Jack's look of concern, he added, "It's to be expected. Those aircraft were flown hard today. The Lancer team replaced a leaking actuator and the Russians pulled an engine. They're coming off the engine-test cell now. But all six teams are indicating up and ready."

It was the most consecutive words Jack had heard from the man in months of working together. Resisting the temptation to say so, Jack nodded his reply.

"Prince Salman requests you join him in the casino control room."

"Thank you, Major. Please pass to your folks that they are doing a superb job."

"Yes. Of course."

"Wonderful. Oh, Major?"

"Yes?"

As casually as he could, he asked, "Have we spotted any threats to security?"

Khalim waited a beat before answering. "No, we have not. Why do you ask, Mr. Warner?"

Khalim had a police officer's distrust of any inquiry. His scrutiny made Jack uncomfortable. "Just curious; worrying goes with the job."

"I see."

The control room was packed with monitors displaying various camera angles covering the casino. Action appeared heavy. In addition to traditional Las Vegas games, guests were encouraged to bet on the competition in every conceivable way, from picking the eventual winner to predicting the results for each event.

"Jack!" Half a dozen heads turned to follow the prince's gaze.

"Your Highness." Jack bowed his head, careful to demonstrate proper respect.

The prince caught himself before becoming too familiar in front of the crew. "Come look at the board."

The electronic tote board, which displayed the running totals summarizing betting on the competition, was changing so rapidly, Jack had trouble discerning the total. When he did, it was impressive.

"Five million dollars? Already? Oh, this must include the Internet tally, right?"

The prince laughed amid smiles from the staff. "No way, amigo. This tidy sum comes courtesy of these deep-pocketed guests of yours. And we've only been open a few hours! They haven't even warmed up; most of the action is on tomorrow's competition. We've got another two million from the Internet, but we're expecting that to take off when the morning papers hit." The prince signaled Jack to follow and led him to the farthest corner of the room. The workers discreetly busied themselves to give the bosses some privacy.

"Jack . . . the council is very pleased. We are well ahead of even our most generous estimates. My uncle called to pass on the king's personal congratulations. How does it feel to be the most popular Anglo since Lawrence?"

Jack grinned, but his stomach—a reliable barometer for trouble—did a familiar flip-flop. The effusive praise, so out of character for his hosts, made Jack wary. Not for the first time he had the gnawing feeling that the stakes were much higher than he was aware. "Thank you. I'm thrilled it's working out."

"But?" The prince was astute. He picked up on Jack's restraint.

Jack instinctively parried the question. "Forgive

me for being conservative. I come from the old
school. It's too soon for me to stop worrying. A million and one things could go wrong. For instance, we
might have easily lost a jet today."

The prince nodded, accepting the explanation.
Yet another old woman. "Very well, my friend. You
go ahead and be pessimistic. But this thing has taken
off. As for a crash . . . well, I think we've reached a
point where a mishap would only spur interest." Seeing
the reaction on Jack's face, he quickly backtracked.
"Take it easy, big guy, that was just an observation.
We're going to do this safely." Escorting Jack out to
the casino floor, the prince leaned close, and whispered, "Try to enjoy yourself a little, my friend. We
could all wake up dead tomorrow, right? Trust me,
this kind of opportunity is a once-in-a-lifetime
phenomenon."

"Son, I've been around airplanes all my life, and I've
never seen a jet do the things you made that sumbitch
do out there today—hell, none of us have. Where'd
you learn to fly like that?" Surrounded by smiling
fans, Mikhail was holding center court at the pub.
The American businessman, on his third Stolie in
honor of his new hero, posed the question loud
enough that it momentarily stopped surrounding
conversations.

Unlike Sergei, who returned to the hangar after
the first wave of well-wishers, Mikhail welcomed the
attention and had kept the guests entertained with

stories and charm. Pausing for effect, he kept his expression innocent, and replied, "As you know, my country is not rich. We have little money for pilots to practice. But we do get the occasional American tourist." Reaching into his flight-suit pocket, he cupped something in his hand, engaging his audience's curiosity with a fist at arm's length. "Yes, I had no choice but to learn the hard way." With a flourish he displayed his prize. "Off the back of a matchbook cover!"

It took a moment for the joke to sink in. When it did, hearty laughter engulfed the beaming Russian.

"Sounds like you're being upstaged, Buckingham," said Hoser, exploiting the opportunity to pull the Brit's chain.

Simon, himself quite popular with the guests, had taken a break from his meandering to join the two Americans. "Ah, yes, the fickle public." Winking at Randi, he said, "One moment they're hungry for bangers and mash, and the next . . . it's borscht."

"Just so long as they want good old apple pie for dessert," Randi said, clapping Hoser on the shoulder. "We don't care if they try the other cuisine."

"And how about you, Ms. Cole? Are you game to try something with a foreign twist?"

"I'm outta here," announced Hoser. "You two are gagging me."

Simon and Randi watched the big man move through the crowd. Men stepped clear, giving him a wide berth. People were still buzzing about his show, but most weren't sure if he was approachable, a dilemma he did nothing to solve.

"That may be the last real fighter pilot," said Buckingham.

"Do you mean that, Buckingham? Or are you just blowing smoke again?" asked Randi.

Simon looked up sharply, apparently caught short by her reaction. His expression changed from bullshit artist to curiosity as he leaned on the table. "I do blow a lot of smoke here, and I told everyone why. But to answer your question, yes, I honestly think fighter pilots are a dying breed, and our friend Hoser is the best of what's left. I suppose you want to know what makes me say that."

"I might be slightly interested."

Simon chuckled. The more he talked with this woman, the more attractive she became. He genuinely liked her, not a frequent occurrence with the birds with whom he usually sparred. "Well, my dear." His voice assumed the tone of a staid professor. "It is quite elementary. You see, over the course of the twentieth century—as we've become ever more civilized—we've systematically eliminated opportunities for life-and-death competition. Don't laugh, madam. When was the last time you heard of a duel for honor? We see skin divers using shark cages. Rock climbers tether themselves with safety ropes."

"Pilots use parachutes," Randi added.

"Very good! As you Americans are fond of saying, mankind has stacked the deck by taking the risk

out of the game. I contend that the last arena for legitimate competition is aerial combat."

"Why not any warfare?"

"Most combat isn't a fight, it's happenstance.
Like one of your drive-by shootings; nothing fair or
honorable about that! In a dogfight, the opponents
have both chosen to be airborne, and the rule of survival is imposed."

"And that is?"

"Kill, or be killed." Buckingham wasn't smiling
as he said it.

Randi, too, dropped the banter. "You said Hoser
was the last of the breed. What's changed?"

"What hasn't? How many MiG kills have Americans scored since you bagged that Fulcrum?"

"None."

"Righto. And none in my country. Sadly, dogfights rarely happen. In fact, both your Navy TOP-
GUN and the U.S. Air Force Weapons School spend
more time teaching how to avoid a dogfight than how
to win one."

"So what makes Hoser different?"

"Simple. He might be the only one here who
would do this with real bullets and nobody watching.
In fact, I'm sure he'd prefer it that way."

"I'm impressed that you would admit that."

"Why not? I'm an opportunist. I freely admit that,
too. Santana is a pure fighter. When the bell rings he's
off the stool and into the fray, no questions asked. No
matter what the odds." Soliloquy finished, Buckingham sat back and contentedly finished his beer.

"Simon?"

"Yes?"

"I was sure you were going to say the profession was ruined when they let women pilots in."

"No, my dear, of course not. It was ruined when they tacked radar and missiles on our kites."

Randi enjoyed his accent. "Missiles" was pronounced, *mis-aisles*. "And women pilots?" she asked.

The antagonist returned. "I only see one problem with women pilots."

"I know I'm going to regret asking this. What, pray tell, is that?"

"Well, it's a simple matter of anatomy and physics, my dear. You see, every time a woman flies inverted . . ."

"She has a crack up." Randi finished the punch line of the old joke. "You boys need some new material," she said as she stood to leave.

Buckingham caught her eye, and with a raised eyebrow, wordlessly suggested they retire together.

She could have pretended to ignore it, but she was tempted. "Not tonight, Squadron Leader. Besides, I haven't spent any time with our extremely attractive Russian comrade."

"Ouch. That shot was below the belt, Lieutenant."

Walking past, she stopped, leaned over, and placed her face inches from his. Her eyes scanned his face, her lips—slightly apart—beckoned. Uncertain, he responded, but as he leaned forward, she pulled back another inch and smiled wickedly.

"There's one last arena of competition left. And you, sir, are an unarmed man." With that, she spun on her heel and left, towing his appreciative gaze and laughter in her wake.

"There is one other thing that has caught my attention, Governor." Khalim had already briefed the elder on the activities of key guests.

"Go ahead."

"Warner and that woman pilot have been talking, but they are being careful to hold their conversations where they cannot be easily observed. I consider their behavior suspicious."

"Don't you think she is still trying to convince someone to let her fly in the competition?"

"Perhaps . . ."

"What is it, Major? I've learned to trust your instincts."

"I am humbled by your confidence, Governor." Khalim kept his head bowed a moment longer until he'd eliminated the effect of the unexpected compliment from his expression. "She has the look of someone who is searching for answers."

"You're right to be concerned, Major. But not about the pilot; she is merely a woman with hurt feelings—no more. We must be focused on Warner. Increase the surveillance on him. I want a nightly report on his activity. And, Major?"

"Yes, Governor?"

"Notify me immediately if there is a meeting

between Warner, this woman, and the prince."

Khalim, attuned to subtle undercurrents, risked probing. "The prince? Is there anything, in particular, I should know, Governor?"

"Yes. Trust no one."

PART 3

EVENT TWO

LIVE
SHOOTDOWN

CHAPTER 15

Official Standings after Event One
1. **Strike Flanker**
2/3. **Lancer and Super Hornet (Tie)**
4. **KFIR II***
5. **Raptor**
6. **EuroFighter**

* 10-point penalty assessed

The order in which teams would fly for each day's competition reflected the previous event's finish. Hence, the morning of Day Two the Russian team found itself with the dubious honor of drawing first blood. Presumably the other teams would benefit from watching, with the greatest advantage going to the last-place team.

Both the objective and rules for event two were deceptively simple. Each aircraft would enter the range, take position on the northern station, and await a vector toward a target aircraft that was being remotely piloted toward them. The clock would start when the two aircraft reached twenty kilometers' separation and would stop when the target hit the ground in flames. Shortest time to kill would win.

The devil was in the execution. No missiles were allowed. It was a guns-only event. And despite the technical advances in developing radar-assisted gunsights, the physics of putting rounds into a moving target were sufficiently complex that aerial gunnery remained a definitive test to judge a fighter pilot's skill.

On Jack's advice, Prince Salman had hired an obscure American company to convert ten surplus Jaguar jets purchased from Oman into remotely piloted drones. It turned out to be an inspired choice. The small band of mechanical, airframe, and engine specialists fell to the task with abandon. A couple of veteran pilots were hired to fly the drones remotely from the command post. Configured with wraparound screens blending live video and three-dimensional computer-generated graphics, the virtual cockpit enabled the pilots to direct high-G maneuvers without breaking a sweat.

The Jaguar was an ideal candidate for modification. Small and built to withstand the rigors of low-altitude combat, the Brit bomber was renowned for its ability to take a beating. However, the boxy-looking machine that had been built in the seventies but survived to see combat duty in Desert Storm was not known as a maneuverable dogfighter. With a green light to enhance the performance of the drones, the Americans, led by a no-nonsense retired Navy maintenance officer, orchestrated a remarkable transformation. They began by pulling all unneces-

sary equipment and stripping each Jaguar's wings
and fuselage of drag-inducing hardware.

Jack had first met Garry Goff, the company's
founder, several years earlier during a high-profile
Navy mishap investigation. Goff, the son of Kansas
farmers, was every bit as taciturn as Khalim. Though
friendly, Jack and Garry hadn't exchanged more than
a few dozen words in the month the company had
been on-site. But Jack was pleasantly surprised when
he took a chance and interviewed Goff about the target drones for his Internet broadcast. For once, the
man couldn't keep his enthusiasm in check.

"Garry, our audience has got to be wondering
what could possibly make this vintage aircraft a challenge for the highly sophisticated fighters we have in
the competition. Can you describe what your group
has done to give these teams a run for their money?"

"Well . . . that's a good question, Jack. You see,
the Jaguar has a couple things going for it already.
It's small and has two afterburning engines. Heck, it
scoots at nearly eight hundred miles per hour on the
deck—that's better than some of these machines
you're evaluating here. But you're right, it was built
as a bomber and couldn't tussle with these fighters,
especially in the state we got our Jaguars—which
was damned . . . uh excuse me, darned sorry, if you
know what I mean. Well, let's just say they'd seen better days. Anyhow, first thing we did was to pull
everything off and outta them that wasn't needed for
drone work. Lightened 'em up considerable: 'bout
fourteen hundred pounds apiece. Now, you take a

look at their wings; used to be, they were covered with weapons stations and pylons. When we got done, they were as slick as a baby's butt."

"I take it that means they can go faster?"

"Well sure. But that's not the real payoff. Where less drag will really count is when these old boys of mine start yanking them around. For starters, they won't slow down, what we call, bleed airspeed, as much. But it goes way beyond that. You understand what I'm saying? Cause what speed they do lose, they'll gain back even that much quicker."

Goff picked up a pair of hand-sized models, angling them so the camera could zoom in for a comparison. "Look here, Jack, think of it this way: For every pound we shave off, we get a triple boost in better performance, endurance, and maneuverability. When the weight we remove reduces drag as well, the benefits go off the scale. For instance, yesterday—after talking with the manufacturer—we were able to bump up the G load. These old airframes we got here can now take nearly ten Gs apiece."

"That is impressive, Garry. I'm not sure that any of the manned aircraft in the competition can pull that much, and even if they can, I'm pretty sure the *pilots* can't. Is there anything else up your sleeve?"

"Well, as you can see, we got 'em painted in a nasty desert-camouflage scheme. Fact is, it's so effective I have to count them every mornin' to make sure they're all still on the ramp." Goff added a wink for the camera. "Then, of course, we did a little tweaking on the motors. Since they don't have to last too long, we're able to bump up the exhaust temperature. That alone ought to improve the thrust by twenty percent."

"Garry, I'm beginning to think the teams are in for a rude awakening if their pilots are expecting the old Jaguar. Is there anything else our audience should watch for?"

Goff looked over his shoulder and leaned closer as if to tell a secret. "Well, I guess I can share this one, as long as you keep it between just us, that is."

Jack was stoked. Who would have thought his crotchety friend would be such a natural on the air? "Garry, I give you my solemn word that our conversation is just between us . . . and a few million of our best friends."

"Well, all right. Long as it's in the family. See, what we did was install a high-capacity chaff dispenser in the upper fuselage. When the pilot hits this button on the console, a couple dozen chaff rounds will be ejected. Chaff is nothing more than foil ribbons cut to a certain length depending on the radar you're trying to fool. The system we got here will explode enough to make a whole darn chaff cloud. It'll confuse the heck out of their radar gunsights. With any luck, we're going to see which one of your boys can shoot straight without all the fancy electronics."

CHAPTER 16

"Sergei, have you got that piece-of-shit weapons system working?"

"Yes, Mikhail. And the new engine and your avionics?"

"It is a miracle. Everything seems to be in order."

"Shall we test-fire the gun?"

"Yes, of course."

The thirty-millimeter gun, biggest in the competition, was a beast. The projectiles were as big as a man's fist. What it lost with a relatively slow rate of fire, it made up for in terrific knockdown power. One round could punch a bowling-ball-sized hole in any airframe.

The big fighter shuddered from a staccato burst.

"God damn it!"

"What is it, Mikhail?"

"Those cretins did not load the tracers properly. Instead of one every ten rounds, they loaded them all together. I've got none left!"

"And this surprises you, my young friend? Last night, I found two men on the job with flasks of vodka tucked into their pockets, but I was so busy supervising the engine change that I couldn't watch the ammo loaders." The rebuke was clear but left unstated.

"You're absolutely right, Sergei." Mikhail's tone was sincere. "I should have been in the hangar helping instead of in the pub. I'm sure you did your best. We will make some changes when we land, I promise. For now, my friend, let's go have some fun, okay?" Contorting his right arm to reach behind him, over the back of the seat, Mikhail extended his gloved hand, palm up, and smiled contritely in the mirror.

"*Da.*" Sergei slapped hands with his hotshot pilot. "Now if you don't mind, please take hold of the stick."

"Strike Flanker on station, ready to play," radioed Sergei.

"Roger that," replied the controller. "Vector one-eight-zero for forty kilometers, angels medium."

Sergei located his prey easily. "Contact one-eight-two for thirty-eight, thirty-five hundred meters."

"That is your target."

"Mikhail, offset west. Come right two-one-zero."

Mikhail made the cut and dropped the Strike Flanker's altitude to get below the target. They'd agreed to offset west to negate a first move by the target into the excruciatingly bright morning sun.

"He's jinked into us, Mikhail, and descended."

"They're not going to let us get any angles, Sergei. Let's just put him on the nose."

"Agreed. Come left one-seven-zero. Range . . . twenty-eight. Angels three thousand meters."

"Flanker, the range is green," said the controller. "Cleared to arm, cleared to fire."

"Flanker armed and ready."

"Stand by for countdown."

"This is incredible, Jack," Randi whispered. "The graphics combined with the sound and video make it almost surreal." They were seated in the upper tier of the domed theater. Above their heads, images of the aircraft streaked toward each other while the audio from the Russian cockpit was piped over the sound system. Projected along the base of the dome were live camera feeds from both cockpits and the range cameras. A graphic listing the results from event one was projected next to a digital clock that would record time to kill for the day's event.

"Our guests seem to like it, don't they?" Jack asked.

Spectators filled every seat. Excited conversations stopped abruptly when the countdown began.

"Flanker, your countdown: three . . . two . . . one. Good hunting, gentlemen."

"Copy."

For several seconds nobody spoke. In the dome, heads turned quickly from one side to the other as the audience tried to track everything at once.

"Mikhail, he's at four hundred fifty knots and holding three thousand meters, at fifteen kilometers. Have you got him in sight?"

"Yes."

At a combined speed of over nine hundred miles per hour, the gap closed in less than forty seconds from the time Mikhail first glimpsed the target. During the interlude, the sound engineer blended a steadily increasing jet-engine audio feed that built to a crescendo as the jets merged. The clock read fifty-eight seconds as they passed.

Immediately, both aircraft pitched up and into each other in violent nose-high turns.

Mikhail was surprised. He'd expected the Jaguar to slice nose low, a classic technique that preserved airspeed. Instead, he found himself wrapped up in a phone booth with a very aggressively flown adversary.

"What the hell?" Mikhail was shocked to see the Jaguar trying to early-turn on the next merge. The bastard was pulling hard, directly into the vertical, obviously to build nose-to-tail separation. Amazingly, the Strike Flanker was defensive.

"Mikhail?" Sergei's voice held surprise. He was virtually helpless in the back cockpit in the close quarters of a knife fight.

Mikhail's labored breaths had the audience cringing. Impossibly, the drone was gaining angles. Both his training and instincts told Mikhail to drop the nose, disengage, and pitch back for a neutral start before he dug himself into a hole, but he refused to sacrifice the time. Truth be told, he would rather die in a fireball than lose to a drone.

Going for broke, Mikhail matched the Jaguar's move. Side by side, the two aircraft were mirrored as they climbed straight up. Both were committed; the first to drop his nose would offer tailpipes to the other.

Sergei was struck by the absurdity of the empty cockpit not fifty meters away. The only two-man crew was getting its butt kicked by the no-man crew.

The airspeed bled off quickly. Mikhail was prepared to tail-slide as long as necessary, risking engine failure, even midair, to outwait the Jaguar.

For his part, Charlie, the drone pilot, was impressed with the Russian's skill and guts. And he had a problem that was only going to worsen. Even with the sophisticated electronics, the time lag between when Charlie made an adjustment via the console and the subsequent activation on the drone was enough to prevent the ultrafine control needed to hold the nose perfectly still. Electing to slice-turn out of the maneuver, he made an understandable, but nearly tragic mistake of not realizing that in a tail slide the rudder would still work, but in reverse. It was a lesson he learned the hard way when he kicked in a bootful of right rudder to drop the nose away from the Flanker and the Jaguar sliced left instead.

Mikhail, Sergei, and the spectators were treated to a heart-thumping moment where collision seemed unavoidable.

"Watch out!" It was all Sergei could think to say as the Jaguar's nose tilted menacingly toward them. He knew that Mikhail had little control authority. Clearly, the aircraft were going to impact, the question was just how hard. Desperately hoping it would miss the cockpit, Sergei reached for the ejection handle.

Mikhail well understood the phenomenon of reverse rudder. In fact, a part of him relished the fact that only he had the awareness to anticipate it and the skill to avoid a collision. Completely twisted around in his seat, he held the aircraft in position for a moment, calculated the arc that the Jaguar's nose would follow, and pirouetted the big machine with subtle inputs translated into movement by the canards.

Like a football slitting the uprights, the Jaguar's nose passed cleanly through the tails of the Flanker. No contact was made, though the audience was treated to a camera angle so close that rivets could be counted.

Mikhail pounced. He ruddered out of the slide to drop in behind the rapidly accelerating drone, selected the dogfight mode on the radar, and was rewarded with a quick lock and an in-range cue as his gunsight settled nicely on the fleeing target. In a moment his thirty-millimeter cannon would rip the drone into shreds.

Since his partner was still shook-up by the near

miss, Pat, the backup drone pilot, reached across the console and hit the chaff button.

The enormous burst of chaff was clearly visible and had predictable results.

"What the hell?" Mikhail watched helplessly as his gunsight meandered aimlessly even as the drone picked up speed.

The drone pilot feinted right, then snap-rolled left and put the Jaguar into a deep, high-G spiral.

Pulling to the limits of the Flanker's airframe, Mikhail could just match the turn. Until the Jaguar eased his G-loading or ran out of altitude, there was no way to gain enough angles for lead. The clock read one minute fifty-two seconds.

"Passing three thousand meters," said Sergei, his voice reduced to guttural bursts as he strained against the G forces.

"I have it," replied Mikhail, letting his partner know that he was aware of the altitude and their rapid descent.

"Good lord, Jack. He's taking him straight down. What's the knock-it-off altitude?" Randi asked.

"There isn't one."

"Oh shit."

Since the Strike Flanker was in the driver's seat, the view in the dome was from the Russian cockpit. It was obvious to everyone how the corkscrew tactic kept the gunsight buried in lag behind the Jaguar's tailpipes. Nor could they miss the horizon filling rapidly with desert.

"Mikhail, pull up! Do it!"

After twenty years in the military, Sergei knew how to bark an order. Mikhail reacted immediately and disengaged from the pursuit. Even so, the Strike Flanker passed through three hundred meters with the nose still having twenty degrees to go. They would make it, but both men knew another second would have planted them in the desert sands.

The Jaguar reacted crisply to the ten-G pull. Since the drone's mission was merely to survive, the pilot leveled out and accelerated, awaiting his foe's next move.

After two such close calls in rapid succession, most pilots would certainly have called it a day and been relieved to do so. The thought of quitting didn't occur to Mikhail. Even as the Strike Flanker bottomed out a mere twenty meters above the desert, he reacquired visual contact with the fleeing drone and pitched his fighter after it, commanding the radar into a boresight mode. Rewarded with a quick lock, Mikhail ignored the engine over-temp warning—his third in three flights—and lined up behind his target. The

Flanker's cannon was installed with a two-degree look-up angle to help reduce the amount of lead required in a turning fight. In this case, it provided much-needed loft to carry the rounds downrange.

Intending to put a thousand rounds on the target, Mikhail squeezed the trigger and was rewarded with a brief burst of gunfire.

The litany of mixed English/Russian curses emanating from the Flanker was so profane that the sound engineer had to cut the audio feed to the dome.

The gun was jammed.

Fifty-four rounds, each nearly as big as a beer bottle, left the muzzle of the thirty-millimeter cannon and traveled blindly across the desert. Fifty-three eventually fell harmlessly into the sand below. One barely grazed a piece of metal before tumbling and joining the others. Hardly a penetrating blow, the damage to the Jaguar's right elevator was slight, merely cosmetic. Jags in combat had taken far worse in stride. But timing and altitude combined to make it a mortal blow.

The drone pilot had commanded an aggressive jink in the split second before the Russian's cannon round arrived. A second earlier, and the target aircraft would have escaped unharmed, able to fly circles around his toothless foe. A second later, and the drone would still have survived with minor damage. But the bobble from the impact amplified the effect of the control input. Not realizing that he'd been nicked, the drone pilot overreacted, his movements abrupt because of the proximity of the desert. The problem compounded when the correction was delayed by the radio link. Another input was sent even before the effect of the last one was realized.

Flight-accident investigators have a name for it. They call the phenomenon, *Pilot Induced Oscillations*, or PIO. In textbook fashion, the drone pilot's corrections grew in amplitude as he fell out of synch with the flight controls. Pilots have a name for it, too. They call it killing snakes in the cockpit, since the stick tends to move in ever-larger swipes. The recovery is simple to teach, but ever so hard to execute. A pilot must let go of the stick. Invariably, the aircraft will settle down. But only if the pilot is out of the loop.

Mikhail's disgust turned to delight when the drone began to wing-rock. After what seemed like an eternity of ever-worsening gyrations, a wingtip caught on a dune top, and the Jaguar cartwheeled into a spectacular fireball.

"Target destroyed."

Mikhail marveled at Sergei's calm and matter-of-fact tone of voice.

"Copy, Flanker. Time hack is five minutes thirty-four seconds . . . good shooting."

"Mikhail?"

"Yes, Sergei?"

"Did you shut down that engine?"

"Yes, I did."

"Good. Please take me home now."

CHAPTER 17

"Salman here."

"Have you made the change?"

"Yes, Uncle. We just made the announcement. I still think this wasn't a good . . ."

"Read it to me."

"Yes, Governor." The prince snapped his fingers and was handed the announcement that had sent a ripple of shock through the compound and even now was being downloaded by the Internet audience. He spoke in measured tones:

"We regret to announce that the Israeli team has incurred a penalty resulting from exceeding the allotted time for the aerial demonstration. This violation of the rules was not caught until our judges reviewed the videotape. In the interest of fairness, we have no choice but to assess the prescribed ten-point penalty. The new standings are: First place, the Strike Flanker; tied for second place, the Lancer and the Super Hornet; now in fourth place, the KFIR II, in fifth place, the Raptor, and in sixth place, the EuroFighter.

All gambling payoffs will be recomputed and your accounts adjusted accordingly."

"Very good. Have there been any problems?"

"Not yet. Warner broke the news to the KFIR team a few minutes before the announcement."

"And?"

"He says that both the pilot and team leader acted as if they expected it."

"May they choke on their arrogance! Nevertheless, we have already been in contact with the Israeli consulate and conveyed our sincere apologies."

"You're kidding!"

"I do not make jokes in matters of state, Nephew."

"Forgive me . . . but apologizing! To them? How can we . . . ?"

"Because we must keep up appearances. Of course none of this would have been necessary if your drone pilots had not run amok. General Majeed himself says that any fighter pilot in the Saudi Royal Air Force could beat the time of the Russian."

"But I explained that. It's not that easy to hit a . . ."

"We are not interested in excuses. It was supposed to be easy. These imbeciles you hired are making it too difficult. And, may I remind you, we're paying them quite handsomely to do it."

"I understand your deep concern, Uncle. But I must ask that you trust me. If it was this hard for Zhukov, everyone else will struggle, too."

"I'm afraid that is not good enough. We cannot afford uncertainty. Now, go make sure your hired guns understand their responsibilities, then call me with your report."

The line went dead.

Nobody was happier with the news of the KFIR's penalty than Simon Buckingham. Without lifting a finger, he'd moved up to a tie for second place. And clearly the Russian team had struggled in the second event. With a little luck, he would take the lead and never look back.

Having flown Jags for years, Buckingham had climbed all over the drones yesterday and even plied the mechanics with binoculars and sunglasses he'd liberated from the guests to get the inside dope. The upshot was that he already knew he couldn't out-muscle the little bomber; he hatched a plan to out-finesse it instead. By bringing the fight down low, his vectored thrust would make a difference. And for that, he'd need exceptional endurance and a little trickery.

With Charlie back at the controls of the drone, a rebuke from the prince still stinging his ears, the two aircraft met at four thousand meters. Charlie executed a slightly nose-low turn and waited to see what the Lancer pilot would do. To the surprise of knowledge-able witnesses—including Randi, Kohl, and White-foot—Buckingham matched the Jaguar's maneuver.

"What the hell is he doing?" Randi asked.

"Is he making a mistake?" asked Jack, unsure why the Lancer's move was unexpected.

"He ought to know he can't match that guy's sustained turn rate. That drone's going to eat him up. And while that happens, it's going to hurt like hell."

Sure enough, the crowd watched as the two aircraft circled. The Jaguar gradually gained angles on every turn.

Inside the Lancer, Buckingham fought mightily against unrelenting high-G load to keep sight of his foe as the drone, sliding from nine, to eight, and then to seven o'clock, moved into the kill zone. It was a brutal experience shared by those listening as his breathing, piped over the dome's audio system, became ever more labored.

"He sounds as if he's giving birth to twins," someone said, to the nervous chuckles of nearby spectators.

Charlie hungered for the kill. His index finger kept tapping the stick where the trigger ought to be. The Lancer was dead meat.

"Good Lord, Charlie, we're supposed to be targets not the shooter," said Pat.

"He can't hit what he can't see."

"Poor bastard. You've been at this nearly three minutes."

"Screw him, that bloke would sell his own mother to win."

*   *   *

The fight had descended to a thousand meters. Simon, who had patiently been sustaining over 7 Gs for nearly four minutes, was nearing the end of his endurance. It was now or never. With a deft move of his gloved hand, he adjusted the exhaust nozzles to vector the thrust down and away from the fuselage, effectively putting on the brakes.

"Oh shit!" Charlie was caught by surprise when the Lancer seemed to freeze and then grow rapidly in his windscreen. He slammed the stick over and attempted a high-G roll away, bleeding off fifty knots in the process.

The jets swapped position so quickly that many in the audience were left to wonder if their eyes had betrayed them. Rather than execute a loaded roll like the drone, Buckingham had pitched his nose forward to dump the Gs and rolled nimbly as the drone lumbered by his right side. The result was that he was positioned inside the drone's turn, nose on, at point-blank range.

The tracers were hardly necessary. Of the 250 rounds fired, more than half found their mark, decimating the target aircraft. The official scorer stopped timing when the biggest of three separate pieces hit the desert.

The clock read, four minutes and three seconds. Simon Buckingham was in first place by nearly a minute and a half.

*   *   *

Jack excused himself when the pager vibrated. He made his way to the casino control room and was met at the door by the kid everyone called Pharaoh.

Motioning Jack to follow him to a monitor in the corner, he whispered, "I thought I'd better give you a head's-up, boss."

At first, Jack found himself matching the kid's dramatic tones. "What is it?" he whispered, before catching himself and restating his question in a normal tone of voice, "What have you got, son?"

"Here. Take a look at the action."

Jack, a touch typist himself, was dumbfounded by how quickly the kid's fingers flew over the keyboard, while on the monitor, page after page of entries scrolled by. "What am I looking at?" Jack asked.

"This is the betting action since the Russian flew this morning. As you can see there are hundreds of entries."

"Who are they?"

Pharaoh tapped out a staccato rhythm. "These accounts are coming in from predominantly the U.S. and Europe. I probably wouldn't have caught it, but you told me to keep an eye out for anything suspicious. Even though they are spread among a wide variety of Internet service providers, there's one thing they have in common."

Warner had to give the kid credit, he knew how to lay out a story—he'd make a good journalist.

"Go on."

"Mr. Warner, every one of these bets is for the max, five grand apiece."

"You've got to be shitting me." Jack did some quick calculations. "What's going on?"

"I think I've found a pattern. That would make it a daemon process." Seeing Jack's puzzled expression, he added, "An automated computer program. In this case it is purposefully chunking out a monster bet into bite-size pieces and spreading those all over. Pretty cool technology. Unless, of course, you think it's plausible that a bunch of moms and pops just decided to max out their credit cards."

"Are the credit-card numbers legit?"

"Yup. And they span the gambit: MasterCard, VISA, American Express, you name it. The numbers aren't sequential, either. I checked."

"But why does it have to be a daemon? Why couldn't it be a bunch of people who were told to lay bets?"

Before spinning his chair around to a second monitor, Pharaoh gave Jack a fleeting glance that could be interpreted as disappointment. But he quickly hid it, if indeed that's what it was. "Check this out," he said while calling up a complex graphic that looked like a pulsating ball of multicolored yarn. "I've done some preliminary analysis. This is a virtual map of the activity in our system. I'm going to isolate only credit-card transactions and color-code those that are in the amount of five thousand dollars in green. This is a playback for the transactions processed an hour ago at triple speed. See if you notice anything."

At first Jack saw only a series of random dots appearing throughout the system. He had no idea what all the squiggly lines meant that periodically bulged and narrowed—he assumed they had something to do with the network—but he was not eager to ask any more questions. Meanwhile, the dots flashed on and off: green, green, red, blue, green, blue, green . . . what the hell was he supposed to see? It wasn't as if they were clustered in one, or even a few locations. In fact the opposite was true; they certainly appeared randomly spaced. Intently, he focused on just one sector. There! It wasn't random at all, he was sure of it. He tapped the screen with each pulse. "There's a rhythm, a beat to their occurrence in each quadrant."

"Excellent, Mr. Warner!" Pharaoh beamed, his confidence restored. "That took me twice as long to figure out. And it wasn't until I ran the tape at triple speed that I saw it. Of course you're absolutely right. These transactions are being fired off on a computer clock cycle. Several actually. I've spotted half a dozen, but there could be more."

"So there are computers out there that are somehow tagging our website, filling out the forms, including a valid credit-card number, and placing bets to the tune of five thousand a pop every few seconds?"

"Yup."

When the next question popped into his mind, Jack was stunned that he hadn't thought to ask it yet. He glanced at the tote board for the answer, expecting to see the odds dropping for a heavily favored team, but the betting profile remained implausibly the same. Although the Russians were favored, they had actually lost ground since their flight this morning. The rest of the pack, with the Raptor in the lead, had closed ranks.

"I give up. Who are they betting on?"

"Strange as it seems, the bets are distributed exactly according to the point spread. What do you make of that?"

"Weird. Whoever is behind it doesn't want to be spotted, but I'll be damned if I can figure out why someone would go to all this trouble if they weren't going to back the eventual winner. Think about the logistics: the computer program, the distribution system, the credit cards . . . it had to take weeks, maybe months, to put together. How about the programming? How good is it?"

"You're looking at pure gold. I'd love to get my hands on it."

The two men made and held eye contact. Pharaoh was eager for the hunt. Jack, the veteran, though wary, was no less committed.

"It could be dangerous."

"I know."

A simple nod sealed their silent pact.

"Where do we start?"

"Lesson one: Start by looking for their motive."

It was an enigma.

*   *   *

Hoser was up next. After watching the Russians from the dome, he, too, had toured the flight line to see for himself the modifications to the Jaguars. After shooting the breeze with a couple mechanics, who needed little encouragement to brag about the hot engines and the chaff bucket, Hoser prepared for a tough fight.

After instructing his partner to slow down the automated betting program by adding a separate e-mail verification process, Jack patrolled the casino. He got an earful while the spectators buzzed about the first two flights. The grumbling about the late penalty had faded with the last flight. He noticed with some dismay that the dome technology was quickly taken for granted. Their appetite for high-tech multimedia was voracious. Conversations centered on the prospects for the other teams. Many in the audience took advantage of the competition to place new wagers, an eventuality the prince's Vegas consultant had anticipated and made convenient by installing betting kiosks nearby. But when the announcer gave a five-minute warning, there was a mad rush as the bettors scrambled back to their seats. The show was a hit.

"Fight's on. Good hunting."

Hoser responded with a double mike click. He was intent upon the kill, not entertainment. Once he had a solid radar lock, he climbed the Hornet steadily. The drone pilot, faced with giving away vertical turning room or matching the climb, chose the latter.

The merge took place at twenty-five thousand feet. Hoser pitched up and into the Jaguar, a move that was again matched by the drone.

The clock read one minute ten seconds.

As soon as he crossed the drone's tail, Hoser overbanked and pulled the nose into a deep slice turn. Having gotten the drone to commit nose high, Hoser would use the extra Gs given by gravity to maximize his turn rate.

"Watch him. He's going down," warned Charlie, now the backup drone pilot.

"Yeah, I see that," replied Pat, who was at the controls for this fight. "We're going straight into an egg."

The drone maintained its arc across the top as the Hornet flew across the bottom. Within twenty seconds they swapped positions. In the dome, it was easy to see why the pilots called it an egg. More speed on the lower half created a bigger turning radius, while at the top, the pilots, using gravity, had the ability to pitch the nose down more sharply.

It was a geometry Hoser intended to exploit. When it came to slow-speed pitch rate, no aircraft could match the Hornet. This was a product of the aircraft's unique design, which placed the horizontal stabilators well aft on the fuselage, behind the vertical tails. As he crested the top, Hoser buried the stick, and the Hornet responded gamely. It cost a bundle of airspeed, but Hoser and the spectators were rewarded with a sight picture framing the Jaguar in his windscreen.

Randi couldn't contain herself. "Nail him, Hoser!" she shouted. Similar cheers echoed throughout the dome; the popular American already had a following. The clock read a mere one minute forty seconds.

Hoser was, above all else, a master of aerial gunnery. Normally, he would acquire a radar lock and let the lead computing gunsight solve the deflection angle. Over the years, he had taught countless students how to shoot by describing the bullet stream as water from a garden hose. To be successful, a pilot had to consider both lead for a moving target and bullet drop due to gravity. Most often these were in two different planes of motion, hence the need for a radar-assisted gunsight. But since he knew to expect radar-confounding chaff, he elected to negate its effect by controlling the angles.

Though he was well out of published range, Hoser had timed it so that the Jaguar was positioned directly below the Hornet, thus neatly solving the problems of both bullet drop and lead. Aiming straight down, the cannon's range was virtually unlimited. And given the lack of a crossing rate, there was no need for a radar lock. It was an all-or-nothing move, since he'd sacrificed all his speed for angles. After carefully maneuvering the gun cross, a fixed symbol denoting the no-gravity bullet flight path, onto the Jaguar, he opened fire.

The Hornet's six-barrel twenty-millimeter cannon spun up in nanoseconds to a sustained rate of six thousand rounds per minute. Each high-explosive projectile was about four inches long and the diameter of a penny. The Jaguar took a couple dozen hits, none more damaging than the round that entered the left engine intake and detonated on contact with the engine fan blades. As metal fragments passed through the rapidly spinning engine, a chunk of white-hot metal the size of a dinner plate detached from the turbine section and burst through the engine casing, severing hydraulic and electrical lines in its wake. It was a mortal blow.

Trailing smoke and flames, the Jaguar tumbled amid debris, much to the delight of the dome audience. Many cheered lustily at the carnage. This is what they had come to see.

"Our hosts aren't going to like this," said Charlie, glancing first at his watch and then at the phone.

"Son of a bitch kicked my ass," observed Pat.

"Have you got any flight-control authority?"

"Not much . . . it looks like I have some aileron, and the right engine is still on line."

"Remember, the clock doesn't stop until it hits the ground."

Pat smiled at the revelation. "Good call, partner." The damage from the exploding engine had decimated the tail of the Jaguar. What was left of the elevators put the drone in a nose-down attitude. Left alone, the drone would have hit the desert in less than a minute, but Pat used his remaining flight-control authority to roll the crippled aircraft inverted and added full power on the right engine. It wasn't pretty, but the drone performed a series of quasi–barrel rolls with the net effect of delaying the inevitable.

Hoser saw for himself that the drone wasn't dying gracefully and tried to position himself for another burst, but the erratic flight path and random debris in its wake made closing too dangerous. He joined the dome crowd as a spectator to Pat's antics.

When the Jaguar finally hit the ground, the clock read four minutes twenty-five seconds.

Whitefoot's muscular torso glistened as he moved purposefully through the kata. The martial-arts routine required a level of precision that demanded total concentration. Whitefoot found the experience meditative. He'd begun the practice in the Academy when beset by ulcers during football season.

Despite his stone-faced persona, Captain Steve Whitefoot was plagued by insecurity. Besides an unruly stomach, insomnia forced him to work until exhaustion before sleep would come. Both conditions worsened as deadlines neared. It was a malady for which he'd learned to compensate by zealous planning and diligent practice. Over the years he'd perfected the formula so that, to the casual observer, he appeared to have ice water in his veins. Nothing could be further from the truth—especially today.

Though he hid it well, Whitefoot had struggled to excel in free-form dogfights since they were too dynamic to script. Fortunately, Air Force training was heavy on doctrine. Air-combat maneuvering was taught in a building-block approach using canned scenarios. In concept, a pilot having mastered the fundamentals would be well equipped to meet any foe. But the peacetime pressures of maintaining flight-safety levels led to a leadership climate that discouraged innovation. Rules of engagement written by staff officers mandated roles of aggressor and defender with the focus upon executing the approved tactical solution. The net result was that training fights flowed predictably, and the outcome was rarely in doubt. Whitefoot thrived in the structured environment. But he had no illusions about today. The rumble in his stomach and yet another sleepless night left no doubt that he was in for the fight of his life. And this time, he was center stage.

CHAPTER 18

While the spectators meandered through the oasis room, enjoyed a gourmet lunch, or added to their bets for the afternoon session, Prince Salman prepared for a televideoconference with the council.

Jack was puzzled by his boss's gruff manner. When summoned to provide the latest tally information, he expected another warm reception.

"We are exceeding all expectations, Your Highness. The casino has already doubled yesterday's take. In fact, with their buddies egging them on, nearly all the winners so far have chosen to let their bets ride. We're recalculating our projections now, but we could be looking at a gross in excess of three times our most generous estimates."

"And the Internet?"

Given the prince's unusual demeanor, Jack decided not to show his cards just yet. He answered as if he'd not spotted the programmed betting. "Beyond expectations. Hold on to your seat, but an hour ago we hit our break-even point. In fact, we've already activated our mirror sites and are scrambling to bring more on line. The appetite worldwide for on-line access to the competition is voracious. And while the subscription audience isn't betting nearly as much per person as our guests, its total will surpass the local tally sometime this afternoon. And just to bring you up-to-date, merchandise orders have been turned over to the American on-line catalog firm we had on contract and . . ."

"What's that? Why wasn't I notified?" The tone was accusatory.

Jack stiffened. Reporter's instincts, honed over years of investigative work, were part of his DNA. It was clear that the prince was being pressured, but for reasons that didn't jibe with the project's stated goals. Given that the whole competition was running smoothly and already a profit-maker, there had to be a hidden agenda.

Jack answered carefully. "We had to divert that traffic off our site to keep the pipes clear. It was an automatic action based on exceeding a threshold. You authorized the procedure, remember?" Jack lowered his voice. "Is there something wrong, Your Highness? Something I can help with?"

For a moment, the prince appeared ready to divulge whatever was bothering him, but he thought better of it. "Just do your job, Jack. Everybody just needs to do his damn job."

"Very well." He was getting closer.

"For two cents I'd tell that arrogant asshole to stick this contract where the sun don't shine," Charlie said.

Pat was more pragmatic. "We should have read that contract better, Charlie. When the good prince showed me that clause about withholding payment for the whole drone contract, I almost dropped my teeth. Our buddies need that money, especially Goff. And I damn sure need the dough. I've already spent half of it."

"Still, he wants us to cheat, Pat . . ."

"Let me put it in simple terms, my friend. Look around you. We're trapped here. These guys could make us disappear and nobody would be able to lift a finger to help. Surely you haven't forgotten how the Saudis stonewalled the investigation of the U.S. barracks bombing a few years ago? And that's with the whole UN on their backs. It's their country, their rules, and nobody is going to give a rat's ass about us. I say, we do it, get our money, and get the hell out of this godforsaken desert."

"That's my plan, too, but . . ."

"But what?"

"What makes you think they'll let us leave?"

"Don't say that. Don't even think it."

"I wish I hadn't."

Moshe Kohl was momentarily stunned when the drone passed down his left wingtip and kept going without making a move. As he cranked his delta-winged KFIR II in a maximum-performance turn to pursue, he radioed his concern.

"Control, KFIR."

"Go ahead, KFIR." He pronounced it *Keefer*.

"The drone is not engaging. Confirm this is intentional."

The friendly voice from the early-morning sessions had been replaced with an authoritative one. "KFIR, the range is green. The clock is running."

Kohl rolled out of his turn, locked the drone, and saw that the Jaguar was just now slicing back toward him. Two kilometers separated the jets. He recognized the classic extend-and-pitch-back fight. Used by U.S. forces in Vietnam, F–4 Phantom pilots developed the technique to take advantage of their forward-firing missiles while keeping their larger, poorer-turning aircraft out of gun range of the nimble MiGs. It was a very effective ploy in combat, particularly over hostile country, and led to the maxim "speed is life." The problem was that neither aircraft had missiles today.

The KFIR II and Jaguar passed again, wingtip to wingtip. Kohl had not gained any angles. Again they reversed course and pointed at each other. This time Kohl tried to early-turn the drone by pitching the nose up, overbanking, and beginning a deep slice even before they merged.

The drone pilot didn't bite. He kept the Jaguar steady for a couple extra beats and pitched back. At the next merge, the fight was back to neutral. The clock read two minutes fifteen seconds.

"Bastards!" Kohl knew precisely what was going on. They were gaming the system to prevent him from getting the kill. Of all the people watching, only a handful would realize what was happening. For most, it would look like the Israeli team simply could not match their counterparts against a high-performance drone.

Kohl's rage quickly gave way to icy detachment. He had to take the drone out. He'd be damned if he'd let them hang the Israeli team out to dry in front of the whole world. The solution, though radical, was really quite simple.

The audience, gaining a measure of sophistication with every session, began whispered conversations about the Israeli's trouble. However, most appraised the difficulty as a pilot-skill problem, unaware that Kohl was being set up.

Jack leaned over and asked Hoser what he thought.

"I don't get it, Jack. With the rest of us, these guys went for the throat. Hell, they almost hit Zhukov. Maybe Buckingham's antics have them wary. Whatever the motivation was for hitting the Israeli team with that penalty, this is total bullshit. With guns, you can't shoot what won't turn."

Randi was equally outspoken. "It's no accident that they're using this tactic against the Israeli team. What I can't figure out is why you are asking us, Jack? Aren't you clued in?"

"I thought I was. I've got to find out who is pulling the strings on this and why."

Hoser put his hand on Jack's forearm. The grip

was powerful, his voice a raspy whisper. "Be damn sure you know what you're getting into."

"I'm not sure I follow."

"You think all this security is just to keep terrorists out? Think again, sport. You do not want these guys to see you as a threat, *comprende*?"

"Okay."

"What's he doing, going home?" asked Charlie as he cranked the Jaguar around only to find the KFIR II still opening distance.

Kohl used a double interval before he pitched back, straining to keep sight. When he had the dot on the horizon in his windscreen, he unloaded to a half G so that the KFIR easily slipped through the mach barrier. As the delta-winged fighter continued to accelerate, he zeroed in on his target.

"I don't know, Charlie. He's got to be really frustrated by now," Pat said.

Kohl put his velocity vector on the drone's nose and held it there. At their closing speed, he had only to wait a few seconds.

"He's got you boresighted, Charlie!"

Kohl surprised himself by not flinching as the jets converged at a combined speed of nearly twice the speed of sound.

The same couldn't be said of the dome audience, or the drone pilots, all of whom cringed at the specter of collision. Traveling among witnesses even faster than the aircraft was the horrifying realization that the Israeli was intentionally going to ram the drone.

Moshe Kohl would have been shocked by the assertion that he'd willingly waste his beautiful jet in such a useless sacrifice. And, of course, he had no intention of dying; he was merely using all the weapons at his disposal. Being a single-engine aircraft, the KFIR II had a highly sophisticated air-intake system designed to control the flow of air into the engine under the most adverse conditions, even when passing through the mach wake of another aircraft. The Jaguar did not.

Kohl wielded the KFIR's supersonic shock wave like a sledgehammer, thumping the hapless drone as the tip of his vertical tail passed within a meter of the Jag's underbelly. The effect was impressive.

Immediately following the near miss, the caution panels in the drone's cockpit lit up like a Christmas tree, while the KFIR II passed through the drone's exhaust wake unscathed.

Sorting through the various warnings, Charlie identified the most serious. "Left engine stall."

Pat read the checklist. "Drop the nose. And shut down the left throttle. We'll need three hundred fifty knots for the restart."

Even as Charlie complied, the audio warning for engine overtemp blasted through their headsets.

"God damn it. Number two just stalled." Charlie checked the status of key systems.

"Better let it hang until we get number one back on line," suggested Pat.

Toggling switches, Charlie was incredulous. "That sonuvabitch did that on purpose!" He glanced at the clock. Three minutes forty seconds. He had orders to stay airborne longer than five minutes.

"Where'd that bastard go?" asked Pat.

Kohl had wasted no time exploiting his advantage. At the pass he pitched the nose up into a half–Cuban eight. Cresting the top of the partial loop, he peered through the canopy to locate his well-camouflaged quarry. He was rewarded by a thin, but discernible smoke trail that fingered the Jag against the desert below. Using the KFIR's narrow-azimuth vertical-scan radar hot mode, he quickly acquired a lock.

"I'm going for a restart on number one, Pat. C'mon baby. Fire up."

"We've got to shut down that right engine, Charlie. It's been in the red for twenty seconds."

"Screw it. Let it cook. Five more seconds, and I can start jinking. Then we'll see how good a shot he is. Besides, I bet he lost sight." He tapped the engine display. "Here we go. We're lighting off."

Kohl waited patiently until the in-range cue flashed. He felt no need to hurry, and little emotion. Having shot down half a dozen MiGs in actual combat made this one anticlimactic. Once in position, the kill was never in doubt.

*   *   *

Charlie commanded a left roll with the stick. The electronic signals were dutifully transmitted, but in the split second that it took them to travel down-range, the drone ceased to exist.

Israeli engineers, constantly seeking to improve the lethality of their weapons systems, had salted the KFIR's twenty-millimeter ammunition with composite incendiary projectiles. Phosphorous-coated zirconium pellets were included to ignite fuel vapor atomized by the impact of conventional rounds.

The effect was a spectacular fireball.

The official scorer held off as long as possible, but the last piece of recognizable debris hit the ground at four minutes nineteen seconds. With two teams yet to fly, Moshe Kohl was in second place behind Buckingham and ahead of the Super Hornet. Much to the consternation of the hosts, the Russians remained in last place.

CHAPTER 19

"Hey, Garry, how goes the war?" Jack asked in response to the drone czar's quizzical look.

"Hi, Jack. Well, we're getting blasted out of the sky on a regular basis, so from your side of the fence, I'd say the war is going just peachy. So what brings you out here to slum with the hired help?"

"Just checking in before the last couple fights. I figure you and your boys are almost out of here, and I wanted to watch one from your side."

"No sweat, GI. Snag a seat and grab a cup of joe. We've got about twenty minutes before show-time."

Jack helped himself and pulled up a chair, casually adding, "And I think you're being modest. Those Jaguars are damn near stealing the show."

Garry's smile froze, then quickly faded. "Is that a problem?"

Jack noted that Garry was expecting a rebuke. "Hell, no! The fights are phenomenal and have pulled in a worldwide audience. Keep putting these teams through the wringer. It's great for business."

"Well, I appreciate your sentiment, Jack, but

we're receiving mixed signals. I'd say there's a disconnect in your organization."

"Can you be more specific?"

"My pilots were visited by the prince and one of Khalim's henchman."

"When?"

"At lunch, just before the Israeli's flight. They won't tell me what was said, but from the way they're acting, whatever it was made Pat and Charlie nervous as hell."

"Well I did notice that the last fight was kind of strange. Any guesses what they were told?"

"I've got my suspicions."

Jack waited for him to expound, but Garry sat back and sipped his coffee, content to let Jack make the next move. Jack shifted gears. "Garry, if you were running a competition like this to pick a new aircraft, what would you do differently?"

"Are you serious?"

"Sure."

Goff seemed to weigh Jack's sincerity before speaking. "Look, you sure you want to hear this?"

"Absolutely. Fire away."

"From where I sit, this whole setup is crazy from the git-go. I'm not sure what the real objective is, but you're certainly not set up to pick the next generation fighter-bomber for this country."

"I'm all ears."

"First off, there's no way the Lancer belongs in the mix. It's a different beast, a short-range weapons system, while these other machines all have long legs."

"Anything else?"

"For the moment, let's assume that the jump jet is a legitimate contender. If I were running this shindig, I'd be a whole bunch more concerned with aircraft maintainability and life-cycle costs than how the jets stack up in a series of jump-through-the-hoop events."

"You wouldn't want the jets to go head-to-head?"

"Not in events where pilot skill is so important. What's that prove? Oh, I'd put them through speed traps, measure their radar cross section, and test their weapons systems, but if I were buying a fleet of the aircraft, I'd be a damn sight more interested in how reliable and easy to maintain they were."

"And how would you judge that?"

"Easy. Break 'em, then fix 'em. You gotta get your hands dirty by performing routine maintenance, like swapping out an engine or hydraulic pump. That way you can see firsthand the quality of manufacturing, check the accuracy of engineering documentation, and actually use the tooling and support equipment. I'd put the jets through some durability tests like flying them on half a dozen successive flights in one day. See how they hold up. And my pilots would fly, not the manufacturer's hired gun. I don't see any of that going on."

"So how do you explain that? Our bosses aren't stupid."

"No, they are not. In fact, I'd say they are about the best businessmen I've ever encountered."

"You didn't answer the question. Any guesses what they're up to?"

"I'd have to say that an *objective observer* would conclude that this competition is not being used to select the best jet on the tarmac. At least not the best jet from the perspective of operating a fleet of them."

Garry's emphasis on the words, objective observer, stung Warner. As a journalist, it was, after all, his vocation. A tremor in Jack's voice revealed his resentment. "Then what are they doing?"

"Why ask me, ace? Isn't it your job to know the inside skinny?" He laughed at Jack's tight-jawed reaction.

"I'm glad you find this amusing," Jack said.

"I wish I had a camera; the look on your mug is priceless." Goff's feet came off the desk as he sat forward to make his point. "Look, buddy, if you want slack, you came to the wrong place. When you decide to quit bullshitting around and tell me why you're really asking these questions, then we can talk."

It had been a while, but Jack vividly recalled the acid sarcasm wielded by career mustang officers like Goff when it suited their purpose. Aboard ship, getting each other's goat was considered an Olympic sport, and Goff was as good as any with a tongue-lashing. "Okay, no games. I really don't know what is going on behind the scenes."

"No shit, Sherlock. What was your first clue?" When he saw that Jack wasn't rising to the bait, Goff throttled back. "You know, I can see those wheels turning in that brain of yours. And if I can, they can, too. Before you get all wound up, mister, you'd best understand your lot in life. This is their ball game, their rules, and their turf. Some questions—hell, maybe all questions about what this crew is up to—are best left unasked. And frankly, as long as they pay up, I don't really give a damn."

Jack knew Garry Goff well enough to know that the man was not easily intimidated. He also suspected that, despite his disclaimer, Goff was bugged by what he saw and was rationalizing the behavior of his drone pilots. He decided not to push it. "Point taken. And thanks, I appreciate your insights. And I promise that I'll keep them to myself."

As they walked to the command post, Goff stopped and spoke with uncharacteristic intensity.

"Jack?"

"Yeah?"

"All kidding aside, I meant what I said. I don't have a good feeling about this place."

"Can you put your finger on it?"

"No, but in thirty years of working in this business I've learned to trust what my wife calls my gutometer."

"That's a new one." Jack poked Garry's belly. "What do you have in there?"

It was Garry's turn not to have a comeback. "I never tell anybody this—and I'll deny it if you shoot off your big yap—but over the years I've grounded a half dozen jets for no other reason than a sour feeling in my stomach. And I'm sorry to say that I've also let a couple fly in spite of it. And I learned to regret it."

"So what is the *gutometer* telling us about the competition?" Though he was trying to keep it light-hearted, Jack surprised himself by how much stock he was putting in the answer.

Garry looked down the flight line, where the last three of his eight drones remained. "Keep in mind, I don't get a vision of the future or anything, just a feeling." He cut his eyes at Jack, checking to see if he was being patronized.

"Believe me, I understand. And I appreciate it. Please go on."

"I think the wheels are going to fall off this cart, my friend."

"You mean like an accident?"

"Could be. Hell, it could be anything. Maybe some wild man will pop over that dune and pound the living crap out of us." He pulled his glasses off and massaged the bridge of his nose. "Ah, for crying out loud, would you listen to me. I've been out in the damn desert too long. I can't believe I brought this up."

"Garry, I'd consider it a favor if you tell me what you're thinking. Out with it. Nobody is listening, and I won't tell a soul."

"Damn it, Jack, I'm not like you, or my wife. I can't really put my feelings into words; that's the problem. It's like . . . like we're in over our heads here. I think people are . . . I think people could get hurt. What with your publicity and the big contract dangling, the stakes are too high. Too damn high for any of these power moguls you got in here, or even the terrorists out there, to leave it to chance. And I can't see our bosses letting you run this thing as a fair fight. There's too much money to be made. I can promise you this much, though. The sooner we wrap this up and vacate this hellhole, the better."

"You think I should leave well enough alone?"

Goff smiled. "Gee, Jack, I don't know why everyone says you're so dumb. That didn't take too long to sink in. Next time, remind me to bring my sledgehammer. In a word, yes. Seriously, you'd better never forget that we're outsiders here."

Though Jack had used virtually the same words in warning Hoser and Randi, hearing them echoed by one of the most levelheaded men he knew gave them added impact.

Garry was still speaking. "If these guys catch you poking around, they're likely to plant your keister out there," he said, nodding to the dunes beyond the compound. "Besides, whose rights are you concerned about? The teams'? Don't bother. You can bet the bigwigs all know the score."

"You really think so?"

"The real competition is going on behind closed doors, buddy. As we speak, you can bet someone's getting squeezed to play ball. This ain't Kansas anymore, Toto . . ."

"Thanks. I'll keep that in mind."

Garry eyed Jack intently for a few seconds. "Why do I get the feeling that . . . oh, never mind. You're hopeless. C'mon, we might as well go watch Pat and Charlie try to pull this out of their asses."

*   *   *

"Alice: prepare to engage. Unarmed single Omani Jaguar, highly modified. Destroy, cannon only. Confirm."

After completing the weapons checks, Whitefoot verbally programmed the automated-dogfight mode. In addition to being programmed for high-G maneuvering flight, the weapons systems and displays of the F–22 would be optimized for close combat.

"Confirmed. Single unarmed category-five aircraft. Cannon only. Destruction authorized. Dogfight modes enabled." The Raptor was ready to play.

Whitefoot tightened his restraints and switched the air supply to 100% oxygen. After a couple deep breaths, he, too, was ready.

"The range is green. Stand by. Three . . . two . . . one . . . fight's on."

The dialogue between Captain Whitefoot and Alice mesmerized the dome audience. "Steve, target heading is steady at three-five-zero, altitude twelve thousand, speed four hundred fifty. Follow HUD cues. Intercept in thirty-five seconds."

"Copy."

The book answer for a one-versus-one turning fight against a high-performance adversary was to employ a mirror tactic. Whitefoot would attempt to match the magnitude of the Jag's first move but in the opposite direction and plane of motion. If the Jag went slightly nose high, Whitefoot would match with a slightly nose-low turn. In what was called a two-circle fight, the objective was to fly the Raptor optimally and either gain angles or watch for the Jag to bleed airspeed for an advantage. The Raptor's next move would depend on the Jag's behavior. It was a classic counterpuncher's tactic.

The black dot in the HUD grew rapidly into a mean-looking, mottled brown fighter. Just before the merge, Whitefoot feinted a left turn.

"He's going left," Pat said. They'd agreed to let Charlie fly the last two missions. Pat would be co-pilot.

"Then so am I." Charlie wracked the drone into a hard left turn, away from the Raptor, the Jaguar's nose tracking ten degrees below the horizon.

"Two-circle, bandit low," Whitefoot notified Alice as he flicked the side-stick control to command a left-hand, nose-high turn. The Raptor's flight controls were commanded to set and hold an optimum turn rate factoring in temperature, altitude, weight, and dozens of other variables. In the dogfight mode, they would function much like an automobile cruise control—the aircraft could hold the turn indefinitely—to pull harder or lessen the turn would require Whitefoot to override by a deliberate and somewhat forceful input. By design, since Raptor pilots would not be required to finesse the pull, they were freed to concentrate on the fight itself.

"He's holding his own, Charlie. And gaining altitude on us."

"I can see that." Charlie bit off the words; he needed help, not a statement of the obvious. The damn F–22 was performing flawlessly, matching his own seven-and-a-half-G pull and climbing to boot.

At the second pass, after both aircraft had completed a full 360 degrees, Whitefoot was gratified to see that he hadn't lost any angles and had gained nearly a thousand feet. All things being equal, that altitude was like money in the bank. He spoke haltingly, combating the Gs with grunting expulsions to remain conscious. "Alice: . . . Target unchanged . . . We're neutral."

In contrast, Alice was unfazed. "Turn rate twenty-five degrees per second, Steve. Prepare to counter."

"Copy."

"What the hell is that boy doing talking when he should be flying?" Hoser asked.

"Shhh . . . keep your voice down," Randi said. They were in their customary seats on the second deck, in what Hoser called the peanut gallery. "And I wouldn't call him a boy, at least not to his face," she whispered. "I read in his bio that he has a black belt."

"Well, I don't care what he uses to hold up his pants, he ought to put a muzzle on that yapping woman."

Randi's head snapped at the insult only to find Hoser grinning in the dark like the Cheshire cat.

"Gotcha!"

"Bite me, old man."

"Time for Plan B."

"Roger that," Pat said.

Charlie released the back pressure on the stick, rolled wings level, and pulled.

"Alice: Target rolling out." The Raptor's heading was opposite that of the Jaguar, but with nearly twelve hundred feet of altitude advantage.

"Continue, Steve."

"Alice: . . . Target going . . . vertical."

"Align heading and follow." Whitefoot had already begun the tactic. He would continue the turn until the Raptor reached a point in the sky where the Jag had pulled through and then match the maneuver. By exploiting his altitude and timing advantage, he could slide in behind the climbing Jag as the fight transitioned from horizontal to vertical. From there he could control the geometry.

"He didn't bite, Charlie." The hope was that Whitefoot would pull directly toward the drone, a common mistake during a transition. By flying a disciplined energy-sustaining fight, the Raptor was capitalizing on every maneuver.

"We can't get slow with the bastard; that damn machine can dance with the best," said Charlie.

"What's Plan C?" asked Pat, as the Jaguar started downhill.

"We see what kind of shot he is."

The clock read one minute forty seconds.

"Target lock. In range, Steve." The egg had gone two full cycles as the Raptor relentlessly pressed the Jaguar into abbreviated dives, forcing the drone to start uphill before recovering its airspeed. Once more, the drone was cresting the top, but this time, the F–22 closed menacingly into the kill zone.

With the target in his windscreen, Whitefoot concentrated on aligning the fuselages. For a high-percentage kill shot, he needed to eliminate any track-crossing angle. He had help. The Raptor's revolutionary gunsight projected a funnel-shaped graphic—open at the top—that moved with serpentine grace on the HUD. Pilots found it much easier to maneuver a target into the snake-sight's gaping jaws than to use the traditional pipper-based symbology.

Despite the nifty technology, the fact remained that cannon rounds are unguided; once fired, their flight path cannot be altered.

Charlie was counting on it. "Pat, call my jinks every four seconds."

"WILCO."

"Jink right!"

Tracers stitched holes in the space vacated by the Jaguar.

"Alice: Target jinking." The Raptor pursued as Whitefoot fought to bring the target to bear once more.

"Jink left!"

Alice spewed information. "Passing eight thousand. Drifting left. Range one thousand. Target heading one-zero-zero."

Before Whitefoot could squeeze off a shot, the Jaguar again shifted clear of the gunsight. Charlie's maneuvers were crisp, in effect hardly more than a sidestep the width of the aircraft, but they were maddeningly effective. Whitefoot tried to respond quickly, but he couldn't align the sight before another jink occurred.

"Jink up!" Charlie temporarily broke the rate of descent.

Whitefoot, who suspected a vertical break turn, yanked the throttles back to avoid underrunning the target and sliding out in front. But it was just another jink. As he pulled the nose up and slammed the throttles forward, he fired a short burst, hoping for a lucky hit. The tracers flew harmlessly beneath and to the right of the target.

"Jink right!"

"Target drifting right. Passing seven thousand two hundred. Range nine hundred. Closure seventy. Target heading one-zero-zero."

Whitefoot, after jinks spoiled his next two shots, was sweating profusely. Overwhelmed with frustration, his stomach on fire, he held the stick and throttles in viselike grips. And with the audience listening in, he couldn't even vent his rage.

The drone was making a mockery out of his skills as a pilot as it skated this way and that, pausing tantalizingly before darting again. At that point, he had no illusions about his ability to hit the target. His miss distances were widening. This torture could go on until he ran out of gas or bullets. Nothing in his training had prepared him for such a wicked defense.

"Oh man, he's got to be going nuts!" said Hoser in his trademark stage whisper. "What a bitch."

"He needs to pull through the target instead of going for the bull's-eye," said Randi.

"I don't think his *copilot* is programmed to think like that."

"You're right," she said. "He needs to tell that damn computer to shut up."

"Jink left!" Pat kept his eyes on the clock, timing his calls to keep the aircraft moving.

"Target drifting left. Altitude six thousand one hundred. Heading . . ."

"Alice: Silence!" Unable to bear it any longer, Whitefoot pulled his nose after the Jaguar and held the trigger down. He wanted it to end, and the easiest way to do that was to run out of ammo. As the rounds counter decremented to zero, the tracers fell below and to the left. In angry desperation he stomped on the right rudder pedal.

The tidy stream of tracers was interrupted by an

ugly-looking flurry of rounds fired off axis by the yawing aircraft. Twelve of the fifty hit pay dirt.

"Jink right!"

"Oh shit . . . we've been hit." Charlie flexed the stick in all quadrants and manipulated the throttles. "And it's real bad. I've got nothing left. What's the time?"

"You don't want to know."

The dome audience erupted in cheers. Whitefoot's struggles were forgotten in the excitement of the fire-ball, vividly captured by the Raptor's HUD camera. The official scorer stopped the clock at four minutes fourteen seconds. The Raptor team was only eleven seconds off the lead.

CHAPTER 20

"The range is green. Three . . . two . . . one . . ."

"EuroFighter copies." Captain Peter Savant acquired a radar lock and allowed the target identifier to confirm his foe. After raising a cover on a guarded control panel, he engaged the Damien weapons system—so named by test pilots who accused the engineers of spawning a creature from Hades—and gripped the handholds on either side of the windscreen. From that point, until presented with a shoot cue, Captain Savant would merely be a passenger.

The EF–2000 was equipped with what its designers coyly classified as an integrated fire-control system. When activated, feedback from the radar, avionics, and gunsight were fed to the primary fire-control computer, which directed commands to the autopilot. The system was designed to destroy targets before an intercept turned into a dogfight.

Since the clock started before the aircraft merged, the EuroFighter team was confident they had a winner.

The success of Damien—the EuroFighter's secretly developed weapons system tallied a gaudy hundred-percent kill rate in twenty live-fire tests—was founded on fundamental physics. By engaging a target that was closing at high speed, the range of the cannon was effectively tripled since the speed of both aircraft was added to the muzzle velocity of the round. Likewise, the destructive power was dramatically increased. At demonstrations, the engineers explained to stunned observers that the force of impact was a function of mass times the square of velocity. And given that a round was likely to hit an inbound target in the engines and/or cockpit and penetrate the length of the aircraft, the cumulative effect was such that it only took one Damien round to destroy a modern fighter. For that reason, Damien was limited to short bursts of fifty rounds. Though it was overkill, fifty was the fewest number of rounds that could be fired without damaging the rapidly spinning six-barreled Gatling gun.

By taking the pilot out of the loop and giving the autopilot full 8-G authority, the Damien system was capable of reacting instantaneously to the smallest deviations in the target's flight path. The handgrips had been added when a test pilot's helmet thumped the canopy after a particularly abrupt correction. As a safety precaution, the procedure called for the pilot to disable Damien at one thousand meters. Left engaged, Damien would initiate an avoidance maneuver the EuroFighter team's pilots termed Mr. Toad's Wild Ride in honor of the EuroDisney ride.

*   *   *

Once more, Charlie was at the controls with Pat in the copilot's seat. There were no jokes; the mood in the small room was grim. Major Khalim, arms folded, was standing directly behind the two pilots. He had his orders. The Strike Flanker could not be allowed to finish last.

"We're going to blow through and make that bastard come get us," Charlie said.

"After the pass, come twenty degrees right for the sun," Pat added. The intercept had been purposely orchestrated to run east–west so that Charlie could bull's-eye the afternoon sun in hopes of making the EuroFighter pilot lose sight.

"Roger that."

The dome audience, apparently wrung out from the day's events, was uncharacteristically subdued. Jack, back from the command post, noted that there were even a few empty seats. Though he would have preferred to watch the fight, he had to check on the Internet activity and look in on the casino and the oasis room via the cameras in the operations center. It would be a long night. Turning to leave, he paused to glance over his shoulder, curious to see what kind of tactics the EuroFighter would employ.

Astute observers noted that the shoot cue in the EuroFighter's HUD began flashing at two kilometers prior to the merge. Most of the audience missed it, being intent upon the aircraft images closing above their heads.

Captain Savant fired Damien by pressing the red button on the control panel.

The Jaguar was completely obliterated. In the silence that followed, the clock flashed an unbelievable forty-five seconds.

CHAPTER 21

"Explain the scoring to me again," said Hoser, after polishing off another lager.

"All right, one last time for the mentally challenged," said Buckingham, who had matched the American beer for beer.

The two pilots had each found his way to the pub only to wind up fending off questions about this new technology that made pilots obsolete. When the onslaught showed no sign of waning, they commandeered a corner table, erected a barricade of empty chairs, and proceeded to drink with a vengeance. Bystanders quickly learned to keep their distance.

Buckingham spoke with the deliberateness of someone lecturing a stubborn child. "With the exception of the frogs, the spread of our times is one minute thirty-one seconds. Since those bastards bested my time by more than that amount, they get a bonus. The upshot of that is that they leapfrog—Ha-ha!—all the way from last place, where they belong, into the lead, where I rightfully belong. Now, I'm in second, the KFIR in third, the Raptor in fourth, the Rooskies in fifth, and you, my sodden friend, are tail-end Charlie, sucking hind teat. Do you understand now, or shall I unpack my crayons and draw you a picture?"

"Go bugger yourself you pompous prick. I still think you're making this up. And I'm not drunk, shit-for-brains. The day has not come that I can't drink you and any of your limey friends under the table. And where do you come off acting so high-and-mighty? I nailed my drone twice as fast as you did and didn't even break a sweat doing it. I can't help it if these morons don't count it a kill until it hits the deck. What a stupid idea."

"I didn't write them, but those are the rules, are they not? Now, if you had paid attention at the brief . . ." He froze for a second in mid-insult, then Buckingham's chair slammed forward with a crash. The Brit slammed the table with his palm hard enough to make the steins jump. "Of course! How did we miss that? Those are the bloody rules! Hoser, you magnificent bastard, you are a genius! We've got to find that bloke Warner."

"I don't know what you're yammering about." Hoser held the empty pewter stein upside down to underscore his dilemma. "But I do know that I'm still thirsty."

"Yes, I see your point. Let us not be hasty. We need to formulate our strategy." The chair went back up on two legs. "Barkeep! Another round, my good man."

Whitefoot acknowledged Randi with a welcoming nod as she prepared to mount the exercise bike next to his. They were alone in the fitness tent. She felt his eyes on her as she peeled off her sweats. Clad in a pair of clinging Lycra bike shorts and jog-bra that bared her taut midriff, she momentarily wished she'd worn a T-shirt. *But if it made Mr. Silence speak, what the hell?* She'd decided to start her private investigation with the other American team.

Surreptitiously glancing at the display on his bike, she noted that he was riding the hill profile at level eight and had thirty minutes remaining. Randi programmed her bike and began pedaling.

At Mikhail's insistence, Sergei left the hangar to get something to eat. Despite their last-place finish that day, the older man was encouraged by the attitude change he saw in the crew and especially his pilot. After Sergei had reamed them out for shoddy work, Mikhail had rallied the troops with a stirring pep talk and his promise of a lavish celebration when they won. From anyone else, the offer would have been laughed off, but the crew knew their hotshot pilot could afford it. As Sergei walked down the corridor, he could hear the men singing while they worked with renewed vigor.

When Jack spied Antoskin entering the Oasis, he left the operations center to join the Russian copilot.

"Mind if I join you?"

"Certainly." Upon seeing Jack's confusion, Sergei

stood, smiled, and bowed in self-deprecation. "Forgive me, Mr. Warner. I meant to invite you to sit. My English has been neglected."

"You are too modest, sir. You are quite skilled at my language. And please call me Jack."

"Sergei." They shook hands, then sat.

Jack pointed at their respective plates and laughed. "Do you see what we have done? I have Mongolian barbecue and you have a cheeseburger. So much for home cooking!"

"Yes, that is a . . . a coincidence of interest. To be honest, Jack, your meal is Mongolian only in name. You should be eating calf brains and borscht . . ."

"I really don't think so."

"That is too bad. You do not know what you would miss."

"I'll take your word for it. By the way, my guys in the communications center said that you have had a tough time getting through to home."

Sergei's expression darkened at the mention of his family.

"I'm sorry, I didn't mean to pry. I thought I might be able to help."

"It is no problem, Jack. I appreciate your wanting to do this. My son . . . our son, Alek, has health problems. Svetlana was to see the doctor, a specialist, two days ago. We are hoping Alek will be accepted for a surgery. I will find out when we finish here."

"Do you mind if I ask what is wrong with Alek?"

"Yes . . . I mean, no. As you can see I have trouble with the phrasings. Again, forgive me." As he spoke, Sergei pulled a wallet from his flight suit, extracted a well-worn photograph, and passed it to Jack. A toddler holding a massive flight helmet grinned at the camera.

"What a doll," said Jack, meaning it. "How old is he, about three?"

"Our son is five years old. As you can see, he is small, quite small, for his age. Alek has a small hole in his heart. It is there since birth. It makes him weak. Without surgery he is not likely to make it through another winter. But we do not have the money. It costs more rubles for the surgery than to buy a home. Surely you have heard of our economy. It is not so good."

"Your family lives in Pushchino, correct? I saw it on your emergency-notification form."

"Yes?" Sergei's tone was guarded.

"Perhaps I can help in a small way. As you know, we have state-of-the-art communications facilities. Since there appears to be a problem with the telephone service in your area, we contacted the university and have arranged for a satellite link. Your consulate here was most happy to help. They have arranged for your wife and son to be at the university for a videoconference"—Jack looked at his watch—"in about fifteen minutes. As soon as you finish your dinner, I will take you to a room where you can speak to them in private."

Sergei was out of his chair in a flash. "This is wonderful!" When Jack stood, he found himself in a bear hug and kissed on both cheeks. Sergei stepped back while gripping Jack's shoulders. "I am no longer hungry, my friend. Can we go now?"

Determined to draw Whitefoot into speaking first, Randi concentrated on riding and soon found herself matching the Air Force pilot's pace. When he accelerated into the hills, so did she. Whereupon he bumped the program up to level nine, gave her a challenging look, and pedaled that much harder. Randi, who was a collegiate athlete herself and had long been into multisport training, tapped her screen and joined him at level nine. In minutes, they were both bathed in sweat, hammering away in a race to nowhere.

Randi stole a glance in hopes of seeing signs of fatigue, but Whitefoot—jaw set, eyes focused on the wall in front of them—looked like he could pedal all night. With her thighs burning from the exertion, she gave up trying to breathe through her nose and panted openmouthed. Determined not to let him dust her, she pushed the pace even harder.

Unbeknownst to either of them, one of the operators spotted the impromptu race from a surveillance camera. With a couple of keystrokes, the image was broadcast to dozens of monitors posted throughout the complex. Curious at first, people quickly deduced what was happening and began chatting and pointing.

Twenty minutes later, as both riders crested the peak climb in the program, they began spinning at maximum speed, their legs a blur. Word of mouth spread and people clustered around the monitors, caught in the moment. Spontaneous betting took place in the casino, with a surprising number of people taking the young woman.

Seeing that he had a hit, the operator scrambled through his extensive CD collection of classical music and dubbed in a sound track. Completely oblivious of the attention they were garnering, Cole and Whitefoot pedaled furiously toward the imaginary finish line in perfect time to the frenetic pace of the *William Tell* Overture.

"What the hell is going on?" asked Hoser when the guests laughingly cheered the racers.

The barman tuned the monitor and turned up the volume. The riders were in a mad sprint, heads down, sweat flying, neither giving an inch.

"I do believe that is your niece on the telly," said Simon.

"You're damn right it is," bragged Hoser. "And I'll bet you a quid she beats that guy."

"You're on, mate. Bye the bye, do you know how much a quid is worth?"

"Not the slightest, but I think it takes two bobs and a bill to make one."

"Just so. A bet with you is like purloining candy from a young child."

"That's 'taking candy from a baby,' dictionary mouth."

"So it is."

At the chime that sounded the end of Whitefoot's session, both riders came out of their tucks. When they looked at each other, chests heaving, legs winding down, each broke into a weary grin.

"You're a tough lady," said Whitefoot, wiping sweat out of his eyes with a muscled forearm.

"You're no slouch, either," Randi said between gasps. "Hear that? What's going on out there?"

"It sounds like a big crowd, but we're too far for it to be from the dome. Was there something scheduled?"

Her curiosity, overcoming her desire to flop onto the floor, motivated Randi to dismount and walk stiff-legged to open the flap on their tent.

"Captain Whitefoot?" She stood aside with the tent flap upheld so that he could see the dozens of beaming faces. "I think we've been had."

"Can I have a moment?"

"Certainly, Jack," said the prince. "Please have a seat. Anything to drink?" Though obviously weary and apparently beset with problems, the prince, in the spirit of his ancestors, was a gracious host when a visitor entered his domain.

"No thanks." Jack sat in the chair indicated. "You look tired."

"I am. Forgive me. Now what is it that brings you here?"

"After speaking with a couple of the pilots, I

reviewed the tapes from today's event. I found a discrepancy with the scoring on the last flight."

"Really?"

Jack noted with some disappointment that the prince was hopeful instead of dubious. Salman's reaction was an indication that he was unhappy with the standings, something that would not occur if the competition were on the level.

"Our timer stopped the clock for the EuroFighter when the target was destroyed. By the rules he should have waited . . ."

"Until the target hit the ground!" Prince Salman finished the sentence with an exclamation. "Yes, of course! Why didn't I think of that?" The prince's fatigue melted as he snatched up the phone and punched a speed-dial button. "And that means the bonus is history." As he waited for the connection, he glanced at Jack. The look he received in return caught him by surprise. He laid the phone back into its cradle. "Why don't you tell me what's put that scowl on your face?"

"I would think you'd be furious at having to adjust the standings for the second time in two days, Your Highness. Unless . . ." Jack let the sentence hang.

"Unless what?"

"Unless the score doesn't reflect what you and the council want."

"I see your point."

"Do your superiors have any idea how much attention this contest has attracted?"

"They can count."

"Money, perhaps. But for every dime we're generating from the Internet, we have ten surfers who are just watching. For every one of them, we have fifty more who read about it in their morning papers. And for every one of them, we can expect a hundred to watch it on the evening news. Do you understand what I'm saying?"

"I'm not sure, Jack. Where are we going with this?"

A lifetime of investigative journalism had attuned Jack's ear to the slightest nuance that would indicate a subject's willingness to unburden a secret. He'd bet a month's pay that the prince wanted to break his silence.

Jack cut to the chase. "What could possibly be worth risking global exposure as a liar and a cheat?"

His frankness caught the prince off guard. After a moment, the prince stood, stepped to the credenza, and opened a drawer. He spoke without turning. "Jack, I have too much respect for you to insult your intelligence by lying to you."

Jack tensed, an adrenaline spike putting him on edge to fight if the prince was reaching for a weapon.

When the prince turned, he held a thin, leatherbound folder in his hands. He smiled at Jack's discomfiture. "What did you think I had in here? A gun?"

"No, of course not."

Jack's denial was unconvincing, but the prince let it slide. "What I have to tell you is very sensitive.

But, I'm willing to risk it since I can't let you get yourself in trouble over something that is out of our hands. How much do you know about the Caspian oil fields?"

"I am very impressed. Thanks for letting me have a look." The F–22 cockpit fit Randi like a glove. After leaving the fitness tent, the two pilots had showered, dressed in clean flight suits, and, to avoid the stares of well-wishing guests, dined on sports bars and fruit juice in the Raptor's hangar. When her host offered to let her climb aboard the world's most expensive and sophisticated fighter, she eagerly accepted.

"Check this out." Whitefoot, who was crouched on a rollaway stand pushed flush against the fuselage, flicked a switch on the console and half a dozen multicolor displays came to life.

"And these are all night-vision-device compatible, right?"

"Yes."

Randi twisted in the cockpit, checking views over the nose, beneath, and behind her. "The visibility is excellent."

"And it's just as good with the lid down. Our canopy is the largest single piece of polycarbonate made in the world."

"She's a beauty, Steve."

"It takes one to know one." At her sharp glance, he flushed. "I'm sorry! That just came out. I didn't mean . . ."

"For a second there you sounded like Bucking-ham." Randi smiled to let him off the hook. "Thank you for the compliment, though." She settled in the seat, gripping the stick and throttles, aware that her new friend was staring with more than casual inter-est. "Steve, do you mind if I ask you a question?"

"Shoot."

"Do you think this competition is on the up-and-up?"

"Interesting question." Whitefoot twisted side-ways and sat down, stretching his legs out so that he and Randi were facing each other. "What do you think?"

She reached out and poked him in the chest. "Nice try, but I asked you first, mister."

"I think it was a raw deal when they grounded you, and I don't understand why your team and the State Department accepted the decision without a fight."

"That's not so hard to explain. There's too much money riding on this for our team to cut its nose off to spite its face."

"So where's that leave you?"

"I don't know. I was pulled out of carrier-suitability testing for this project. Depending on what happens here, I suppose I could be reassigned. I haven't given it much thought. Right now I'm just trying to help any way that I can."

"Including spying on the competition?" Though he was smiling, there was more than jest to the ques-tion.

"No. This is personal." As soon as she said it, she realized how it sounded. It was her turn to be uncomfortable. "I really didn't mean that as a . . ."

"Relax, Cole. Neither of us are big talkers. I like you, though. I guess that's because we're really two of a kind."

"How so?"

"I'm an outsider, too. It seems as if I've had to prove myself every step of the way and always under the glare of a big spotlight. Sound familiar?"

"I see what you mean. If you failed, people would judge not only you, but everyone like you."

"Exactly. And I know people think I'm rude or mysterious because I'm quiet and don't show emotion, but I just can't afford the distraction."

"Well it's working. You had a great score today."

He turned away. "I don't know about that."

"What do you mean? You were in second place before the Euro team came out of the woodwork."

"It was a lucky shot."

Randi realized that if his statement wasn't false modesty, it was a confession. "We make our own luck."

Whitefoot's head was bowed. When he glanced up, his eyes were brimming with shame. "I gave up out there. Not once in my whole life have I done that. But I just couldn't hit that damn thing. I can't tell you how badly I wanted it to end. I don't know why I'm telling you this, but I swear I just held down the trigger and kicked the rudder. It was stupid and irresponsible." He cupped his head in his hands. "I'm fooling myself and everybody else. I don't deserve to be here."

Randi slid out of the cockpit, stepped across to the platform, and crouched beside him. "Look at me."

The tortured expression revealed the depth of his pain.

"You ran into a tough situation, and you got lucky. That's no big deal. Not long ago, I came within an inch of putting my number one test bird in the water on a bonehead decision. And you saw what Santana did yesterday. He's been at this longer than you and me put together!

"We're fighter pilots. When shit happens—and we make it through somehow—the best tactic is to offer one up, learn from the mistake, and press on. Otherwise, we can lose our edge. Bottom line: What happened out there today isn't nearly as important as the fact that you learned something about yourself."

"That I'm a quitter?"

"No. That you still have your integrity. Even though all those people think you scored a kill based on skill, they're clueless about what we do. Most wouldn't know a good snap shot if it hit them in the ass. What matters is that you didn't fall into the trap of believing your own bullshit. As long as you have that, Steve Whitefoot is still in control, not his ego."

Whitefoot smiled gamely. "Thanks, Mom."

"Don't mention it." She stood up, hands on hips. "Now, if you're ready to quit moping around, I can show you how to counter that defense."

"Seriously?"

"Yup. We've got a desktop simulator in our hangar. The question is: Can you pull your head out of your ass long enough to learn from a woman?"

He stood up and offered a mock salute. "Second Lieutenant Whitefoot reporting as ordered, ma'am."

She laughed. "Move out, mister."

"So this is about oil? You're going to have to bear with me. I'm afraid I don't see the connection with this competition," Randi said. She'd left Whitefoot engrossed in the simulator and met Jack in the bath area of the Oasis where they shared a hot tub. Pharaoh had revealed that the steam and ambient noise of the jets made it impossible to listen in on conversations. That it had the side benefit of helping them both relax only served to further enhance the young man's status as a genius.

After briefing Jack on what little she'd learned about the F–22 team—namely that they felt that they had the inside track regardless of how the competition ended—Randi wasted no time in asking to be brought up-to-date. Concerned about their safety, despite the prince's apparent trust, Jack had reluctantly agreed, insisting on the condition that she stop poking around on her own. They agreed to work as a team.

"How's your geography?" he asked.

"Pretty good."

"Okay, what's significant about the Caspian Sea?"

"Let's see . . . it's landlocked. Iran to the south,

Russia to the north and west, and what is it, Kaz . . ."

"*Kazakhstan* to the east. Very good. What country lies east of Kazakhstan?"

"That would be China?"

"You got it. Now what you might not know is that the Tengiz oil field in the northern Caspian is enormous; latest estimates put the reserves at two hundred billion barrels. That's as much as in the North Sea or the Persian Gulf fields.

"Yeah, and I bet everyone is trying to get a piece."

"Sure. China and the U.S. have steadily pumped cash into the region, along with the usual institutional investors. Just to make it complicated, they are all hedging their bets by covering every horse in the race."

"But it's not working?"

"Extracting the oil is only one part of the equation. You can't change geography overnight."

"In other words, what good will it do if they can't get it out of there?"

"Bingo."

"So they build a pipeline, right?"

"Great idea. So good, in fact, that there are six different pipelines in various stages of construction. Iran, Turkey, Kazakhstan, and Russia are all seeking to become the portal through which Caspian oil gets to the world market. The problem is that there are only a handful of companies in the world that can handle the logistics and engineering of building a pipeline in that type of terrain. And they work for the highest bidder."

"Where does our little contest come in?"

"Most people forget that the Russians used to be the world's largest oil exporter. Now it's Saudi Arabia. The Russians are cash-starved, but they already have major segments of a pipeline to the Black Sea in place. The problem is that it leaks like a sieve—so bad, in fact, that the UN is boycotting any oil shipped through it. The Russians need big bucks to repair and upgrade it. The Saudis have more money than God and want even more. It's a marriage of convenience."

"So they can raise prices?"

"Eventually. Right now, they'll settle for controlling them. OPEC is becoming increasingly fragile. Iraq and Iran desperately want to increase production. And every day, the Brits find ways to squeeze more for less out of the North Sea. For the past few years, Saudi Arabia has been held hostage by the threat of someone pushing prices down by sending more than their share to market. But with their hand on the spigot to the Caspian, the Saudis could literally flood the market, absorb the losses, and put their competition out of business once and for all. Or, if they get a little tired of the way they are treated internationally, they can put a stranglehold on two-thirds of the world's oil. Think anyone will want to go toe-to-toe with them?"

"Take me back to the competition. How does it fit?" asked Randi.

"Given the strategic implications, the Saudis can't very well walk up to the Russians and hand over seventy-five billion dollars, or more. Over the years—ostensibly for the sake of peace and stability—they've milked all sorts of concessions from the international community as a sort of quid pro quo for not trying to make a grab for the whole enchilada. To pull this off, they can't risk the exposure until they have taken control. Not only would the United States and China take it to the UN Security Council, but OPEC would crumble overnight."

"What could the UN do?"

"Agree to buy from Iran, the Brits, the U.S., even the Iraqis; anybody but the Saudis. They could block the engineers from working, and they'd probably slap severe sanctions on both Saudi Arabia and Russia, particularly on high-tech equipment."

"And OPEC?"

"If they get wind of the strategy, the other OPEC players, most of whom are hungry for cash flow, would open the taps. The end result would be that the price of oil would plummet before the Saudis were ready to go to the mat. Believe it or not, despite their apparent wealth, until the pipeline is in place, the Saudis remain vulnerable. The nineties have not been the boom years they expected when they set up their incredibly generous domestic social security system."

"So this whole thing is a ruse to funnel money into Russia?"

"So it would appear."

"Appear? What's that supposed to mean?" She maneuvered around the tub until she was facing him, steadying herself by holding on to the tiled edge on either side of his head. Her cheeks, flushed from the heat, framed big blue eyes that Jack found irresistible.

He was acutely aware of her nearness and struggled to keep his eyes glued above her neck.

"Jack Warner, there's something you're not telling me. We have a deal, pal. Now spill it."

"I'm not convinced that the prince wasn't just feeding me a convenient answer. Nothing I can put my finger on, but I'm suspicious. I don't doubt that the Caspian angle is part of the explanation, but I think there's a good bit more to it."

Randi considered the ramifications of his answer. For effect, she pursed her lips while arching her back, knowing full well that she had her friend on the ropes. When his knee touched her side he pulled it away as if her skin was scalding hot. "Like what?"

Jack had reached his limit. He ducked beneath the surface of the water—stealing a forlorn look at the shimmering body he'd love to entwine—and escaped to the far side of the tub.

"I don't know yet," he answered from a safe distance. "But I'm going to find out."

"You mean, *we're* going to find out, don't you, *partner*?" She stood up in the waist-deep center of the tub and gracefully swept her wet hair back with one hand, the water sheeting off her bare shoulders.

"Whatever you say, Lieutenant."

PART 4

EVENT THREE

STRIKE MISSION

CHAPTER 22

Official Standings after Events One and Two
1. **Lancer**
2. **EuroFighter ***
3. **KFIR II**
4. **Raptor**
5. **Strike Flanker**
6. **Super Hornet**

* Score recomputed (timing error)

Pilot Briefing/0630

"Excuse me, Mr. Warner."

"Yes, Colonel Kohl?"

"How can we continue this charade? Each morning we meet, not to discuss flying, but to adjust the standings. Where does it end?"

"I can answer that," said the prince, stepping up to stand next to the podium.

"It ends here. For consistency's sake, posted scores will remain unofficial until confirmed by the videotape-review process, which I will personally supervise. You have my solemn promise that the rules will be enforced fairly and swiftly."

"I'm afraid that's not good enough, mate," said Buckingham, who sat with his boots propped on the next chair. To the surprise of witnesses to his late-night pub antics, he showed no aftereffects from the rousing drinking games that had gone on past midnight. Neither, for that matter, did Hoser, though many of their victims had already called guest services pleading for all manner of hangover remedies. "We've still got the problem of how you plan to run the last event."

"Can you be more specific?" The prince's icy tone revealed barely contained anger.

"Certainly. Allowing the fly-by-committee team to use that gimmick of theirs in the dogfight competition makes a mockery of the contest. With the computer awarding a ninety-five percent probability of kill, all they have to do is point and shoot. The rest of us might as well not show up."

"Captain Matsasuta? You have something to add?" asked the prince.

"Yes, thank you. I speak on behalf of the EuroFighter team in conveying that, as pilots, we are sympathetic to what has been said. But it is of no consequence. Again, I must point out that we are here to pick the best aircraft, not the best pilot. The EF–2000 has amply demonstrated that the integrated fire-control technology is reliable. Frankly, it is a lethal weapons system with a performance record that justifies an even higher probability of kill. There can be no argument about this fact." He bowed and sat down to approving nods from his team.

"Bloody bollocks!"

"I had a feeling that you might have a rejoinder, Squadron Leader."

"Then you are perceptive, sir. As much as I disagree with the entire premise of their spokesman's logic, I am more than willing to base my objections on fact." He paused for effect before continuing. "The Damien system has never performed in combat."

The prince signaled for silence, and said, "That can hardly be used as reason to disqualify it since neither has your Lancer, or for that matter, any of the other aircraft we have assembled."

"You miss my point, sir. Though our aircraft may be new, the weapons we will be using in the dogfight event have all been observed in combat."

Captain Matsasuta stood and spoke forcefully, the deference of his previous statements replaced with frustration. "This is ludicrous. Already this man has cost us the lead in the competition with his complaints. Certainly no one here believes that he makes a sufficient argument to prohibit the use of a new technology. Obviously, his problem is that it makes our aircraft superior."

Buckingham smiled, clearly happy to have gotten a rise out of his foe. "Throttle back, Captain. I'm not suggesting that we ban it, I'm just saying that there are countertactics for every weapon. We simply have not had the opportunity to develop them for your little toy."

"Go to hell," said Matsasuta.

Several voices demanded order.

Buckingham waited for the clamor to subside. When he spoke, the amused tone was absent. "You say you deal with facts, bloke. Then deal with these: One, Damien has had one and only one public demonstration; two, the target it engaged was not maneuvering; three, to assign such a high probability of kill based solely on that record is total bullshit; and, four . . . I'll be happy to meet you, or any of your mates, anytime, anyplace to discuss this further."

"Knock it off!" Hoser's use of the universal command used by pilots to cease a dogfight cut through the raucous arguments that followed Buckingham's challenge. "Everybody take a seat and listen up." When quiet was restored, he spoke calmly. "Each of us has a mission to fly today. It's time to focus on that, or someone is going to plant one out there. But I can see that ain't going to happen until we stick a fork in this debate. So here's what we're going to do: I'm going to make a suggestion. There will be no arguments or discussion about it. Every team and the prince get a vote. It's all or nothing. If we fail to agree, we cancel today's schedule and stop flying until the problem is solved."

Several people started to object. Hoser cut them off. "Maybe I didn't make myself clear. If you don't like it, vote no. That will be the end of it."

"Go ahead, let's hear it." Kohl's support silenced

the others. The most experienced combat pilots commanded a great deal of respect.

"Thanks, Moshe. Now just hear me out. This afternoon, after we finish with event three, we test this Damien system again against another drone. If it can repeat yesterday's performance, the probability of kill goes up to ninety-nine percent. If it doesn't, we average the two tests. Regardless of the outcome, the standings for the first two days stand as they are now. That's it. Now, let's see a show of hands."

Kohl, Santana, and Buckingham voted for it immediately. Whitefoot glanced at Randi, winked, and raised his hand as well. After a brief discussion with his pilot, Sergei voted in support for the Russian team. The prince raised his hand as well. All eyes were on Captain Matsasuta. Though he knew he should seek approval from his superiors, his desire to silence his enemy was overwhelming. It was unanimous.

"Shit hot, gentlemen. That's more like it. Jack, give us the skinny on today's mission and make it snappy. We're almost out of time."

Jack quickly consulted his notes. He had worked very hard to put together a professional-sounding brief, and now he had to turn it into a sound bite. He did his best to hit the high points. "All right. In a nutshell, we have set up the live-fire range as depicted in your briefing packet. Major Khalim's crew has worked with each of your support teams to ensure that the ordnance is safely handled, loaded, and expended. He will be available after I'm finished should you have questions.

"Once you arrive on station, you will receive a target briefing that covers the three targets you will attempt to destroy. We will make this as realistic as possible by forcing the attack heading and weapon for each target. You are free to use whatever delivery tactic you see fit; however, be advised that each target will be defended by a simulated missile battery and mobile antiaircraft systems. Should they successfully engage you, as judged by videotape proof, you will be penalized fifty points. Your baseline score will be a composite of your accuracy for both hits and timing computed in feet and seconds. Your total score will include penalties if there are any. Therefore, a perfect score would be zero. Are there any questions?"

"Yes, Captain?" Everyone turned in surprise that the American was volunteering to speak.

"To show respect to our international friends, I'd be willing to have my miss distance measured in meters instead of feet," said Whitefoot. He almost pulled it off, but he couldn't keep a straight face.

"Cole! What have you done to that young man?" asked Hoser. "He made a joke!"

"Nicely done, Jack," said Randi when she joined him in the dome.

"What do you mean?"

"Your briefing, silly."

"Oh that? I wish you'd seen the one I prepared. I had slides, photos . . . and what's so funny?"

"You, you big ham. Was there anything that you

left out that we couldn't find in our preflight packets?"

Jack replayed the brief in his mind. "No, I guess not. But it was so rushed, it's just that I could have done a much better job covering everything if I'd had some time. Why are you laughing at me, damn it?"

"What a knucklehead you are. You just gave one of the great briefs of all time, and that includes ones I've given, and you don't even know it. Thank goodness we had that mess with Buckingham and Matsasuta; otherwise, we'd still be sitting in there listening to the great orator."

"Bite me, Cole."

CHAPTER 23

"Lancer, stand by for the nine-line brief for your first target." The pilots had agreed to use the American standard nine-line brief format for passing key information about the targets. Because the information was broadcast in shorthand and in a specific order, the pilots could readily input the data into their systems.

"Ready to copy."

"First target: TOT twelve-eighteen Zulu, IP Charlie, bear one-eight-zero for thirteen-point-six, camouflaged tank, negative mark, two Mark-eighty-two conventional bombs on a single pass, attack one-seven-five, egress east, area defended by SA–6 and Stinger missiles. Come up thirty-five-forty-five for Yankee control, over."

After Buckingham finished scribbling down the specifics, he repeated them to his controller for confirmation. He received a noncommittal, "unknown," when he asked if the tank was a mobile target. The "negative mark" instruction meant that he wouldn't have a mortar-fired smoke round to help locate it. The SA–6 radar-guided surface-to-air threat forced him to use low-altitude tactics, which, in turn, put him in the handheld Stinger missile envelope. Since they were wielded by two-man teams, it was likely that he wouldn't spot the shooters. All told, it meant that he'd have to get in and out quickly.

It took Simon nearly a minute to enter all the data and work out the attack geometry. That gave him barely more than three minutes before he'd have to push out. And there were still two more targets to brief.

"Lancer standing by for second target."

The dome audience had a bird's-eye view courtesy of the Saudi Royal Air Force surveillance aircraft and its geostabilized telephoto cameras. In all, three angles were provided: a big picture of the target area, a zoom-in on the aircraft, and the target camera, which had been calibrated with rings for scoring the hits. Also projected on the perimeter of the dome— along with the countdown timer that had a column for each target—were video feeds from the aircraft's HUD and the land-based range cameras.

The target set was comprised of surplus tanks, obsolete artillery pieces, and highly maneuverable, remote-control dune buggies. Each aircraft would attack the armor with a pair of conventional, five-hundred-pound iron bombs, and a smart weapon of the team's choice. They would also be challenged to strafe the nimble dune buggies, which were capable of speeds up to fifty miles per hour and equipped with an acoustically triggered evasion system that programmed a hard turn away from a near miss.

*   *   *

The little jump jet skimmed the floor of the wadi—
nothing more than a funnel depression snaking
between the dunes—as Buckingham threaded his way
toward the target. Occasionally he would leave one to
cross to the next, a mottled brown speck momentarily
visible against the morning sky, but only to an
observer looking in just the right spot—so fleeting
was the exposure that a blink would obscure its passing as the diminutive fighter darted back into the protection of the arid riverbed.

Though the Lancer was equipped with a flight-
path computation system that could be coupled to the
autopilot, Buckingham preferred to use the navigation cues as a baseline from which to deviate,
remaining flexible by controlling the speed himself.
Such skill couldn't be taught. It required an innate
sense of timing and direction. And of those so gifted,
Simon Buckingham was in a class of one.

"He flies so low, he kicks up sand." Jack cringed, as
did most of the audience, when the view switched to
an aircraft close-up.

"I've never seen anyone routinely operate with less
margin for error," said Randi. "He flies like a surgeon."

"How come his HUD says to come left and he
goes right? Wouldn't that screw up his timing?"

"I honestly don't know; it's as if he has a need to
increase the degree of difficulty. But it looks to me

like he's got it under control. Okay, he's entering the target bowl. Now watch this, he's going into the pop."

The range camera picked up the Lancer as it cut hard to the right, suddenly reversed, and pulled obliquely into a climb. The aircraft's attitude never stabilized as the bomb-laden fighter snaked first left then to the right, leaving decoy flares in its S-shaped wake. As suddenly as the climb began, the jet rolled onto its back and sliced back toward the bowl-shaped target zone.

"There it is." Randi elbowed Jack and pointed at the HUD view. "And look at that, the bastard is heading exactly one-seven-five, right on his attack heading."

Mesmerized, Jack watched the HUD attack symbology as Buckingham dragged the bomb cross squarely across the turret of the half-buried tank.

"Bombs away!"

The HUD picture jerked in response to the loss of the twin five-hundred-pounders. Instantly, the horizon rotated to the right, well past ninety degrees, as Buckingham pulled hard left to make his eastward escape. Two seconds later, the tank disappeared in a double fireball. Concussive waves shook the range camera. A view from the airborne camera clearly showed the billowing smoke column dead center in the target ring.

The countdown timer for the first target flashed three zeros: a perfect score.

*   *   *

In contrast to the Brit's Zen-like approach, the EuroFighter left the IP Delta—as it had the previous two—with full autopilot engaged. Given the irregular height of the dunes, the terrain-following radar had been secured for the flight. A minimum altitude of one hundred feet above the highest elevation was established. From the IP, the EF–2000 would proceed to a predefined pop point, execute the climb, and surrender flight control to the pilot for the strafing mission. For his protection, the automated dive-recovery mode remained active, as did the countermeasures suite.

At the prescribed time and place, the EuroFighter executed its pop-up maneuver. Peter Hartmann took control passing five hundred feet. He quickly flipped the aircraft on its back while still in the climb so that he could spot the mobile target. Fortunately, the speeding buggy kicked up enough sand to be visible. On cue, Hartmann pulled the aircraft's nose to the buggy and designated it a target with his helmet-mounted sight. The ground-attack radar locked, tracked the machine's metal frame, and commanded the laser range finder to slave to the radar beam. Fire-control information, precise to less than a centimeter, was passed via the mission computer to the HUD.

Cues in Hartmann's native tongue began the countdown to fire: "*Drei . . . zwei . . . eins . .* "

One heartbeat before firing, the buggy locked all four brakes. The radar processed the change in forward motion and notified the mission computer, which, in turn, depressed the range finder, shifted the targeting solution, and notified the autopilot, which calibrated the appropriate flight-control input. However, commands were not relayed because the aircraft was in pilot mode. In the meantime, Peter saw the target drop to the bottom of the HUD well beneath the pipper. He immediately bunted the aircraft's nose by pushing forward on the stick—steepening the dive—and struggled to maneuver the free-floating gunsight back to the target. With only a couple seconds left in his dive, Hartmann flicked the left wing down to increase momentarily his rate of descent and adjust his tracking solution. The gunsight swung beneath the target—exactly as he intended—allowing him to let it drift up as he rolled out. It would be close, and require an extra hard pull-out, but with any luck he would have a decent snap shot.

The EF–2000 mission computer was programmed to be keenly aware of the fallibility of its human interface. Hartmann's last-ditch maneuver generated a sufficient target-tracking error that, when combined with the dive and mission parameters, matched a pattern of behavior in its extensive library. With more than eighty percent certainty that the pilot had become boresighted on the maneuvering target—a fairly common phenomenon among less-experienced pilots—the automatic dive-recovery mode activated to halt the rate of descent.

"What happened? Did he fire?" asked Jack, as the HUD filled with sky.

"No. It looks like he aborted," said Randi. "Geez, that's too bad, I thought he was going to make a helluva play there. That's going to hurt their score, big-time."

"Alice: Target confirmed. Cleared to engage."

"Copy, Steve. Stand by for bomb release."

In contrast to the others, the F–22 team chose to attack the armor from altitude. At fifteen thousand feet, the Raptor's stealth characteristics left it virtually invisible to the SA–6, and its engine exhaust was likewise engineered to keep the infrared signature low. Whitefoot would have to dive steeply for the strafe pass, but that tactic would actually improve his scoring chances since the track-crossing angle was naturally reduced.

Truth be told, this event was tailor-made for the F–22. In fact the only complaint from the Raptor team was voiced by the lead weapons system engineer when he sniffed that dropping iron bombs from a Raptor—an aircraft designed from the ground up for smart weapons—was like serving Budweiser in Waterford crystal.

After rechecking the switchology for the umpteenth time, Whitefoot had little to do but wait.

"Approaching target, Steve. Bomb release in three . . . two . . . one . . ."

CHAPTER 24

"And you're sure that *none* of our systems were able to track that son of a camel?"

"Yes, Governor. I am quite sure. The Lancer posted a nearly perfect score that will only solidify his position in the lead." Prince Salman was numb from lack of sleep. But as a side effect he was no longer worried about the effect bad news would have on the council during his televideoconference.

"I see. And the others?"

"The results are still preliminary, but the Super Hornet looks solid for second place. He was the only one to destroy the mobile target. The Raptor and Flanker are tied for third."

"And our Hebrew guest?"

"The KFIR ran into some bad luck. We've got clear footage of him flying directly over one of our Stinger teams. He never saw them."

"Well that's something at least. What about the EuroFighter?"

"Last place. Both for the day and the competition."

"So it is possible for a team to drop that far on the basis of one day's event?"

"Yes it is, given that the others perform significantly better. And, of course, it works the other way, as it did yesterday."

"And what about you, Nephew? How are you holding up? You sound tired."

Normally the prince would have been alerted to the elder's uncharacteristically calm reaction to bad news and the sudden interest in his well-being. But with his mind dulled by fatigue, he sought only an end to the conversation.

"I'm fine. I'll get some sleep after the flight test this afternoon."

"Good. Do that."

"How's the action?" Jack asked Pharaoh.

"The programmed betting dropped off when we put in the verification loop, but overall, the Internet betting has increased steadily. Mostly small stuff in the twenty-five- to fifty-dollar range, but lots of it. Most people like the Lancer."

"Has there been anyone showing special interest in the tote?"

"Well, yeah, now that you mention it. Major Khalim has been all over us. He's been pulling reports every twenty minutes or so."

"And his attitude?"

"At first, when the big action dropped off, he was really uptight. But when the total continued to scale up, he seemed relieved. Of course, it's tough to tell with that guy; I don't know about you, but he is one dude I don't want pissed off at me."

"Stay beneath his radar screen, okay? Don't do anything to make him suspicious of you."

"Roger that."

Jack had to laugh. Pilot jargon was penetrating everyone's language.

"Where's Simon?" asked Randi, noting that the Brit was the only aviator—other than the Frenchman flying the EuroFighter—not in the auxiliary control room, where the group had assembled to watch the flight test of the Damien system.

"I haven't seen him all day," said Jack. "I wouldn't be surprised if he was sleeping, though, given the reports I've heard about last night."

"Lightweight," said Hoser.

"You don't look so strong yourself. Maybe you should take a nap," chided Randi.

"You know what you can do with your nap, young lady."

"EuroFighter is up and ready." Captain Savant's voice was tinged with boredom. In his mind, and those of his team, the outcome was a foregone conclusion.

"And the drone?" asked the controller.

Pat nudged Charlie, who himself was suffering the ill effects of a vicious hangover, having celebrated the completion of the drone contract into the wee hours. That he and Pat were promised a bus ride to Riyadh as soon as it was done and an upgrade to first-class tickets, along with a healthy bonus, barely made the throbbing in his head tolerable.

"Drone is on station," he transmitted without even opening his eyes.

"Don't you want to see?" whispered Pat.

"Why? You've seen that EuroFighter shoot. The stupid bastard is going to get his lights drilled out. And I couldn't care less. All I really care about is that they don't find his carcass until we're halfway to the States."

"I don't believe he's doing it. And I really can't believe we let him talk us into it. Goff is going to kill us when he finds out we launched the test bird. And God help us when he finds out about that maniac being in it."

The test bird had been left human-compatible to iron out the bugs in the system. And Goff, unaware of the last-minute add-on mission, had left early to coordinate paperwork for getting his team out of country. Pat and Charlie were supposed to close up shop and meet him in Riyadh that night.

"I told you. I covered our tracks. The spare has an electrical problem." Charlie mimicked a pair of wire cutters with his hand. "Besides, what choice did we have? It was either do this or fork over every dime we made here." He shook his head. "I still say those dice that asshole was using were loaded."

"And I told you to stop betting with those guys when you were only five thousand in the hole. I'm pretty sure that big guy was in on it."

"To hell with them both then. Now for God's sake, shut up. You're giving me a headache."

*   *   *

Buckingham had nearly killed himself before the first round was fired. The slicked-down Jaguar had almost gotten away from him on takeoff. Overcontrolling, he'd started a nasty oscillation, but the jet quickly recovered when he let go of the stick. Once he was airborne, though, being back in the cockpit of the little warbird felt like old times. The elegant simplicity of the controls made the Jaguar effortless to fly. And did it fly! His warm-up acrobatics hadn't even touched the jet's new performance envelope. Buckingham decided right there and then that he was going to take this machine back to the Empire Weapons School as an adversary aircraft. It would give the Tornado pilots fits. Smiling beneath his mask, he knew he'd never have to buy his own drinks again.

The only fly in the ointment for that day's mission was the Jaguar's lack of radar. Buckingham's simple tactic had only one prerequisite: He must *see* the EuroFighter *before* it fired. Screw that up, and there wouldn't be any more toddies in the pub. Without radar to point the way, Buckingham had to locate his adversary the old-fashioned way. Manning up, he'd personally made sure the canopy was squeaky clean.

"Radar contact. One-eight-three for twenty-eight kilometers, angels one-five."

"That's your target."

"Roger."

"The range is green."

"Copy green range."

"Stand by for countdown."

Savant engaged Damien and confirmed that the master-arm switch was on.

"Trois . . . deux . . . une . . ."

"C'mon, mate . . ." Buckingham coaxed, as the fighters closed. "Show yourself." He risked another quick turn to the left, forcing the geometry so that the EuroFighter would appear to the right of his nose, away from the clutter of the windscreen-mounted HUD. Once more refocusing his eyes by deliberately staring at a distant dark spot in the desert, he began the search pattern again: left to right; top to bottom.

There! A glint of sunlight—probably off the frog's canopy. Right where he was supposed to be. In the back of his mind, Buckingham noted the effectiveness of the EuroFighter's camouflage. He'd let the bastard get inside eight kilometers. Too damn close anytime and nearly fatal that day. Taking a deep breath and holding it, he willed himself to remain focused as the dot in his windscreen grew into a sharp-featured silhouette. Eyes burning, he couldn't risk blinking.

For his part, Savant watched Damien align the gunsight with quick, sure movements. With a finger poised over the firing button, he would wait until the solution was perfect.

*   *   *

"What are they waiting for?" asked Mikhail. "I thought they were going to maneuver the drone this time."

"Watch and learn," said Hoser, winking discreetly at Randi's questioning look.

The in-range cue began flashing. Savant gave it an extra second and pushed the red button. After the first burst, Damien was programmed to fire repeatedly until the target was destroyed. So accurate was the system, this feature had never been needed. The EF–2000 cannon spun up and fired fifty rounds.

The instant he spotted the burst of smoke from the EuroFighter's cowling, Buckingham pulsed the stick. The Jaguar responded with a leap, immediately gaining seventy-five feet. The cannon rounds closed with breathtaking speed—a supersonic horde of angry crimson bees—but swept below the aircraft. Too late, Simon realized that he'd focused on the first salvo instead of watching for a second. Smoke from the second burst was already clearing. Instinctively, he pushed the stick forward—the negative-G maneuver slapping his helmet painfully against the canopy.

Peter Savant's own neck popped with the force of Damien's correction. Since the Damien system actually tracked its own bullets, in addition to the target itself, the system recognized a high probability of miss, initiated a correction, and fired again. In less than two-and-one-half seconds, two bursts of fifty rounds hurtled toward the drone.

Had the Jaguar been a twin-tailed aircraft like the Hornet, or the size of the Flanker, or had Damien fired even ten more rounds, the results would have been devastating. As it was, rounds from the second burst passed cleanly overhead the diving jet, bracketing the Jag's tail by scant inches.

Buckingham had no time to consider his good fortune. The bunt put him directly in the path of the onrushing EuroFighter. It was the third deadly threat he'd faced in a mere six seconds.

The severity of the EuroFighter's escape maneuver was programmed as a function of time to impact. In this case the mission computer determined that a maximum-performance evasion was warranted. The nine-G pull lasted only three-quarters of a second, but the rate of onset took the aircraft to its structural limits. Savant, who was gingerly raising his head from the force of the first correction, felt something in his neck snap as his chin buried itself in his chest. The hard-edged oxygen mask dug into the bridge of his nose while searing pain shot the length of his left arm.

"Christ, what happened?" The pilots huddled around the console—Savant's anguished cry still echoing from the speakers.

"EuroFighter, say your status."

The HUD view showed the nose twenty degrees above the horizon in a slow roll to the right.

Matsasuta grabbed the mike from the technician. "Peter! Come in!"

"My ne . . ." The transmission was garbled.

"Say again, Peter."

Several seconds passed. The aircraft continued to roll as the nose slid lower. "Peter!"

"Cannot . . . raise head." His voice was weak. "My neck . . . my neck won't move."

The news stunned the pilots, who exchanged horrified looks.

Randi was the first to speak. "Get a doctor in here." One of the technicians grabbed a handheld radio and spoke urgently.

Kohl asked, "How do we get the autopilot on?"

"Peter. Peter, engage altitude hold."

The nose passed through the horizon with the right wing down.

"I can't see it. Something wrong with my left arm. I can't feel my fingers." His fear was palpable.

"My God, his neck is broken," said one of the EuroFighter pilots.

"Let me try." Hoser took the mike from Matsasuta, using his shoulder to move the much smaller man aside. "Peter. This is Hoser. You've got a pinched nerve there, buddy." He spoke with a trace of amusement in his voice. "Happens all the time. Don't sweat it. Your arm will be fine in a second. Right now you're going to have to use your right hand to find that switch." He toggled off the mike, and asked, "Where the hell is it?"

"Left console, behind the throttles," said Matsasuta, who, with eyes closed, found and manipulated the imaginary control. "First . . . no, second row, middle switch. Move it forward."

Hoser nodded. "Just reach over with your right hand, find the throttles, and work your way back. Locate that second row of switches and slide your fingers to the middle one . . ."

Another painful yelp accompanied the aircraft's recovery to level flight.

"Peter. Talk to me, buddy."

"My God, it hurts bad."

"That's normal. In fact it's a good sign. Means your body's electrical system is working, that's all. Now we're going to get you back so we can have the doc take a look at it."

"But I can't see outside or the instruments."

"No sweat. Remember, we can see through your HUD from here." Turning to the technician, he said, "Get another radio up on thirty-thirty."

Kohl spoke as he moved to the door. "Call my hangar, tell them to scramble the KFIR."

"Belay that." Hoser held up his hand.

"We need another set of eyes up there, Santana. My team can have me airborne in five minutes."

"Hold on. We've got someone already there."

"You're up on three-zero-three-zero on number two, sir." The technician handed Hoser a second mike.

"Jaguar, base."

"Who the hell is he talking to?" whispered Whitefoot. Randi could only shrug.

"Go ahead." Buckingham's voice—instantly recognizable—dropped jaws throughout the control room.

Hoser spoke with deliberate calmness. "The kid in the EuroFighter torqued his neck. Probably busted. He can't raise his head, and he's lost the use of his throttle hand."

Buckingham responded in kind. "I see. I'm about four klicks away. It will take me a moment to rejoin. In the meantime, it would be helpful if you could ask him to throttle back a tad. And you might want to consider turning him toward the field."

"You've got to be shitting me!" Mikhail was the first to find his voice. "That idiot was flying the drone against Damien?"

"It's a long story; for later. First we have to get the kid down." Hoser keyed the number one radio. "Hey, Pete, we need you to throttle back. Can you see your engine instruments?"

"No."

"We've got you at four hundred knots. Take a stab at setting about two-fifty. We'll let you know if you pulled too much power." To the others he said, "Let's get his heading squared away. Matsasuta, you work the scope and call it."

Matsasuta slipped into the chair vacated by the technician and slipped on a headset so that he could also talk with the control tower. "Okay. He's heading one-nine-zero. What are the surface winds?"

Kohl opened the door and checked the wind sock. "Westerly at ten."

"Then we bring him in from the east. Come left to one-zero-zero. What scale is this scope in?"

"Nautical miles, sir."

"Of course it is. That figures." Matsasuta glanced up at the Navy pilot to let him know he was kidding.

"Damn straight." Hoser knew he had picked the right man.

"He's thirty miles north."

Holding down both mike keys, he said, "Peter, I'm going to call a left turn. Just roll her in and roll out nice and smooth, okay? Buckingham is joining up on the outside."

"Yes."

"Good. Peter, start turn. That's it, just hold that angle of bank . . ."

As the EuroFighter came left, its radar—still searching diligently in dogfight mode—spotted and locked a previously identified hostile target at close range. The mission computer deferred to the Damien system since it had not been disengaged and overrode the altitude hold command. In the span of a heartbeat, the aircraft nose snapped up four degrees to center the gunsight.

Matsasuta caught the HUD symbology change out of the corner of his eye, and shouted, "Damien!" just as the cannon spun up and fired.

*   *   *

"Bloody hell!" radioed Buckingham upon recovering from yet another near miss from the relentless weapon system. "What say, blokes, we turn that nasty bugger off? I do believe I shat my trousers."

"Peter, are you still with us?"

"Yes. Damien is secured. And you were right about my arm. After that last one, it doesn't hurt anymore. It just feels numb."

Hoser exchanged glances with Randi, and mouthed the words, *not good.*

"That's exactly what happened to me in '82, partner. I was flying an air show and popped my neck just like you. After a minute, my arm fell asleep. It was just a pinched nerve. The doc fixed me right up. But we'll square all that away when we get you on deck. First things first; we have to get you heading home so you can buy the beer, son. Now . . . start turn . . ."

Sergei asked, "He can't eject with his neck like that, can he?"

"He's not. We're going to trap him in the short-field arresting gear. It's going to take all of us working together."

"Isn't that going to hurt his neck?" asked Randi.

"It's not like a shipboard trap; there's twice as much pay-out. And it's a damn sight better than ground-looping it."

"Steady up," said Matsasuta.

"Stop turn, Pete."

"What's the plan?" asked Mikhail.

Hoser was silent for a moment, then barked instructions in rapid-fire order. "Matsasuta, you're going to talk him through the landing checklist. Sergei, you work the scope for the approach. Kohl?"

"Yes?" Randi and Moshe answered at the same time.

"No, Moshe. Find a jeep and radios, then come get me. Mikhail?"

"Yes?"

"You get Khalim's crash crew out there, but keep them out of the way. We need a lot of room. Also see if you can get a couple roller stands from the hangar. Randi, go find that goddamn doctor. And you four," he said, pointing at the rest of the EuroFighter team, "go with her. Get a brief from the doc. Mikhail, don't let those crash apes manhandle the kid. Use these guys. Have them open the canopy, dearm the seat, disconnect his gear, and unstrap him. Carefully! But don't move him or even touch his helmet until the doc says okay. And just in case, have them brief the crash crew on what they need to know about that jet if this gets ugly. Whitefoot?"

"Yes, sir?"

"Get up in that tower and do whatever it takes to keep those idiots from screwing this up. Do you need any help?"

"No."

"Good. Questions? No? Shit hot. Don't stand here, people; let's get this show on the road!"

*   *   *

"Twelve miles, on course. Level five thousand." Sergei had the advantage of using both the ground-tracking radar—now piped to his scope courtesy of Whitefoot—and the view from Peter's HUD. The tower supervisor had strongly objected to having his field taken over, but quickly acquiesced when Whitefoot demonstrated that his only other option involved extreme pain. Nevertheless, to cover his ass, the civil servant was recording the entire process.

The crash crew, under Mikhail's control, was standing by. Randi located the doctor, an orthopedic surgeon, by commandeering the public-address system. He'd been lost in the maze.

"Radio check?" Hoser and Kohl were in position at the approach end of the runway. Hoser, a former landing signal officer, would talk the kid down in the last half mile.

"Loud and clear," responded Matsasuta.

"Tower? Confirm the arresting gear is in battery."

"Confirmed," said Whitefoot. "Maximum speed for his gross weight is one hundred sixty knots."

"Roger one-six-oh. Crash crew?"

"We're up. The doctor is here," said Mikhail.

"Good. Peter. Are you ready for the landing checklist?"

"Ah . . . yes." Savant's voice had weakened considerably in the last few minutes.

"Walk him through it, Hiro."

"Lower the gear handle, now." The EuroFighter was equipped with autoflaps that would program when the gear came down.

"Peter?"

"Mmm?"

"We need the gear down."

"Oh . . . yes, I . . . I'll try."

"He's drifting right," said Sergei.

"Peter!" It was Buckingham. His voice was high-pitched.

"Yes?"

"I've got a serious problem. One of your rounds must have nicked me after all. There's a fire light and my cockpit is filling with smoke." He coughed for effect. "I have to land on your wing. You've got to bring me in, mate."

Sergei raised his eyebrow at Matsasuta. Nothing the Brit said or did surprised him anymore.

"Roger. Stand by for gear." There was newfound purpose in Savant's voice.

"Three-quarters of a mile. I have control," Hoser announced. With eyeballs calibrated from controlling thousands of carrier landings on a dozen deployments around the world, he alone could coerce the ever-finer control inputs required to put the jet into the landing zone. Since Matsasuta had talked him through engaging the autothrottles, Peter had only to concentrate on the stick.

"Peter, don't think about being smooth. Just follow my commands exactly, and we'll get Buckingham down safely."

"I'm counting on you, mate," Buckingham added.

"Okay." Savant sounded determined.

"Come right . . . steady up. Good. You're a little high, push the nose down . . . now catch it. Good. A little left . . ."

The confident and subtle nuances in Hoser's voice were mesmerizing. From his bird's-eye view, Buckingham marveled that the American caught deviations before he could see them from his own cockpit.

"How's he do that?" Mikhail asked Randi.

"It's a gift. He's recovered more crippled jets than you can count."

"Hold the nose up . . . a little more . . . Good. A little left . . . steady there . . . Hold it. Good . . ."

Buckingham leveled off at one hundred feet.

Hoser and Savant—one with the eyes, one with his hand—flew the aircraft directly into the runway centerline. There was no flair; this was a Navy landing. The tailhook left a trail of sparks as it skittered down the concrete.

"Throttle back."

The engine noise cut to a whisper but was immediately replaced by the sound of the crash trucks racing to meet the jet.

"Good trap!" The tailhook snagged the two-inch cable, stretching it like a giant rubber band as the fighter slowed.

"Peter?"

There was no answer.

"Peter, this is Hiro. Are you okay?"

"Yes. I . . . I'd like that beer now."

CHAPTER 25

"Please? Will somebody *please* get me down from here?"

"C'mon, Hoser." Randi pleaded Jack's case. "Let him down. He's learned his lesson."

"I don't know. Simon! Mikhail! What do you say? Do we let him live?"

The three pilots gathered at the base of the chair-and-table pyramid they'd built as Jack's funeral pyre. Jack was perched atop it, mummified to a chair by a hundred yards of duct tape. Over his head was a pilot's helmet bag. Mikhail gave a table leg a kick that sent a tremor through the rickety, twenty-five-foot stack.

"Earthquake!"

"Stop it! That's not funny."

"Perhaps 'tis time to set it aflame," said Buckingham. "We owe a sacrifice to the gods for our good fortune. What do you say, Hiro?"

Hiro had been drinking sake. A great deal of sake. With a scarf tied around his forehead, he looked like a samurai. Teaming with Whitefoot, the two had destroyed several pieces of furniture while demonstrating their martial-arts prowess. He punctuated his answer by snapping another piece of lumber. "I say, *Banzai!*"

The entire pub picked up the cry: *"Banzai! Banzai!"*

Jack would swear later that he felt flames licking at his boots.

"So what do you have to say for yourself?" demanded Hoser. "And remember, this is your last chance." It was his third "last chance" of the hour.

Jack, sensing that the rate of alcohol consumption would soon put these maniacs beyond caring, made his apology as sincere-sounding as possible. "I was wrong to get mad that nobody called me about the rescue. I was selfish. Instead of thinking about your safety, all I thought about was getting my story on the air."

"And what else? Let's hear this part loud and clear, mister. Shhh!" Hoser held his hand up to silence the rowdy crowd.

Jack resigned himself to the loss of all dignity. He repeated the confession they'd been coaxing him to make all night. "You are all fighter gods and I am just a slimy, maggot, has-been reporter leeching off society."

A cheer erupted from the crowd as the jukebox was turned back on.

Jack's voice was barely audible above the din. "Now, can I come down?"

*   *   *

"That is all, Governor." The prince, dressed in traditional garb, bowed, and spoke with great deference. "May I answer any questions?" After requesting an emergency meeting, he had commandeered a helicopter to fly to Riyadh for an audience with the elder. Two governors, who happened to be in the city, joined them.

"I can see that you believe passionately in this new plan."

"Yes, Governor, I do. I humbly submit that we risk too much by orchestrating the results of the contest. I beg your forgiveness for not bringing this to the council's attention earlier. It is clearly my fault." By identifying himself as the culprit, the prince gave the council a convenient scapegoat to justify a change in plans. It was a calculated move on his part, part of a larger strategy.

The elder exchanged glances with the men on either side. "Please excuse us for a minute."

The prince bowed further and left by a side door.

"Gentlemen, your thoughts?"

"I am pleased to see he takes his responsibilities so seriously," offered the junior governor, not wanting to commit until he knew which way the elder was leaning.

"Very true, and, of course, perfectly useless information. And you, Governor Jalawi? Are you willing to take a stand?"

"He makes good points about the difficulty of controlling the outcome now that the contest has so much visibility. Two-hundred and fifty million people! It is unbelievable the attention this man Warner has brought upon us. Still, we must not let the Russians lose. We have too much riding on the outcome."

"I agree. We will implement the contingency plan. I also find our young heir's sudden change of heart suspicious. This bears watching." To the junior governor, he said, "Summon my nephew. We will not discuss our plans for tomorrow with him. Let the arrogant one think he has won this round. In fact, this is working out to our advantage. He will be that much more convincing when dealing with the participants."

"Socks check!" Buckingham stood atop a table, his flight suit around his ankles.

While several people familiar with the British RAF tradition hastily dropped their pants and flight suits, many more stood mouths agape, wondering what the madman was up to now.

"We must see the color of your socks, but only from the top down," Simon lectured. "Last one to peel down, goes up in the chair!"

In a flurry of flying buckles and trousers, the crowd disrobed. Randi grimaced, glanced at the chair from which Warner had recently been rescued by Sergei. After considering her options, she shrugged out of her flight suit.

"Holy shit!"

The coordinated set of black panties and low-cut bra, worn just in case tonight turned into something interesting, were obviously a hit. With hundreds of eyes burning holes in her, she said, "Don't stand there looking like an idiot, Captain. Shed that suit."

"Uhh . . ."

"You better hurry, Steve, there're only a couple people left."

"I'm going to kill that limey bastard," he said, dropping his flight suit to a chorus of hoots.

Captain Steven Whitefoot was not wearing any underwear.

Lieutenant Randi Cole executed the only response that was proper for the circumstances. She came to attention and returned the salute.

PART 5

EVENT FOUR
THE GAUNTLET

CHAPTER 26

Official Standings after Events One through Three
1. **Lancer**
2. **Super Hornet**
3/4. **Raptor/Strike Flanker (tied)**
5. **KFIR II**
6. **EuroFighter**

Pilot meeting

"That sun is killing me. Somebody close those damn shades."

"Sun? We're underground, Einstein."

"Oh."

Jack surveyed the pitiful excuse for a pilot cadre with a growing sense of satisfaction. It had taken him an hour of painful swabbing with Randi's fingernail-polish remover to clean off the adhesive residue from the duct tape. Worse yet were the numerous bald spots, where massive hunks of hair from his arms and legs—he'd been stripped to his skivvies before the ceremonial mummification—had been yanked out by the roots. While Sergei had proven to be an adept rescuer, his draconian method of untaping left a good bit to be desired. So it was with unadulterated pleasure that Jack signaled the beginning of Day Four with a blast on a portable air horn borrowed from the equally resentful crash crew.

"Egad!" Hands clasped ears throughout the room.

"Welcome to the zero-six-thirty pilot briefing for the fourth event. I trust that each of you has had a suitable night's rest. I'm sorry, it doesn't look like you can hear me."

Jack made an adjustment to his microphone. "HOW IS IT NOW?"

"Oh God, make it stop . . ."

"We should have burned the bastard when we had the chance."

"Bugger off, Warner, you bloody sadist."

"Now, now . . . I am only here to help. By the looks of you, it's time for damage control." Jack signaled to his assistants, and carts of fresh coffee, orange juice, bottled water, and plenty of aspirin were wheeled in. "I'm sure this will break your hearts, but by order of the show's director, today's first launch has been delayed by one hour. Drink up, boys and girls."

"Given the, ahem, energy levels of some in our midst, does anyone have a problem if we juggle the starting lineup? No? Then who would like to go first?" While the gaggle had vastly improved from his first glimpse—once again, Jack marveled at the recuperative powers of fighter pilots—the ringleaders would clearly benefit from more downtime.

Moshe Kohl raised his hand. "I'll go."

"Any objections?"

"I'll take second," Whitefoot said.

"Bless you both," said Buckingham. "Did anyone get the license of that sake truck that hit me last night?"

"So that's it." Jack started the wrap-up. "Allow me to recap. Each of you will receive your sealed instructions at the aircraft. In them you'll find the coordinates for three checkpoints and target-specific information. You are free to choose any route of flight that will get you to the target on time, but the more checkpoints you hit—each is worth two points—the better your score. As long as we're on the subject, a direct hit on the target is worth eight points, a near miss—inside twenty-five meters—is worth five, and a wide miss three. If you make it to the target, but don't drop, it's worth two, the same as a checkpoint. You will be opposed by Saudi Royal Air Force F-15s. If you bag an Eagle, it is only worth one point.

"Again, the objective of the gauntlet is to make it to the target unscathed, drop your single inert bomb, and return. If, at any time, you are nailed with a valid kill shot, you're done for the day and your total is debited three points. Any questions?"

"Can you tell us if the target has ground defenses?"

"That's a good question, since it may drive your tactics. As stated, the mission is a sneak attack. The target is a command and control center. If you make it cleanly through the air-defense net and are not picked up by the site's own surface radar, the target's defenses will be minimal. If you are spotted, they will be put on alert. Specific information is in your target packet. If there are no further questions, that wraps up the brief."

The pilots started to disperse.

"If I could have just one more moment, please." The prince had joined the brief only minutes earlier.

"I left Riyadh this morning, where Captain Savant is recovering from surgery to fuse three verte-brae. I have good news. Your friend has regained some feeling in the fingers of his left hand, and the surgeon described his prognosis as excellent."

"That's beautiful."

"Before I left, Peter asked me to transcribe this message and read it to you:

Dear friends,

I cannot tell you how much I appreciate your efforts to save me. Without you, I would be dead, and worse yet, our beautiful airplane would be pranged again. That is a joke. Bless you all. They tell me I will never fly again. That is no joke. I want you each to know that as much as I love to fly, this is okay for me. Thanks to you, I have my whole life to treasure the memories. So do not worry about me. Just fly safe and think of your

friend Peter from time to time. Oh, and do tell
Simon that he is a much better pilot than actor.
    Sincerely,
    Captain Peter Savant"

The group broke up quickly without making eye
contact.

"So, how did it go in the city?" asked Jack when he
and the prince were alone in the ready room. Jack's
suspicions were running overtime.

"Much, *much* better than I expected. I took your
advice and asked for permission to run the contest on
the up-and-up."

"Could you run that by me again?" That Jack
couldn't remember offering such advice added to his
surprise that the prince would take such a risk. Then
again, it could be total bullshit. Odds were building
that it probably was.

The prince lowered his voice. "All right, maybe
you didn't say it in so many words, but after our discussion I couldn't forget that look you gave me when
I told you about the Caspian Sea deal. Remember
when you asked if anything could be worth being
branded a liar and a cheat?"

"Yes, I suppose I did."

"And you're dead right. We have no business
jeopardizing our reputation no matter how much oil
is involved."

Jack had to admit that the young man gave a con-

vincing performance. He certainly looked as if the
weight of the world had been lifted from his shoulders. For the first time in days, he looked energized
and enthusiastic, despite having gotten little sleep.
"It must have gone okay; you still have your head
attached."

"I was surprised at the reception. The council let
me explain my reasoning, then asked me to step out
of the room. I don't mind telling you, I was worried
when I was summoned back in only five minutes. But
when the governor who came to get me gave me a
smile of encouragement, I began to get my hopes up.
Then the elder explained that my brief had convinced
them. Jack, I know it sounds far-fetched, but we've
got the okay to finish the contest fairly, no matter
what the outcome."

"And there were no conditions imposed? At all?"
Jack was especially uneasy with the suddenness of
the council's apparent reversal. It simply didn't fit
their pattern of behavior. He'd long ago learned that
habits—like a tradesman's penchant for squeezing
the most out of every deal—were nearly impossible
to break. When they were, an extraordinary reason
must be present. Protecting the council's reputation
didn't seem to be a likely candidate. Careful to keep
his expression upbeat, he wrestled with his suspicions, very much wanting to believe in the prince's
integrity.

"There were no ifs, ands or buts. Isn't that amaz-
ing? I tell you, pal, this whole experience has been
remarkable. You're going to think I've gone soft, but

when we took off from the palace this morning, the sun was just coming up. The city, my home, Jack, was peaceful and beautiful." He closed his eyes and smiled at the memory. "I feel a deep pride for my country and my people. It was as if the dawn symbolized the new opportunities that we're bringing them." He put an arm around Jack's shoulder and led him out. "I've become completely rejuvenated. By the way, how's it feel to have transformed a culture? And don't think I'm going to let you off the hook, buddy, when this competition is over. No way, José. We have only just begun!"

Despite Jack's suspicions, the prince's enthusiasm was contagious. It felt mighty good to be appreciated. And they *had* been incredibly successful, by anyone's standards. But when Jack left his boss to grab a bite to eat, his smile faded. For better or worse, Jack Warner had been cursed with a mind that refused to believe its own bullshit.

"Sorry about that, but you had it coming."

Jack had joined Randi in the Oasis for a bite and returned a nearly empty bottle of fingernail-polish remover. He was disappointed in her lack of sympathy.

Between bites of melon and pastry, Jack filled her in on the prince's startling news. He tried to present the story objectively. Her skeptical reaction reinforced his feeling of unease.

"Jack, from what we know, it doesn't seem likely

that the Saudi council would so easily give up their plan of controlling the competition."

"That's astute. And I don't think so, either."

"Is the prince lying, or just naive?"

"He might be legit. I hope so; I'm inclined to cut him some slack. He's worked himself to exhaustion. If you think about it, these are men whom he respects, and it would be natural for him to seek their respect in return. Perhaps they see that as a weakness and blew some smoke up his ass. Who hasn't been there?"

"Well, the jury is still out. In the meantime, do you have any guesses at what the council might be up to?"

"They don't have much time to help the Strike Flanker make a big move in the standings. Their plans, if there are any, have to involve today's mission. As I see it, the wild cards in the gauntlet are the Eagle drivers and the AWACS. Either or both could be involved. I wouldn't be one bit surprised to see everyone bagged today with the exception of the Russians."

"Even so, Simon's lead is huge. The bettors have him at even money. If he comes in second today and tomorrow, he'll still win."

"You may have just answered your own question."

"You mean that they have to make Simon finish worse than second? That sounds ominous. What are we going to do?"

"Talk to him, I guess. But I know he'll blow me off."

"Jack, I don't think you've given enough thought to your own vulnerability. If something is going down, then you are the wild card as far as the council is concerned."

"We still have to warn Simon."

"Better let me talk to him. Besides, I speak his lingo."

"Well, you're certainly better equipped to hold his attention. What are you going to say?"

"I'll tell him to check six."

CHAPTER 27

The AWACS commander was incredulous. The prince's decision not to feed his airborne command and control system the data from the contestant's telemetry pods meant that his controllers would have to rely exclusively on their own onboard radar and those of the Eagles. It was lunacy! Even so, he was careful to phrase his objection so as not to overstep his authority and offend a member of the royal family. "I understand the instructions, Your Highness. And we are honored to serve in any capacity. But, as you know, several of these aircraft have stealth technology. We may not be able to pick them up, especially at low altitude."

The general lowered his voice. "I hope you will understand that I am not just concerned about how that makes us look to my superiors. There are national-security ramifications of exposing our weakness."

"Your candid observations are right on target, General. To ensure that you are not held responsible, you will receive written verification of this conversation via satellite fax within ten minutes. I appreciate and value your advice, as do all of our countrymen. Please understand that this decision was not made lightly and has the full support of the council.

"It is in our best interest to conduct this mission with scrupulous integrity, and that means both the AWACS and the fighter pilots must rely on their organic systems. I would urge you to seek the silver lining in this cloud. You are the very first to observe these new technologies in an operational setting. From that perspective, it is a wonderful opportunity to assess our own capabilities and make recommendations for enhancements, don't you agree?"

Mollified by the compliments and written orders, the general throttled back. "Yes, Your Highness. I should have known that you saw a bigger picture. Thank you for setting this old warrior straight. I will keep an eye out for the orders. Peace be upon you."

"And on you."

The KFIR II employed several stealth and deception technologies adapted from the Americans, with a couple twists courtesy of Israeli engineers. Even so, it could not fly with impunity into the teeth of an integrated air-defense net manned by eight F–15s coordinated by an airborne search radar. Moshe Kohl needed another angle.

When the controller called, "Fight's on," to signify that the clock had started, Moshe took a slight twenty-degree heading cut into the defenders and waited for the Eagles to show their hand. By coupling very little closure with low altitude, he knew—from extensive tests with the Israeli's own F–15 force—that the KFIR's composite airframe would not show up on the Eagles' radar until just inside fifteen kilometers. If he turned head-on, he'd reduce his radar cross section, but the increase in closing speed would highlight him on the AWACS Doppler system. Given that the KFIR was not a fully stealth aircraft like the famous F–117, Kohl would need advantageous geometry to offset the huge disparity in numbers. Especially since he couldn't rely on his own radar to track the Eagles because it would highlight his position.

As he glided northeast across the nearly featureless desert, the KFIR's signal processor cataloged the hostile radar signals and displayed their sources in a tactical picture. Six Eagles were southbound in pairs, oriented in three zones east to west. The fourth pair was likely staying close to the target as a goalie and to keep an eye out for an end run.

At twenty-five kilometers from the target, three radar symbols dropped off Moshe's display almost simultaneously. The pairs had split into an opposing racetrack pattern. While one Eagle flew back toward the target, the other would head outbound for a predetermined mileage, at which point they would each reverse course. In this way the lanes—each of which just so happened to hold a bonus checkpoint—would always be protected by radar pointed south.

Though it presented difficulties, Moshe was not

discouraged since each Eagle would now have to scan that much more sky. The Israeli Air Force preferred to keep their pairs together to keep the search responsibilities more focused.

"Can't they see him on their radar?" asked a guest seated in the row below Matsasuta.

"You'll know when they do," he whispered. "That's when things get interesting."

The KFIR's tactical display marked the paths and turnaround points used by the F–15s. After a lazy turn to the west, heading back across the lanes, Kohl timed his approach to intersect a point just outside the fifteen-kilometer limit when the westernmost Eagle would start his turn back. With luck, he would be well positioned for the next phase of his plan.

"We still have no contacts. Nothing to report." The general kept the frustration out of his voice by tapping the single-page fax safely tucked into the breast pocket of his flight suit. Let the young prince explain. Even a general must follow orders.

Moshe caught a glimpse of the Eagle as it began its turn to the north. Eschewing the bonus points, he accelerated and closed, but remained low. By placing himself directly beneath the Eagle and matching its speed—even though they were vertically separated by twenty-five thousand feet—the AWACS Doppler system would have trouble distinguishing between the two. That left the wingman with which to contend. By now, the frustrated pilot had no doubt opened up his scan, which, while covering more space, gave the radar only a couple sweeps to locate and synthesize a return before it moved to another chunk of the sky. Even if it did pick him up briefly, the target return on the scope would, hopefully, be superimposed beneath his partner.

It was maddeningly difficult for Kohl to head directly at an opponent who, by virtue of his altitude advantage, had significantly better missile range. In the parlance of fighter pilots, the Eagle had the longer stick.

The oncoming Eagle's radar remained low for several sweeps as the kilometers counted down toward fifteen. For a moment, it looked as if he'd been spotted. But it was a false alarm. The signal faded once more. As the two Eagles passed, they acknowledged each other with a wing rock.

Now it was time to circumvent the goalies.

"He's slipped inside the gate. That was pretty crafty," said Matsasuta. He'd been narrating the event to an enthralled group of nearby listeners. "But I'll be surprised if the AWACS doesn't pick him out now that he's going to lose that cover. And there we go. The inside Eagle is turning south. Let's see what the man with nerves of steel does now."

With twenty kilometers to the target, Moshe weighed his chances. He was carrying an inert bomb that could be delivered in a dive, from a pop, or with a lay-down. Since accuracy counted, he would prefer a dive or pop because they gave him a chance to make adjustments, but his exposure to the area's defensive systems would be greater. It would have to be a lay-down.

"He's lit 'em up!" Matsasuta pointed to the HUD airspeed readout as the KFIR quickly accelerated. "And it looks like he caught the backcourt with their pants down; they're heading the wrong way."

It was indeed a mad dash. One that would have worked but for the general's decision to put an experienced pilot onboard the AWACS.

"Slash five-one split-S now! Bogey inbound come to one-niner-zero. Go vertical scan. Select Sparrow and launch on lock!"

Only the voice of his operations officer—a man with whom he had flown as wingman for three years—could have elicited such an immediate and faithful response by the pilot of Slash 51. Without a second thought, he snap-rolled the F–15 and pulled, simultaneously thumbing back on the radar-select toggle. The Sparrow missile was already selected. Halfway through his maneuver, the HUD symbology flashed as the radar locked a high-speed target. Without waiting for a shoot cue, he fired. One second later, the minimum-range warning flashed. It didn't matter.

"KFIR, you're dead. Vector two-seven-zero to vacate the area." The controller transmitted on the flight-safety frequency that all pilots monitored.

Just that quickly, the Israeli team's chances of winning evaporated. Yet Kohl was gracious. He'd been bagged fair and square. "Acknowledged. Please pass my sincere congratulations to Slash five-one. He must have eyes in the back of his head."

There was a pause during which the KFIR made his turn and began to climb. Then the general himself came on the air. "Colonel Kohl."

"Go ahead."

"You, sir, are a most worthy opponent."

A series of double mike clicks followed as the Eagle pilots echoed their agreement.

CHAPTER 28

"So there you have it. The bottom line is that Jack and I think you may be in danger. Personally, I hope you don't take it lightly." Randi had tracked down Simon in his hangar.

To his credit, the Brit had stopped joking long enough to listen to her intently. "We have reached much the same conclusion, but, of course, had not ferreted out the underlying reasons. And I appreciate your concern, professionally and . . . personally. We've been vigilant. The Lancer has been under twenty-four-hour guard, and we have run independent tests on our petrol. We also fostered the plan to shift our launch to last so that it will be more difficult to stack the deck against us."

At her look of surprise, he added, "I hope you didn't buy that little charade," he pronounced it, *sha-rod*, "about my being too hungover to fly."

"Well, it was a convincing act."

"Dear Randi, I'll let you in on a little secret." Buckingham motioned her closer, and whispered, "I've been nursing beers since that first night. Frankly, I don't know how Hoser can keep it up. The man is an animal. Of course if you tell him, I shall deny it. You do understand?"

"Your secret is safe with me."

He stepped back. "Very good. Now, unless you can think of some other precaution, I think we are prepared."

"I'll make sure that Jack runs a backup tape on the mission recorder."

"Righto then." His serious demeanor gave way to a mischievous grin. "Now on to more important issues. After I have thoroughly waxed everyone's tail today and tomorrow, are you prepared to take a celebratory holiday to the English countryside with an officer and gentleman of the Royal Air Force?"

"Absolutely!"

Buckingham's grin widened.

"Be sure to let me know when one shows up."

"My dear, you have the most venomous tongue."

"Alice: Compute best route via checkpoints to target. Minimize exposure. Present options."

"Copy, Steve. Stand by. Do not maneuver. Estimated time to compute is thirty-three seconds."

Alice was being stretched to her operational limits. While fusing the data from her sensors with the stored threat information in her library, along with the navigation parameters and priorities Whitefoot had programmed, her parallel processors would crunch the numbers at several million calculations per second. Once Whitefoot chose a plan, she would shift to tactical mode and use sensor data to make real-time decisions.

"Alice: Select Plan B. And recommend minimum-detection altitude. Factor the following: visibility ten miles, no clouds."

Alice computed the altitude at which contrails would form and extrapolated a shadow index to determine a likelihood of being spotted against the desert background. Her answer surprised Steve.

"Steve: Recommend medium altitude."

"Alice: Justify choice."

"Shadow index is eight-point-five. Contrail band extends from twenty-eight thousand to forty-five-plus. Medium altitude presents best chance of minimum detection and will not be expected. Recommend fifteen-thousand-two-fifty." She didn't wait to be asked to explain. "This altitude targets boundary of typical F–15 high and low search parameters."

"Alice: Medium altitude approved."

"Raptor, fight's on."

"Steve: Coming right to three-five-five, descending to altitude fifteen-thousand-two-fifty, setting three-hundred-sixty knots, control-stick steering engaged. Radar in sniff." Alice had control of the guidance, altitude, and speed, but in a mode that enabled Whitefoot to input changes without disengaging the system.

* * *

"That's a new one." Randi had joined Jack in their customary seats.

"You mean his altitude?"

"Yeah. I honestly thought Steve would be the one to come in high. But he wouldn't give me any hints. They must have terrific confidence in their stealth package."

"It looks like he's heading for checkpoint three."

"After Moshe got skunked, I think everyone is going to make sure they get a couple points in the bank before making a run on the target."

"By the way, how did Simon react?"

"He actually listened to what I had to say, but he's going to fly anyway."

"Well, we didn't expect him to back off. At least he took it seriously."

"I promised I'd ask you to run a backup tape on the mission."

"That's a good idea."

"Can you do it without alerting anyone?"

"I'll have my young tech buddy do it."

"You have a way with people who work for a living. They all seem to like you."

"Well, as my ex is fond of saying, 'There's no accounting for tastes.'"

Whitefoot monitored Alice's decisions via the high-resolution tactical display. Attached to the F–15 symbols were balloon-shaped graphics that depicted their likely radar and visual-detection envelopes. Alice zigzagged to keep the Raptor outside the coverage, all the while progressing toward the valued checkpoints.

"This is maddening," said the general. The defenders had not so much as a hint of where the Raptor was hiding. "The Americans sell us this technology, then promptly build an invisible strike fighter that can waltz through it unfazed."

"He's not invisible, sir," said Major Jadin. "Just stealthy."

"And your point?"

"Put all our radars into sniff mode. They're doing us no good anyway, and he's using them to plot our position."

"And then what? Tuck our tails and go home?"

"No, sir. Stack the fighters in around the target. If he gets close, we'll spot him before the bomb run. And if he uses his radar, even for a moment, we'll get an azimuth cut and send half a dozen Eagles right down his throat. That still leaves a pair to stay put and protect the target."

"You must stay awake at night thinking of these tactics . . . and I must be crazy to listen to you. May Allah help us both if this fails, Major. Make it so."

One by one the F–15 symbols changed to red, indicating a loss of data. "Alice. Say target status."

"Steve: Signals dropped on four . . . five . . . stand by."

"What the hell is going on?"

"Steve. All targets have stopped radiating."

"Alice: Recommendations?"

"Steve: Unable to estimate detection probability. Need more information."

"I don't. These guys are being pretty cute. Alice: Proceed to the last checkpoint. Expedite." Whitefoot searched the sky for predators.

"So let me get this straight." The American investment mogul was incredulous. "We've got what? About two billion dollars' worth of hardware up there? And they've all turned their systems *off*?"

"So it would appear." Randi was equally stunned.

"Straight up. What do you think of his chances?"

"With no radar? It's eight pairs of eyeballs to one pair. And they know precisely where he's going. With the visibility today, I don't give him more than one in ten."

"What would you do in that situation?"

"With six points in the bag, if I didn't think I could get in there, I'd abort. As tough as these guys are flying today, that looks like a score that could hold up."

"Please don't take offense, but that's not the answer I expected. Fighter pilots are, by nature, risk takers. From what I've read about you, young lady, you fit that mold to a tee."

Randi was flattered that Warren Keating, introduced to her by Prince Salman as one of the world's most successful investors in high technology, had taken time to learn more about her. In his sixties, and, from all evidence, happily married, there was no indication that his interest was anything but genuine. As a measure of respect, she gave him a thoughtful answer. "You have to balance the value of one target against the future targets that aircraft and pilot can destroy if they survive. Today, the objective is to score the most points. If I was up there and they pulled that stunt, I'd back off."

"I think this might be an example of how you approach things differently as a woman. Don't you think Buckingham or the Russian would rather slit their wrists than give up? Hell, you saw what the Israeli colonel did."

"Maybe so. But I can guarantee you that Santana wouldn't wade in there either."

"Why are you so sure?"

"He's the one that taught me that a professional knows the difference between courage and foolishness."

"That's not bad." He pulled a worn pad and pen out of his breast pocket and jotted it down. "I'm going to use that one with my folks." On the spur of the moment, he asked, "Listen, what are you doing for lunch?"

"Nothing special."

He stood. "Please join me. I've got some people you should meet and a couple things to discuss with you."

"Aren't you going to stay and watch the fight?"

"Maybe later. First, I've got to get a bet down. Seems I just got a hot tip."

"Steve: Recommend burst transmission to build target picture."

"Alice: Initiate two-cycle sweep."

"Spike!" The operator eagerly highlighted the Raptor's signal on the command and control display.

"Slashers: Threat bears one-seven-zero, execute heart attack with stinger." Turning to the general, Major Jadin explained, "The lead two pairs will take thirty-degree cuts away from the bearing line, separated high and low, hold it for twenty seconds, and then turn to parallel. The geometry is heart-shaped, hence the name."

"And the stinger?"

"The third pair will take a ten-thousand-foot split and run right up the middle with their radar on. They should sweep the American into the pincers on one side or the other.

"Steve: Multiple targets in proximity of target."

"Altitude?"

"Various."

"Damn. Let's see if they come out to play."

Three seconds later, a single radar illuminated. It was heading directly at the Raptor.

"If there's one, there's probably two of the wily bastards. Alice: Narrow scan, one sweep."

The tactical display showed a second target, above and to the right of the first.

"Gotcha! Alice: Offset west, engage dogfight mode. Let's get us some Eagle meat."

Several members of the dome audience whistled and hollered warnings, but to no avail. Captain Steven Whitefoot, United States Air Force, died in a virtual fireball at the unseen hands of Slasher 61.

Once more, the target remained unscathed.

CHAPTER 29

"Hoser is up."

"Copy, Super Hornet. Fight's on."

The F/A–18 was stealthy, but not ghostlike. Hoser had a different game plan in mind than his peers.

"That's him! Still nothing on radar, but he's transmitting intermittently. There's another spike. I've got a solid bearing at one-eight-five." The AWACS controller was ecstatic to have hits on his scope right off the bat.

"Slasher four-one and four-two, vector one-eight-five." Major Jadin wanted to keep the American at arm's length. "Let's go lead trail, high-low. Slasher four-one, you transmit; four-two, use sniff."

"One copies."

"Two copies."

"Warning. Threat radar. Classified F–15. Range undetermined . . ."

"Shut up, Betty."

"Say again. Command unintelligible."

Hoser scanned the cheat sheet of commands Randi had taped to the top of his knee-board. "Betty: Mute."

"Mute enabled."

"Betty?" There was no response. "Shit hot. Why the hell didn't somebody tell me about this before?"

The dome audience roared with delight.

"Still nothing, sir. He's gone lights out."

"Slasher four-one, give it another ten kilometers and then return."

"Four-one. Two, keep a sharp lookout. Plan to stagger back to cover my turn."

"Copy."

Hoser picked up the high Eagle first. As soon as he knew they were coming down the bearing line, he'd taken a ninety-degree cutaway and hustled ten miles east—tagging a checkpoint in the progress, thank you very much—before reversing. The move put the sun at his back, and with his nose perpendicular to their flight path, the Super Hornet's radar signal was no longer aimed toward the snooping AWACS.

The lead F–15 obligingly flew onto his scope. Hoser put the radar back into sniff and searched visually for the wingman. Finding him in trail put a smile beneath the oxygen mask. "You thought you had old

Hoser." Timing his pull until after the lead and then
the wingman had completed their reversals, Hoser
plugged in the burners and flew a belly intercept on
the wingman.

"What's he doing? Why would he get that close?"
asked Jack.

"I have absolutely no clue. He could have nailed
both of them by now."

Hoser loved formation flying, particularly the slot
position, where you tucked the nose of your fighter
right up under the exhaust nozzles of the lead. In
years past, he'd made a game of challenging his
wingmen to try to shake him; nobody could. Yet,
stuck beneath the flying tennis court they called an
Eagle—by fighter standards it was huge—bordered
on dull and boring. Nevertheless, the HUD camera
literally provided the dome audience with a riveting
perspective that had many sliding down in their seats.

It helped that Slasher 41, the lead, was in a hurry
to get back to station. No fighter pilot likes to have
his tail to the threat.

Four-two had already asked to cut the power
once, but was hesitant to call for another reduction,
especially since speed in a hostile area is a lifesaver.

It was poor form to leave your wingman in lag,
where he couldn't be visually cleared, but the flight
lead rationalized that if the Super Hornet tried to run

them down, he'd be forced to go supersonic and the AWACS would spot him.

Just to be safe, the wingman kept his head on a swivel, completely ignorant of his remora-like partner.

Inside fifteen kilometers to the target—after overflying a second checkpoint—Slasher 41 continued his thoughtless behavior by throttling back without so much as a courtesy head's-up.

Hoser almost swallowed his gum when the wingman's big speedbrake deployed—unbeknownst to him since it was located on top of the F–15—and he found himself directly beneath the Eagle and rapidly skittering out in front. His own speedbrake was no match for the Eagle's barn door. Borrowing an old Blue Angel technique, he porpoised the aircraft violently. The maneuver immediately shed fifty knots.

Several audience members later claimed to have suffered vertigo and neck injuries.

Enough of this nonsense, thought Hoser. Leaving the nose down, he dived several hundred feet, then plugged in the burners and pulled into a raking gunshot, stitching the underbelly of his host. Knifing through the Eagle's exhaust, Hoser pirouetted the Super Hornet 120 degrees, put the lead Eagle on top of his canopy, and pulled.

"Slasher four-one, four-two are dead. Vector west."

"Damn it!" Later, Jadin would have a scalding rebuke for the pair's lookout doctrine. "Six-one, six-two, snap zero-eight-zero for twelve. Disregard exiting Eagles."

The former Slasher 42 couldn't help himself. "He's heading for the target at twenty-five thousand!"

The next voice was Prince Salman's. "Silence! Dead men do not talk."

Hoser gave the target area a once-over and counted four hits on the scope. There was no way he'd make it, at least not in broad daylight. He had six points. If he could bag the last checkpoint on the way out, it might be enough. With a snappy roll, he neatly split-S'ed, heading southbound and down.

The Super Hornet's flight dominated the lunchtime discussion among Keating and his wealthy peers. Randi enjoyed listening in.

"I think they should give it to him. He caused it as much as if he'd pulled the trigger."

"But all he did was run away. At least the other guys died in a blaze of glory."

"Lieutenant Cole, what do you think?"

"Please keep me out of it, gentlemen. I'm not what you would call an objective observer."

An immaculately dressed man Randi recognized as a career statesman summed it up succinctly, "The man tagged three checkpoints, bagged two Eagles, and got away scot-free. And I agree. He ought to get credit for the third Eagle that six-one shot by mistake. I've been in combat, gentlemen. There's no such thing as friendly fire."

*   *   *

"So what do you make of all this?" asked Keating as he and Randi strolled through the Oasis.

"You mean the competition or the accommodations?"

"Both."

"Part of me—the part with a stack of bills to pay—thinks it is an absurd waste of resources, while the other part thinks it is pretty neat. I just wish I were flying."

"What, no angst about pilots being treated like court jesters for our benefit?"

She stopped and stared hard at him, gauging if his comments were intentionally dismissive. "Is that what you think?"

He was still smiling. "I think that you all are immensely talented, remarkably courageous, and stunningly . . ."

She was sure he was going to say, beautiful, and decided not to let him get away with it. "Stunningly?"

"Gullible."

"Gullible?"

"Yes. You and your peers want to believe that your efforts here are noble and worth risking your lives for."

His bold characterization put her off-balance. "And they aren't?" It was all she could think to ask.

He perched on a rock, looked around casually, and said, "Randi, how much is Hoser being paid?"

"I'm afraid that's none of your . . ."

"Look, I'm not going to offer you a bribe, and

I'm not going to repeat what you tell me. I'm just trying to make a point."

"He's paid about seventy-five dollars an hour.
Why?"

"And of course all the beer he can drink." Again,
the smile was believable and dulled the sarcasm.

"Yeah, that too."

"Then let's recap. Today I bet a hundred grand on
the Super Hornet for the gauntlet event at three-to-
one odds. So while our friend is up there killing himself for a couple hundred dollars, I stand to make
roughly two hundred thousand."

"Oh my God."

"Don't be surprised. You gave me the tip."

"But what if he loses?"

"I can't lose, Randi."

"Don't be so sure. Buckingham and Mikhail
haven't flown yet. Either of them is capable of beating his score."

"I don't doubt it for a second. But you're not listening. I can't lose. None of us can."

"I'm afraid I don't understand."

"That two hundred is pocket change compared to
what I'm going to walk away with thanks to your
pals."

"So you must mean that you know who is going
to win. You're telling me that this thing is rigged. Is
that it, Mr. Keating?"

"Call me Warren."

She stood silent, hands on hips, working up a full
head of resentment.

He shrugged. "Suit yourself. I wouldn't doubt that it's rigged for a second, knowing our hosts as well as I do. But I couldn't care less. The betting is just a smoke screen."

Randi couldn't resist putting him in his place. "You must mean the oil."

"Oil?"

"Yes, the Caspian fields. The Saudis gain control of the Russian pipeline by funneling money into the right hands via the fighter contract. Maybe we're not as naive as you think, Mr. Keating."

"We?"

Randi caught herself. "Just a figure of speech."

He stood, and laughingly patted her on the back. "No, ma'am. You've got me. I didn't think you'd uncovered that angle. The question is, what are you going to do about it?"

"Probably nothing. Supposedly the head of the Saudi council of governors agreed this morning to let the contest be run on the level. I have my doubts, but that's where it stands."

"Well, good for you. Hey, let's get back to the dome. I want to see if our boy's score holds up to the competition."

She stopped before entering the dome. "Warren?"

"Yes, my young friend?"

"That was it, wasn't it? The oil? Somehow I get the feeling that if I hadn't shot off my big mouth, you were going to tell me about something else."

He smiled again and pulled her aside. "You are a refreshing piece of work, Lieutenant. And I like your style. What I'm about to say wouldn't be appreciated by the others. But first I need to know if you can keep a secret."

"It depends. I can if it's for a legitimate reason."

"Do you really think that things like this are that black-and-white?"

"Yes, I do, Warren. And deep down, I bet you do, too." She felt a momentary tinge of regret that she hadn't played along.

"Well, I hope you'll understand, but your silence is a little too open-ended for me. I can't lay it all out for you, but I'll tell you this much: Anytime you put this kind of money and these kinds of people in one place, there's liable to be more maneuvering than a bushel of snakes in a phone booth. And you're right. Oil is king in this part of the world; that's for sure. Nobody would ever go broke betting on the Saudis cooking up an oil deal." Then he winked. "But that's old school. The margins are ultrathin. I encourage you to open your eyes." He gestured to the Oasis. "This is a completely new game."

She gave him her best smile. "C'mon, Warren, you can do better than that. Give me a hint, at least."

"You're very persuasive. If you ever decide to get out of this racket, promise me you'll let me offer you a job."

"Deal."

"Excellent. Here it is: Real money doesn't have to be pumped or even dug out of the ground anymore. In today's global market, it can be made out of thin air—providing someone has the requisite vision, guts, and timing. And think big, my dear. Real big."

"But what about the contrails, Mikhail? They'll know we're up here." The Strike Flanker was passing thirty-five thousand feet and still climbing like a banshee.

"No, my friend, they'll *think* we're up here."

"But how will we get down without marking? Even with the engines at idle, we'll leave a trail."

Mikhail chuckled but did not respond.

"Mikhail? Surely you are not . . . No! Listen to me, you insane Bolshevik, I order you not to even think of it!"

"Strike Flanker, fight's on."

"Yes, it certainly is."

The next sound Sergei heard was a quiet rumble as both engines flamed out.

"Slasher five-one has a visual on a contrail at twelve o'clock long. He's going for the moon."

"Copy, Slashers. Elevate."

"Sergei, think of all the gas we're saving the Rodina." Mikhail was speaking in a normal voice, with his mask off. The silence in the cockpit was a novelty.

"Don't you talk to me, you crazy bastard. You better hope those engines restart, because I will hack you to pieces with my survival knife before you even think of ejecting."

"Not to worry."

"Not to worry? Our blood could have boiled at that altitude!"

"No, comrade. I talked with the engineers, and they assured me that the seals would hold. Don't you trust them?"

"On second thought, I am going to kill you anyway."

"Well, let's have some fun first. Bringing the number one throttle around the horn."

"What did I miss?" Whitefoot slipped into the chair next to Randi's.

"They took it into the cons and then, catch this, Mikhail shut down both engines to sneak back down."

"No way!"

"Yes, *way*, my savage friend. And he's already tagged two checkpoints."

"Hey! Who you calling 'friend,' lady?"

Jack caught the flirting but pretended to ignore it. A little pang of jealousy struck, but quickly passed. Truth be told, he was glad she'd found someone worthy.

"He's fooled you. That machine is not invisible. Go to surface map and look for high-speed targets." The prince's radioed orders on the private channel were unequivocal.

The controller looked to his general for confirmation.

He responded wearily, "Do it. May Allah protect us if this Russian does not win today."

"Contact! Single target heading zero-zero-five, five hundred forty knots, eighteen miles south of the target."

Of the eight Eagles, six fired simulated missiles at the lone intruder. On the dome ceiling, the Strike Flanker looked like a slowly moving dartboard.

"Strike Flanker is dead. Vector two-seven-zero."

"What is the EuroFighter carrying, sir?" the tower lookout asked, handing the binoculars to his supervisor.

"Decoys. I saw plenty of them used by the Americans during the war."

"Should we notify the operations officer? There are no decoys on their manifest."

"Screw it. They want to take over my field? Then they can get somebody else to be their eyes."

"EuroFighter, fight's on."

The small, unpowered decoys had a terrific glide ratio and were equipped with radar reflectors that made them appear as full-size aircraft when viewed head-on. Released from twenty-five thousand feet, they could cover nearly fifty kilometers in a straight line. But the engineers added a devious twist by programming alternating S-turns. Heading northbound, Captain Ytong dropped both decoys, confirmed that the wings deployed, then dived for the deck. On battery-powered autopilot, the first decoy took a slight cut to the west, while the second immediately turned hard to the east.

"Radar contact! Bearing one-eight-five, fifty-two kilometers, angels twenty-four. He's in a left turn and fading. Okay, I lost him."

"Slasher Six-one, six-two, commit."

"There he is again."

"Slasher six-one flight, come left one-seven-five for forty-eight, angels twenty-three-five."

"He must have circled. He's fading and drifting right this time."

"Sir?"

"Yes?" answered the major.

"He's popped up to the west again. For some reason, he seems to be running a racetrack perpendicular to us. He's not getting much closer."

"Slasher five-one, five-two, vector one-niner-zero. Six-one, six-two, continue to come left one-seven-zero. We'll bracket him. Expedite."

While the Eagles pursued the baffling decoys, the EuroFighter had slipped inside the outer perimeter. Captain Ytong briefly considered tagging the third checkpoint but decided to launch his weapon instead. At twelve kilometers and 540 knots, Ytong engaged the loft-delivery mode.

The EF–2000 was immediately picked up by AWACS and the backstop Eagles as it broke away from ground clutter.

The EuroFighter's defensive-countermeasures system functioned autonomously. Detecting an F–15 radar, it ejected the first of a half dozen small transponders loaded next to the chaff bucket. The disposable transponder was aerodynamically designed to spin at nearly ten thousand revolutions per minute. Its circuitry used the resultant energy to transmit a decoy signal nearly irresistible to radar-guided missiles.

"Bomb's away." Captain Ytong thought it only fair to announce that he'd pickled a thousand-pounder on a ballistic trajectory that would take it to nearly eighteen thousand feet with a time of flight of almost a minute. The loft technique wasn't precise—it was designed for nuclear weapons—but in this case, a wide miss was still worth three points. He continued the pull into a half–Cuban eight that quickly had him heading south.

"Heads up in the target area! Incoming bomb. That bastard is trying to kill somebody!"

"Slasher three-one has a tally-ho. Five miles in trail."

"Nail him!" The Eagle, though large, was one of

the fastest fighters ever built. But the EuroFighter was no slouch and was already at full steam. With the safe zone only twenty-five kilometers away, it would be a close call.

"Request permission to go vee-max."

The velocity-maximum switch was installed in Eagles to allow a pilot in a combat emergency to boost thrust by fifteen percent. Use of vee-max in the Royal Saudi Air Force had never been approved in peacetime because it required the engines to be replaced.

"Permission granted."

The Eagle pilot grinned beneath his mask as he was pressed hard against the seat by the boost in power.

"EuroFighter is dead. Continue south."

CHAPTER 30

The Lancer was small, but it was not a stealth aircraft. Buckingham had no choice but to come in low.

Major Jadin deployed a pair of Eagles to orbit each checkpoint and put his best pilots overhead the target at ten thousand feet. The AWACS crew would sanitize the skies above.

"This doesn't look good for Simon," Randi said.

Hoser had joined the group in the back row. "You're right. I don't know who they have calling the shots, but the guy is good. I'll give him that."

"Comrades!"

"Oh, make way for the walking pincushions," said Hoser, welcoming Mikhail and Sergei.

"Bite my shorts, Santana. At least we didn't run away. Here you go, you ungrateful bastard." Mikhail held out the pewter stein filled to the brim.

"Like I said, make way for the ace of the base."

"Hoser, you are such a whore."

"No, dear. Just thirsty."

*   *   *

"Lancer, fight's on."

"Righto."

Buckingham had plotted his strategy carefully. Orbiting at the extreme southwestern corner of the range, he painted each of the checkpoints and the target area, noting the low altitude of the lurking Eagles. He wasn't surprised. He'd have done the same thing.

"Spike! One-niner-zero for fifty from the target."

"Slasher four-one has a solid radar contact, twenty-five miles. He's northbound and descending through five thousand."

"Four-one, prosecute. Four-two, hold your position."

"Four-one."

"Four-two."

When the F–15 detached from its mate, Buckingham leveled off at three thousand feet and activated the Lancer's electronic-countermeasures suite. The signal augmentor, used in training to amplify his radar reflectivity, automatically switched off. Then he throttled back.

"Four-one. Broke lock; searching."

"He has countermeasures. Don't lock next time.

Plan on using a Sidewinder." The heat-seeking missile would not need radar support.

"Copy."

Onboard the Lancer, a special transmitter fired up and bounced a target return signal off the dune tops four miles distant.

"Radar contact!" The Eagle pilot held his altitude until six miles, then performed a deep slice turn out of the sun. Without a lock, he didn't have a HUD diamond superimposed over the target, but he was confident that he would quickly spot the Brit. The Sidewinder seeker head growled menacingly in his headset as it searched for a heat source as the altimeter wound down. *Where the hell is he?*

"Slasher four-one is dead. Vector two-seven-zero."

Simon couldn't resist rubbing a little salt in the wound. "Jolly good. Do be so kind as to send along another."

"Four-two, radar contact!" The wingman's voice betrayed his eagerness for revenge.

"Hold your position, four-two. We expect him to come your way. Seven-one, seven-two, vector two-zero-zero. Be advised we suspect he's using terrain bounce. Run a cold intercept and keep one radar in search. And Slashers: Any wingman that lets his lead be shot at close range will find himself flying a desk."

After making certain that he'd attracted plenty of attention, Buckingham put his radar in sniff, dropped to the deck, and scurried east.

"Bogey dope?"

"Negative contact. Keep your eyes open, four-two. He's going to want to cross that checkpoint."

In point of fact, Buckingham had no interest in the checkpoint. He wanted the target. More precisely, he wanted a direct hit on the target that all five of his competitors and their gold-plated airplanes had missed. And he had a perfectly reasonable plan to get there. He would follow the yellow brick road.

"Why is he going only eighty knots?" Whitefoot asked.

"I don't know, unless . . . Hey, anybody got a chart handy?" Hoser asked.

"Here." Sergei pulled one out of the leg pocket of his flight suit."

Hoser thumped the unfolded map with his fingers. "God damn it, why didn't I think of that?"

"Think of what?" asked Randi and Moshe simultaneously.

"The damn road, that's what. He's scooting down that road they use to bring the equipment and VIPs in from Riyadh. See here? It runs along the eastern border of the range. You can bet the AWACS and the Eagles have their systems calibrated to ignore the traffic."

"I didn't see it out there," said Mikhail. "And besides, how fast can they go? Surely not a hundred miles per hour."

"It's tough to see because it's covered in sand," Jack said. "And they do drive that fast. The trucks have Head's Up Displays . . ."

"Get out of here."

"And there's a signal transmitter embedded in the road. The drivers get a bonus for making good time."

"But is there much traffic?"

"Not normally. But the vendors started shipping out gear about an hour ago."

"Hoser, how close does it get to the target?" asked Whitefoot.

"About that close on the back side." His thumb and index finger were separated by an inch. There was no need to explain. On the pilot's chart that measure translated to six miles, a perfect distance from which to pop. "Lady and gentlemen, we are in the presence of pure genius. Let's watch the show."

*   *   *

"Your Highness, I implore you. Please feed us the telemetry. We've got nothing on our system since the first kill."

"Negative, General. You have your orders. I suggest you collapse your perimeter and stop him before he gets to the target."

The general was a good leader and a man to whom the prince had looked for approval and guidance when he was flying. It pained him to hear the man nearly beg.

"General."

"Yes, Your Highness?"

"I will remind you that the Lancer does not employ stealth technology and that there is no indication that your systems are functioning abnormally. Nothing should be taken for granted."

"Major Jadin."

"Yes, General?"

"Let's go through it one more time. Give me a rundown on every single contact you have."

Buckingham held the Lancer within a dozen meters in the wake of the fifteenth and last truck in the convoy. He had climbed to ten meters to escape the billowing sand from the convoy.

The turbine whine, just audible over the roar of his own diesel, caught the driver's attention, but he couldn't tell where it was coming from. In any case, he had his hands full staying focused on the taillights of the truck in front of him.

Even though the trucks were nearly maxed out at slightly less than one hundred miles per hour, the speed was terribly slow for the Lancer and required judicious use of vectored thrust. Buckingham had his hands full, too, since his ground-attack system was displaying an error message. Unable to take his left hand off the stick to reprogram it, he would either have to climb or put the bird down.

"I can't believe he actually landed the damn thing."

"How the hell did he know they were on to him?"

"I don't know that he did. Maybe he has a problem, but, in any case, the guy has brass balls and luck like you read about."

"Oh would you look at this? It's like he scripted it. The Eagles have slowed to a crawl."

"They're probably eyeballing some trucks we can't see."

"You're right; they have their flaps full down."

"And check this out! Simon is airborne."

"The lucky bastard has a HUD full of Eagles."

"Slasher seven-one has a column of trucks in sight. There is no sign of the . . ."

"Slasher seven-one and seven-two are dead. Vector east."

"Damn it! What are your men doing out there, Major?"

"Their very best against a damn good enemy, sir."

*   *   *

Buckingham delighted in demonstrating the Lancer's uncanny acceleration from 100 to 550 knots.

In the dome, the graphic image of the little jump jet sped toward the target with cartoonlike acceleration.

Approaching six miles, he climbed sharply, alert for defending Eagles while scanning the desert for the target. In his pop maneuver, the countermeasures system automatically dispensed chaff and flares, preventing the Stinger missile crews—still wary from the EuroFighter's wild bomb attack—from getting a solid track. The minute he'd spent on deck troubleshooting his tactical display had also given Buckingham time to sweeten the navigation system. As he rolled the little fighter onto its back, the target symbology was perfectly superimposed over the tent that represented the command post. It was like shooting ducks in a barrel.

"Direct hit."

The dome audience erupted in a standing ovation as the tent collapsed in a burst of sand.

Now to escape. Buckingham put the nose down and firewalled the throttle. He was short on fuel—the heavy use of vectored thrust had exhausted his reserve—making a climb before reaching the border necessary.

*   *   *

Lieutenant Muhammad Sadairi, pilot of Slasher 42, was a distant cousin to Prince Salman, but his bloodlines were not sufficiently pure to join the royal elite. The previous day's summons had actually been his first visit to the inner sanctum of the palace. While he orbited in wait for the Lancer, he reached toward the glareshield and touched the picture of his son with a gloved finger, once more reliving the most remarkable experience of his life.

"Your father must be very proud of you, my young cousin."

Sadairi had not allowed himself even to dream that the elder governor knew of his existence though, for his entire life, he had secretly hoped for simple recognition from someone in the palace. But there were literally thousands of distant relatives, and he'd long ago resigned himself to anonymity. Now, to be referred to as a *cousin* of this great leader was a dizzying experience. He answered carefully. "My entire family is humbly honored to serve, Governor."

"Yes. One certainly can see that. Why, the king himself has mentioned his pride in your accomplishments."

The young man's eyes widened; he did not trust himself to speak. *The king!*

"He regrets not being able to meet with you himself, but he asked me to offer you this token of his respect." The elder clapped his hands and a servant emerged carrying a pillow upon which sat a jewel-encrusted gold-handled dagger with the distinctive charcoal blade of handcrafted Damascus steel. After handing the pillow to the elder, the servant backed away to disappear once more into the folds of the hanging tapestry.

"This knife was a favorite of the king's father and has been in the royal family for generations. Here, please take it."

Sadairi rose to his knees and bowed until his head touched the floor. "Forgive me, Governor. Only a prince may possess such a treasure. It . . . there must be a mistake."

"There has been no mistake." In point of fact, the knife was but one of a dozen recently made to order as gifts for visiting dignitaries. The elder's hand rested lightly on the young man's quaking shoulder. "We do not have much time, my son. This very special knife is intended for your son. He will soon be our family's newest prince."

Sadairi looked up, his face radiant with emotion. "But, how? I am his father. And I am no prince, sir."

"Not yet."

Sadairi's jaw hung slack in shock.

"You have been selected, from among all the pilots in the Saudi Royal Air Force, for a mission of the utmost importance to our homeland." He lowered his voice. "It is of such a nature that you will not survive physically. But . . ." He clasped Sadairi's shoulders and seized the young man's frightened eyes with a penetrating stare. "If you are successful, *Muham-*

mad Sadairi . . ." The emphasis on his Muslim name was unmistakable; each word the elder spoke struck with the force of a hammerblow: "If you are successful . . . your soul . . . will be . . . martyred!" The elder's eyes beamed with the joy he felt for the honor accorded the young man. Then he nodded, seemingly overwhelmed with satisfaction at the wisdom of his choice. "For thousands of years, Arab fathers have chosen their son's names to imbue them with the strength of their namesake. I can see that the courage of our prophet—*May His Name Be Praised*—runs through your veins, my son.

"As you know, the Koran advises . . . no, *requires*, that the family of a martyr be honored. Even as your loved ones are told of your sacrifice, the king himself will decree that you have been elevated, posthumously, to the status of prince. In the days that follow, throughout our land women will sing your praises. Arrangements have already been made so that your own son—your *legacy*!—will come to live in the palace, where he will grow in splendor while learning of his father's heroics. And your own father—a man who has lived his life in humility, as you say—in addition to the pride he will bear, he will be accorded high status, with a stipend to live the rest of his years without working."

The elder released his grasp to signify freedom of choice. "All of this awaits if you accomplish your mission. But first, you must tell me. And here, my son, you must be absolutely truthful. Do you have the heart for it?"

Tears streaming down his face, Sadairi reverently picked up the knife and kissed it.

"Allah Be Praised."

"Uh . . . oh. He isn't out of the woods yet," said Matsasuta. "That last F–15 looks like it has a bead on him."

Sadairi had no trouble picking up the little fighter streaking across the desert. His radar was optimized for high-speed targets. Nor did he have to struggle to catch up. The Eagle had nearly twice the top-end speed of the jump jet. And none of the witnesses were too surprised to see him forgo a missile shot in lieu of a guns attack. Buckingham had humiliated the Saudis, and he had to be nearly out of fuel. Truth be told, he was due for a taste of humble pie.

Simon's electronic-warning gear lit off when the Eagle illuminated him. A quick glance over his shoulder revealed that he would not be able to escape. But Simon had no intention of dying without a fight. He would take on this bastard, and, just before the gas ran out, he'd plop the jet down on the nearest flat spot and worry about it later. So, with the Eagle streaking in from his six o'clock, Simon grinned beneath his mask in anticipation and pitched back.

*   *   *

"That kid better watch out; Simon is reeling him in."

"Man, he's got a lot of smack. He's going to over-shoot like a big dog."

"Here comes the skid . . ."

"Watch it, asshole!"

"No! God, no!"

"Oh Jesus . . ."

"Get on the radio and get that helicopter inbound!"

"Lancer . . . come in. Slasher four-two . . . come in."

The silence was broken by the high-pitched beeping of an emergency locator beacon on Guard frequency. After a few moments the audio technician filtered it out.

"Slasher five-one has smoke. Stand by one."

"Angel two-four, vector zero-niner-three for thirty-five. Possible downed aircraft."

The search-and-rescue pilot answered to the staccato beat of the helicopter rotors, "Two-four en route."

"Range control. Slasher five-one." The pilot's voice was restrained. "We have the wreckage from both jets in sight. It was definitely a midair."

"Any sign of survivors?"

"No . . . none."

CHAPTER 31

"I want to thank you all for coming."

In reality nobody had come to the ready room for the evening pilots meeting as requested—Jack found them at the pub—but it was a good ice-breaker.

"Anytime, my good man."

"Yes indeedy."

"Just give that secret decoder ring of yours a twist, and the boys will muster up."

"Say, mate! Have you a spot of duct tape?"

Jack had been to a couple fighter pilot wakes, enough to know that he needed to get to the group before they got wound up. "Before we start, I thought you'd like to know that the RAF confirmed that Simon's family has been notified."

"I should think so . . . it was on the bleedin' Internet!"

"But it was a jolly good show, eh?"

"The man said he wanted to be famous, righto?"

"Nothing like a splattering oneself on the telly in front of God and everybody."

The fake British accents and forced laughter of

the few guests sitting on the perimeter lent a surreal quality. Unfortunately, Randi was missing. Jack could use an ally. For a moment he debated finding her, but he judged their mood as precarious, and he didn't have much time.

"I won't beat around the bush. Prince Salman has a televideoconference in an hour with Riyadh. The topic is canceling tomorrow's event. I came here to elicit your support."

His announcement met with silent shrugs.

"Maybe I didn't make myself clear. There's talk of canceling the rest of the competition."

"Well you be sure to let us know, mate."

"Speaking for m'self, I was planning on getting merely shit-faced, but if I'm not flying, then I can aim for comatose. Barkeep!"

Jack was incredulous. He'd been certain of rousing the pilots into angry support. But they hadn't even asked who would be declared the winner. It was as if they couldn't care less. "Hoser, can I talk to you? Privately?"

Santana wore a pained expression, but after studying Jack, he muttered and followed him out into the Oasis. When they were facing each other, he waited for Jack to speak.

"What the hell is going on? Why don't they care? Have they given up because of what happened to Simon?"

"Nobody's given up in there, Ace. If you walk back in and say there's a zero-six-hundred brief, they'll nod and drink a little faster, that's all."

"I don't get it. He was their friend. You'd think they'd want to finish this thing so . . ."

"So his death wasn't in vain? Is that what you mean?"

"Well, yeah."

"You think Buckingham's death is meaningless if there's not some grandiose cause associated with it?" Hoser didn't wait for an answer. "Christ, Jack. You, of all people, should know better. Look, we came here to fly and fight; it's what we do. This is a dangerous business. People die. We can't control that. And if you or somebody else cancels it, we can't do anything about that either. It's simple; stop trying to make it complicated."

"But what about the competition? Listen to me, there's never been anything like this. There are literally *millions* of people watching and thousands of jobs on the line." Jack's voice rose, gathering looks. "And what about pride? Don't tell me that it doesn't matter who wins, because I know it does, God damn it."

Hoser's voice glinted with a metallic edge. "You could pull the plug on this shindig of yours, schedule tomorrow's fights in a black hole, and every one of those hired guns would be there." He turned to leave, but stopped and faced Jack with the resigned expression of one expecting his message to clang off the hull. "It's not pride, Jack; it's honor. You'd do well to recalibrate your eyeballs."

Watching Hoser return to the group—one to which he had mistakenly thought he belonged—Jack's eyes stung with the impotence of defeat. The

Oasis was nearly empty. Workers were busily dismantling some of the displays. A third of the guests had already checked out, taking advantage of the king's offer to spend the night in luxury accommodations in Riyadh. The rest were probably packing.

It was all falling apart.

"Meet me in the film room." She didn't wait for an answer.

Jack pocketed the phone and made his way to the briefing area. He had provided the pilots with a room stocked with audiovisual equipment as a debrief room.

"I didn't see you at the pub."

"How's the crew doing?" Randi asked, without looking up from the monitor as she manipulated a large dial on one of the tape machines.

"It sounds like a British pub in a bad movie. And it's going to get uglier. How are you doing?"

She looked up sharply. "Why do you ask?"

"Oh, for Christ's sake. I didn't mean it like that! I know you're as tough as any of those guys." His frustration boiled over. "Why the hell can't any of you pull your head out of your ass long enough to admit that it hurts to lose Simon? And that this whole thing we're doing out here actually matters." He turned his back to her, embarrassed by his outburst, alarmed at the torrent of rage he'd discovered.

Randi walked around the console and placed her hand on the back of his neck. "You okay, buddy?" she asked in a small voice, peering at the side of his face, a sad little smile tugging at the corner of her mouth.

Jack's breath came in ragged gulps. Suddenly he was as close to bawling as he'd been since childhood. The onslaught of emotions was disorienting.

Guiding him to a chair, she stood behind, kneading the muscles in his neck and shoulders. "Close your eyes for a minute. You haven't slept for days, have you?"

He shook his head.

"Simon was a good man. You lost a friend today, and your defenses are down. Take a deep breath. Now let it out. You know, it's probably a good thing in the long run. At least you're facing the grief head-on. But I don't want you to think it doesn't hurt every one of us to lose him. Another breath . . . good. You've just got to understand what that midair represents. He was the leader of the pack, know what I mean? Most of us are probably struggling with the fact that if he's the best, and he can die . . ."

"But this is nothing new. You face death every day you strap in."

"No. You've got that completely wrong. We face risk, sure, but not death. In fact, most of us do a great job of pretending that death doesn't exist. We talk about mishaps that destroy airplanes, but almost never about the human being in the wreckage. Even when something like this slaps us in the face, most pilots will bury the emotions."

"But you don't know what's going on in the real world right now."

"No. I haven't thought much about it since the accident."

"Our web site is choked with people talking about Simon. Hundreds of thousands of strangers are on-line this minute because they're devastated by his loss. And they didn't even know him. But we're his friends, and those assholes are in there making jokes and . . ."

She spun his chair around. "But, but, but . . . bullshit, Jack Warner. Enough of this. You're a reporter, bub. You may be hearing me, but you're not listening."

He couldn't maintain eye contact.

She cupped his chin in her hand and forced him to look at her. "I need help figuring out why Buckingham died. Something is fishy about that midair. What I need to know right now is that you are going to be able to suck it up. So, are you?"

"Okay . . ."

With a flash of her eyes, the word "but" melted in his throat.

"The tape stops there." The last frame showed the Lancer nearly centered in the HUD.

"Okay. What should I be looking for?"

"First question: Why did it stop three seconds before the midair?"

"Maybe that's all we got signal-wise?"

"I doubt it. Given the relay antennas, there would only be a few milliseconds' delay at the most. Second question: Why is the pipper not tracking the target?" She tapped the monitor with a rose-colored fingernail.

"I see what you mean. It's not on the Lancer, is it?"

"Bingo. Now, look at the velocity vector. Remember, it shows the actual flight path of the airplane, while the pipper shows where the bullets are going. And the gun on the F–15 is canted up nearly three degrees."

"The velocity vector is on the tail of the Lancer. But then it would have to be if they hit, wouldn't it?"

"Absolutely. Just *before* they hit, but not three seconds early. That's an eternity in a dogfight. We'd expect to see it arrive just before the impact. This means the Eagle pilot was boresighted. And that means he either froze, or . . ." She left the sentence unfinished. "I'm going to run it from the start of his dive. Watch the symbology."

Not once in the pursuit did the pipper settle on the Lancer, but throughout the intercept, the velocity vector danced around the aircraft. When it drifted off, it appeared that the pilot deliberately brought it back on target.

"Son of a bitch! It looks like he did it on purpose," Jack said.

"Hold on, Sparky. You can't jump to that kind of conclusion. Hell, he could have been distracted by a caution light. Who knows? But it's a stretch in anyone's book to think he deliberately took a header into Buckingham's jet."

"Stay here. I'll be right back."

"Jack, in forty minutes the council will decide whether or not to cancel the competition. Why am I here?"

"Randi?"

"Your Highness, this is the tape from Lieutenant Sadairi's HUD camera." She started the tape from the first time the Lancer appeared in the HUD. "Note the velocity vector."

"What the hell is he doing?" Salman became agitated and nudged Randi aside to run the playback himself. "Where's the rest of the tape? Does he say anything?"

"That's the official copy," Jack said. "He doesn't speak during this run. But it's been edited. The last three seconds were cut off."

"What do you mean, edited? What are you saying?"

"Cue it up, Randi. I had a backup made, Your Highness. Whoever edited the master didn't know about it."

They ran the last three seconds in slow motion. As expected, the velocity vector never wavered as the Lancer grew rapidly until impact.

"You can see that Buckingham is using vectored thrust. Maybe the maneuver fooled Sadairi." The prince didn't sound convinced by his own logic.

"Now turn up the volume and run it at normal speed, Randi."

Sadairi's breathing was rapid, but there was a murmured phrase two seconds before impact.

"We can't make it out. It sounds Arabic."

The prince appeared stunned. "I can. It's ancient Arabic. We call it the martyr's prayer." He rolled his chair back and stood. "My cousin knew he was going to die. My God, that was no accident."

Randi spoke forcefully, her anger barely in check. "Accident? That was murder! That was a good man who died out there. I want to know what the hell you are going to do about it?"

"Randi . . ." Jack cautioned.

"It's all right, Jack. She's right. But I just don't know, yet." He paced to the wall and back.

Randi and Jack exchanged glances.

"Of course this means my uncle lied to me. He has to be behind it. The council had no intention of letting the competition finish once Buckingham nailed down first place. That's why they called for the halt after the acci . . . the midair."

"Is the king involved?" Jack asked.

The prince looked up sharply, then shook his head. "No. He would be protected from something like this. In fact, most of the council won't know the details. This involves the elder, Governor Jalawi, and one or two others at most."

"What would happen if the king found out? Sadairi was part of the family."

"Hell, Jack, half the country is related. I'm not

sure what his reaction would be personally, but he wouldn't be inclined to blow the whistle and create a scandal, if that's what you mean. Don't get me wrong. I know it sounds brutal, but I can see the logic in their decision-making. They picked a distant member of the royal family to deepen the tragedy. With two deaths, especially of the front-runner, the competition can be canceled without losing face.

"From where they sit, in the end, the Russian team doesn't win, but they don't lose either. In a month or two, they'll announce that they've made a decision and selected the Strike Flanker. I'm sure they're renegotiating the pipeline deal as we speak."

He stared at the two of them. "I'm sorry I got you into this. If my uncle finds out we know, we're all dead. I know you don't want to hear this, but we've got to destroy that tape."

"No." Jack surprised himself with the firmness of his answer. He opened a locker, removed a video camera, and mounted it on a tripod.

The Prince and Randi exchanged puzzled looks. "Jack, this isn't California. Look around. We're trapped in the middle of the desert with no way out."

"You know something? I've been told that since I arrived, but it's just not true. This is a glass house, and we have a couple million sets of eyes on us. And by the way, that includes Khalim's. Just so you know, the kid who made this tape for me told me that our rooms are bugged and the surveillance crews have been tracking us with orders to notify him if the three of us ever met alone."

"And you brought me here knowing that?" asked the prince.

"Yup. Consider us even. I had no choice; I needed to know what was on that tape. And more importantly, I needed to know where you stood."

"Jack, do you really think they'd risk taking us all out?" asked Randi.

"He's right about that. Put yourself in their position. Given the stakes, they can't take a chance."

"Then we need a plan," Randi said. "Any ideas?"

Jack noted that she didn't waste time bemoaning her fate or worrying about whom to blame. "Right now, we're going to make a little video. Randi, you handle the camera. Your Highness, cue the HUD tape and play it on my signal."

Jack smiled, suddenly rejuvenated. The uncertainty and fear were replaced with a calm sense of purpose he recognized as an old friend. Once he'd committed, there was nothing to do but see how it played out.

"Oh, and Randi?"

"Yes?"

"When we're done here, go pull the plug on that party. Tell the boys there's a zero-six-hundred brief."

"Consider it done. Anything else, boss?"

"Yeah. How do I look?"

"Let's see . . ." She gave him the once-over, and, leaning close to brush some imaginary lint off his shoulder, whispered, "I have more to tell you . . . later."

CHAPTER 32

"We cannot afford to wait any longer. Major Khalim will locate Warner. In the meantime, Nephew, the council has concluded that we must postpone the competition indefinitely. The king will make the announcement shortly. It is unfortunate, but this tragedy has cast a pall over the event. After the funeral we will, of course, hold a full investigation to see what part of *your* system failed."

The message was clear: The prince would be the scapegoat. No doubt youthful enthusiasm would be blamed for an overly aggressive plan. Salman appreciated the elegance of the tactic. The king had chosen him over the council's objections. His uncle's position would be strengthened and a potential rival eliminated. In the meantime, the council would enjoy the spectacle of the cocky young man's comeuppance. Prince Salman smiled politely into the camera.

It wasn't the reaction they expected. Looks of consternation appeared on the televised faces of the council.

"Perhaps you do not understand the seriousness of the situation," said Governor Jalawi.

"Oh, I most certainly do, Governor. I also appreciate irony. It was my uncle who warned me about bringing a viper into our tent, do you remember?"

"Obviously you are distraught," the elder said. "But we have no time for this. From this point forward, Major Khalim will assume command and you will—"

"Forgive me, Governor. I have something to show you that you might wish to consider before making a final decision. This will only take a minute." He started the videotape via remote control.

Randi had framed Jack from the waist up, giving the scene the look and feel of an on-site report.

"Ladies and gentlemen. Jack Warner reporting to you from the highly classified Shaybah airfield in Saudi Arabia with a late-breaking story. We have learned, through an unimpeachable source, that the FLY-OFF competition that has captivated the world's attention this week has been a complete sham. A very-high-ranking member of the Saudi royal family confirmed that the Russian team was picked to win by Saudi government officials who are involved in a complex geopolitical conspiracy to place two-thirds of the world's oil supply under their direct control."

The camera zoomed in until Jack's face filled the screen.

"But as shocking a discovery as that is, it pales in comparison to the revelation that today's tragic accident, which took the lives of competition leader Simon Buckingham and Lieutenant Muhammad Sadairi—himself a member of the royal family—

was deliberate. In a moment you will see the startling evidence for yourself. Further, our ongoing investigation indicates that this murder-suicide mission was ordered by the head of the Saudi council of provincial governors."

Jack nodded, and the camera panned to the monitor. The tape was cued to the beginning of the dive. "Those of us who have watched the flying events of the past four days have learned a great deal about fighter aircraft. You are looking over the nose of the F–15 flown by Lieutenant Sadairi through his Head's Up Display camera. Please note the position of the aircraft's velocity vector and gunsight during this film clip. I will remind you that the velocity vector displays the aircraft's true flight path. For a pilot to score a simulated kill, the gunsight must track the target for two consecutive seconds. However, instead of using the pipper, Lieutenant Sadairi holds the velocity vector on the Lancer. His intent becomes clear when you hear him utter a Muslim prayer for martyrdom seconds before deliberately crashing his F–15 into the British aircraft."

After the clip, the camera returned to Jack, who spoke with the seriousness of a seasoned anchorman. "The official copy of the F–15 tape was altered. Fortunately, a backup was secretly made. This tape and the documentation of the conspiracy behind it have been posted on the Internet at a dozen sites around the world. The reason for this should be clear. Obviously, my life and those of my colleagues are in jeopardy. Should something happen to us, I urge everyone who hears my words to demand a United Nations boycott of Saudi Arabian products and a freeze on their internationally held assets until a full investigation has been conducted and the criminals brought to justice.

"This is Jack Warner, deep in the great desert, the Rub Al-Khali, signing off."

The door to the studio burst open. Khalim, followed by three guards armed with short-barreled assault weapons, shoved Pharaoh, his face mottled with red welts and lower lip bleeding, into the room. The prince calmly remained seated with his hands on the table. Khalim spoke to the council while holding the terrified youngster by the shirt collar. "This vermin confessed to making a duplicate of the flight tape for Warner."

The elder spoke. "They are bluffing. They have not had time to put anything on the Internet. We must find Warner and the tape." He looked at the prince. "You have five seconds to tell me where he is or the boy will be shot."

"No, he will not." The king strode into the palace conference room flanked by several guards, who positioned themselves behind the council members with weapons drawn. Speaking into a cell phone, the king said, "Mr. Warner, please join Prince Salman in the studio so that all of us may speak." He turned to the camera. "Major Khalim, unhand that boy and have your men secure their weapons. You will take your orders directly from me, or you will be replaced. Do you understand?"

Khalim bowed. "Yes, Your Majesty."

"There will be no more killing."

Jack entered the studio and joined the prince at the table. He laid the prince's phone in front of him.

"Your Majesty, these men are traitors!"

At a nod from the king, guards quickly gagged the elder and bound him to his chair. "Mr. Warner, rest assured that this man and his minions will be dealt with. But I must know. Did your report air?"

"No, Your Majesty. My report has not aired."

The king visibly relaxed.

"But it will."

"Come again?"

"A toned-down version of the report, less inflammatory, but no less damaging, has been prestaged at several sites with instructions to release it to the wire services in twenty-four hours."

The king's eyes narrowed, accompanied by a humorless smile. "You would attempt to blackmail me in my own country?"

"No, sir. Please consider it an insurance policy."

"And payoff is contingent upon what, exactly?"

"Your Majesty, I have spent the past six months in your country. During that time, I have been impressed by the talent and thirst for knowledge of your young people." He nodded first at the wide-eyed teenager sitting to his right and then to the prince. "I'm afraid that certain members of your government have failed to understand the significance and incredible power of ArabNet. You have captured the collective attention of millions of viewers, who became swept up in the compelling drama of the competition. And right here, five hundred of the world's most influential people experienced firsthand the generosity and creativity of your country even as they were dazzled by technologies mastered by few in the world. In less than a week, Saudi Arabia has reshaped its image and emerged as a visionary leader in a world connected by communication.

"You've asked me to tell you what my conditions are for killing this story. Your Majesty, the story was embedded within tomorrow's update to the press. We used a technique computer programmers call a Trojan Horse. Inside the code there is a triggering mechanism that will launch it on the Internet in"—he looked at his watch—"less than twenty-four hours. I assure you that it cannot be stopped."

"I do not understand your motives, Mr. Warner. You said it was an insurance policy. Why are we having this conversation if there is nothing to be done?"

"You Majesty, the insurance policy isn't for me. It's for your country."

"My patience is at an end, Mr. Warner. I expect that you know that I am not a man you would wish as an enemy."

Jack ignored the threat. "Your Majesty, you own the newest information broadcast system on the planet, and at this very minute, you have the entire world tuned in, including your competition. I have a simple question: Tell me, sir, what does a man with such power do when he has just been given a twenty-four-hour exclusive on the hottest story of the year?"

"You must be mad," said Governor Jalawi.

The king did not speak for several moments. Then he pointed to Pharaoh. "You there . . . young man."

"Yes, Your Majesty?"

"Is he right about this Trojan Horse? Can it not be stopped?"

"No, Your Majesty. I . . . I wrote it myself. There is not enough time to track down all the copies and kill it before it activates."

"Grandson?"

Prince Salman answered, "Yes, Your Majesty?"

"Effective immediately, you are the new minister of information. As your first order of business, you will see that ArabNet exploits this . . . this opportunity before anyone else."

"I understand."

"Mr. Warner, may I have your word that this conversation will remain private?"

"Yes, Your Majesty. On two conditions."

The king reacted as if he couldn't believe his ears. "For the love of *Allah*, there must be Arab blood in your veins. I hesitate to ask, but go on."

"Number one: The competition will not be canceled."

"Prince Salman?"

"I think he's right. We should finish this thing."

"If it can be done safely, then I approve. And the second condition?"

Jack picked up the phone and stepped out of earshot. The king listened intently but replied to the camera. "And if I approve, I have your word that what has transpired here will remain off the record?"

"Yes, Your Majesty."

"Your motives are inscrutable to me, sir, but you have a deal."

CHAPTER 33

Jack had just turned out the light, nestling deep into the cool sheets, when there was a soft tapping on his door.

He eyed the clock—9:35 glowed in angry red numbers; too early to get away with claiming to be in a dead sleep. "Yes?" he asked in a weary voice.

"Jack? It is Sergei. Are you awake?"

Biting off the automatic sarcasm, Jack snapped on the light, and said, "Of course. Just a second." Then he climbed out of bed, pulled the covers up, put on his robe, and opened the door. He found Sergei framed by the corridor's dim light, but there was just enough to spot reddened eyes and a curious expression that could be the result of either joy or sadness.

Sergei waited a moment, then stepped forward and wrapped Jack in a powerful bear hug that lifted him off his feet. The man was happy.

Weak and caught by surprise, Jack was stuck on an exhale with no chance of catching a breath in the Russian's steel-band grip. Fatigued, he faded quickly; the numbness that overwhelmed him not altogether unpleasant.

Meanwhile, Sergei exclaimed, "Jack! You have made me very happy." When he felt Jack wilt in his arms, he released the American, only to have to catch him before the limp body crumpled to the floor.

Jack's shoulder felt like it was in the jaws of a large predator. His eyes fluttered open revealing the bear-like visage of Sergei—a part of his brain marveled at the man's finger-thick, single eyebrow—hovering over him with a worried expression. It took Jack a moment to realize that the large head wasn't moving; he was being shaken senseless.

"I'm okay," Jack said, not at all convinced that he was.

"Are you sure?" At last, the movement stopped.

"Yes." His whole body tingled as feeling returned.

"You fell asleep in my arms, Jack. Are you ill?"

"No, I don't think so. Just dizzy. But, why are you . . ." Jack caught himself. He had no desire to hurt the man's feelings. He sat up, swinging his legs over the side of the bed, while motioning for his guest to take the nearby chair. Rubbing his hand through his sleep-tousled hair, he asked, "Enough about me. What can I do for you?"

Sergei beamed. "Nothing! You have already done me the greatest of favors, my good friend. This is what I have come to tell you tonight."

"I'm all ears."

"Pardon?"

Jack laughed at the puzzled look his expression

garnered. "That's a saying that means I'm ready to listen."

"Oh, of course. Very good joke. Since you are nothing but ears, I will talk, and you will listen, right?"

Jack nodded and smiled, wishing secretly for nothing more than solitude and bed.

"I have again used your communications system to speak with Svetlana, my wife. She tells me that arrangements have been made to take our Alek to Moscow. Jack, he is to have the operation he needs to repair his heart! An American team of doctors will visit Moscow next week. Alek's records were sent to them by the university, and these doctors accepted our son as their patient." Tears pooled and ran down rugged cheeks.

Jack was simultaneously moved by Sergei's gratitude and chagrined by his previous desire to shuffle his visitor out the door. Thankfully his entreaties through the State Department to get Alek on the list of candidates had been effective. The breakthrough occurred when one of the guests, the chairman of one of the world's largest health-insurance companies, brokered a virtual introduction to Dr. Hooker, the lead surgeon on the American team. Dr. Hooker, a down-to-earth North Carolinian, had made no promises, but was receptive and agreed to review the case on behalf of his fellow volunteers. Jack made a mental note to show his gratitude.

"Sergei, this is the best news I've heard in a long time. Will you be leaving tomorrow after the last flight?"

"*Da*. I mean, yes. Mikhail and I are scheduled to fly out in the afternoon. Hopefully, the Iranians will be more cooperative this time."

"I'll make sure we get on that clearance first thing. Is there anything else I can do to help?"

Sergei stood. "No, you have done enough, my friend. I wanted to say thank you and ask if I could be of some help to you?"

Jack stood and braced himself for another hug. "No thanks are necessary. It was a simple matter of contacting the right people. I appreciate your offer, but I can't think of anything I need right now."

"Are you sure? I think I am not wrong to have noticed your interest in the . . . the goals of the Russian team." His eyebrow raised in question.

Despite the language barrier, Jack was alert to the nuance of Sergei's offer. He was willing to shed some light on the conspiracy. It was an enormous risk, and one Jack knew the military officer could ill afford. "Sergei, you should know that the plot between the Saudi government and certain elements in your government to have your team win has been discovered." He watched carefully for the reaction.

Sergei's jaw clenched, but he did not feign ignorance or surprise. "This we suspected. To warn you of this conspiracy is the other reason I was coming here to see you, Jack. But Mikhail and Sergei . . ." he patted himself on the chest. "We are not part of this. You believe, no?"

"Yes, of course. There are greedy people in every country. But what about you? Are you in danger?"

"I do not think so. After the accident, our superiors seem no longer worried about where we finish in the competition. But we are not giving up. The Russian team still plans to win tomorrow."

Matsasuta had given him the same confident answer when asked about his chances. In fact, give any fighter pilot in the group half a chance, and each would claim the ability to snatch victory from the jaws of defeat. "So after you win and fly home, what's next? Another assignment?"

"Perhaps. I am also considering retirement, but the economy is not so good as you know. I am afraid I will not find work, but I am also getting too old for flying." He stroked an imaginary beard and grinned. "And because of my old age, I need to sleep." Sergei reached out tentatively for a handshake. "Thank you and good night, Jack."

Jack shook hands fondly, then, on the spur of the moment, pulled Sergei close and squeezed him as hard as he could. "Good night, comrade."

"Do you mind if I sit down?"

Moshe Kohl looked up in surprise to find the American F–22 pilot, Whitefoot, standing before him. Surprised because he'd purposely taken a table in the most remote corner of the nearly empty pub, the late hour, and also because nobody had spoken to him since his skunking on the gauntlet event. After encountering his disappointed ground crew and fielding a call from an obnoxious government bureaucrat full of recriminations, Kohl's mood had darkened steadily throughout the day.

"Suit yourself."

They sat in uncomfortable silence for three long minutes. Whitefoot was clearly nervous and kept glancing away.

Kohl finally broke the ice. "What's on your mind, Captain?"

The American took a deep breath before saying, "Most people know I'm not much of a talker. But here goes. I believe I know what you're thinking right now, and I respectfully want to say that you're wrong, sir."

Kohl wasn't accustomed to anyone calling him wrong to his face, particularly not someone so junior to him. "Captain, after today's abysmal performance, I'm certain you'll find me unpleasant company. That is precisely why I chose to sit back here."

"Forgive me, sir. This will just take a minute."

He shrugged in resignation. "If you must. Get on with it then."

"You may not have gotten any points, today, but you came within one second of winning the whole thing. What's more, you didn't resort to lobbing your bomb in from six miles out or taxiing down a highway to sneak in the back door. Not that I should talk, I didn't even get that close. I just want you to know that I think you're a true warrior, sir. And I'm honored to have flown against you." Whitefoot stood and extended his hand.

Kohl paused for several seconds. The corner of

his mouth tugged in a smile as he shook hands with his foe. "Sit down, please, Captain."

"Steve."

"Okay, Steve, take a seat. You know, son, that's the second time today that an adversary has taken the trouble to give me a compliment. I've never experienced that before. Most of my adversaries are . . ."

"Dead?"

"Well, yes."

"Colonel Kohl?"

"Moshe."

"Sir, I'm in no position to address you informally. You are a war hero and a lieutenant colonel."

"You put a lot of stock in my kills, don't you, Steve?"

"Yes, sir."

"You want to know something?" He didn't wait for an answer. "I regret every one of them."

"I don't understand."

"None of my victims escaped by parachute. Each of those men died at my hands. I don't see it as something of which to be proud."

"But, sir, they were trying to kill you! You won honorably defending your country. If you hadn't, they might have killed your wingman or strafed your field. You had to destroy them. It was your duty."

"Yes it was. But you should know that you can't take a life without giving up something in return. A part of your soul dies as well. If it happens to you, you will see what I mean."

"I've never known a MiG killer to talk like this."

"Of course not. I don't talk like this in my own ready room either. They'd ground me." He tried to lighten the moment with a half smile that didn't sell. "Steve, I'm trying to tell you something I've never put in words. I'm not sure why; you just caught me at a difficult time. I've been at this business too long, I guess."

"That's not true."

"That remains to be seen, but hear me out. We both come from cultures—tribes in fact—where our people have been pushed into a small corner and have to struggle like hell just to keep it. But in America, there is no enemy for your people to battle. While in my country, we are threatened with death every day. And so it has been for my entire life. Steve, in my heart, I am a teacher, not a warrior. I belong where I can help others by sharing, not killing."

Whitefoot was silent for nearly a minute before saying, "Honestly, I'm stunned to hear you speak like this, Colonel. All my life, I've prayed for a chance to pit myself against a worthy opponent in a fair fight. I consider your many victories to be the highest form of accomplishment. Maybe someday, after I've shared your experiences, I will feel the same way, but today, I can't imagine it."

"I thought you might say that. And it's given me an idea. I have a suggestion for you."

"What's that?"

"Why don't you come fly with the Israeli Air Force?"

"Pardon?"

"I'm serious. Come fly with us. With your skills, I can get you into the KFIR II program on my team."

"But there's no way our Air Force would let me go."

Moshe waved off the objection. "Not true. Over the years, we've had a dozen requests from your State Department to accept an exchange pilot. They would jump through hoops to get someone inside our training program. We've always turned your government down because, frankly, we weren't sure the pilot would measure up, particularly in combat. And if he didn't, just imagine what problems that would cause. But you've got great hands, you're a test pilot, and you've got a burning desire to fight. We could use you. And who knows? Maybe I could teach you a few things before I retire."

"I don't know what to say."

"Do you want to do it?"

"Yes, sir. Absolutely. I'd give anything for the chance."

"That's good enough. Let's go put a letter together."

The pounding finally penetrated Jack's consciousness. He stirred, and answered with a sleep-thickened tongue, "Yes?"

"Open up." It was Randi.

"Go away!"

More pounding.

Yawning, Jack rolled over stiffly and checked the

time. It was just past midnight. He growled while climbing out of bed, then slipped on a robe and unlocked the door.

"Nice hair."

Jack tried smoothing down his pillow-induced cowlick, but gave up and hobbled barefoot back toward the bed.

"No you don't. I need you awake, sport." Randi deftly guided him to a straight-backed chair before perching herself on the edge of the bed.

"What is it? I was fast asleep." He rubbed his eyes for effect.

"The story just went out over the net. Pharaoh said the entire Internet is bogged down with the traffic. All the wire services picked it up, too."

"Who did the report?"

"The prince, along with a live statement from the king. They even showed the three governors being led off in shackles. Oh, and you'll like this: You were given credit for breaking the story. They used some of our tape, though not the part where you called the competition a sham." She poked his bare shin with her flight boot. "So, you're famous again. How's it feel? And who knows? There could be another Pulitzer in it."

"Fat chance, but thanks for giving me the head's-up. Now, if you'll excuse me, I'd like to get some sleep. Which reminds me. Why are you still up? You have a big day ahead of you, Lieutenant Cole."

"And just how did that happen? Don't tell me that's what you coerced from the king? Surely you didn't give up that golden opportunity for me?"

"That's none of your business. Now, please, go to bed."

"Don't you want to know what else I found out?"

"Not unless it's earth-shattering."

"Well, okay . . . it's just that I thought you'd like to know that the whole oil thing was a ruse."

That caught his attention. "Come again?"

She lay back with her head on his pillow and pretended to be inspecting her nails. "I have it on good authority that the oil angle was a cover for something bigger."

Jack rubbed his face hard, trying to clear his thoughts. "Okay, you've got my attention. Spill it."

She sat up, eager as a kid to share a secret. "As you know, I met with Warren Keating. What you don't know, because we haven't had time to talk, is that he said some things that are going to blow your mind."

"I'm all ears." Somewhere in his brain, he realized he'd used that phrase before.

"I watched him bet a hundred thousand dollars on event four."

Jack whistled. "I know he's loaded, but that's a bundle. And he doesn't strike me as a man who is in the habit of pissing his money away."

"When I cautioned him about the risk, he said there was no risk."

"No risk? Then he must have been tipped off. I take it he bet on the Russian, right?"

"That's part of the surprise. He bet on Hoser."

"Get out of here."

"No shit. And he did it based solely on my saying that Hoser wouldn't be likely to wade into the target area against all those Eagles."

"That's pretty thin for laying out a hundred grand. First off, he had to know you were just guessing, and secondly, anybody who did make it to the target would be likely to beat his score."

"That's what I said. But he said that he knew all about it and didn't care. Then he said, 'I can't lose; none of us can.'"

"*None of us?* Who the hell is he talking about?"

"I'm not positive, but I'm pretty sure he was talking about some of the guests."

"Now let's see if I got this straight. He bets against the Russians, admits that anyone could win the event, and still says he and his buddies can't lose?"

"You got it. On top of that, I got the distinct feeling that he was going to clue *me* in on how to make some money, too, before I shot off my big yap."

"What did you say?"

"Well, first I told him about the Caspian oil thing. I knew it was a dumb thing to do as soon as the words came out. He clamed up immediately. I'm sorry, Jack. Truth is, I was just showing off because he called all the pilots gullible."

"That's a strange thing to say."

"Yeah, I thought so, too. And he wasn't being mean-spirited. He said we were risking our lives for something we thought was noble and wasn't."

"Okay . . . you said that was the first thing. What else did you say?"

"Well, before we got back to the dome, I tried to make up for it. And he was all ready to talk. But when I told him I could only keep it a secret if there was a legitimate reason, he refused to give me the skinny. Dumb, huh?" She eyed him through her bangs.

"Nope. He wanted it off the record, and you couldn't comply. It would have gained us nothing for him to tell you something in confidence that you couldn't share with me. And it would frustrate the heck out of you. The first rule of a professional journalist is to never apologize for being honest."

Randi flashed him her best smile. "Thanks for understanding. I was dreading telling you. But there was no way I could sleep until I did. So, what do you make of all this?"

"It's getting curiouser and curiouser. When you think about it, the king caved in awfully quick this evening. And I've always suspected that the prince ponied up that information about the Caspian Sea too readily. Damn it, I must be slipping. If I had been on the ball, I would have seen the pattern before this."

"But what about the council? That wasn't a fake. Those guys were really hauled away in chains."

"We're looking at a power play of some kind. The prince admitted that they were going to use him as a scapegoat. He's a sharp guy and probably saw it coming from day one. Which reminds me, what's this about the Caspian Sea oil shtick being a smoke screen? What did you mean by that?"

"Keating was playing it cute, but he said that it was no longer necessary to make money by pumping it out of the ground. According to him, it can be made out of thin air. And he said to think big. Really big."

"Geez, what's bigger than oil? Any other clues?"

"Not much. He did say that oil was traditional and that the margins were too thin."

"Son of a . . ." Jack jumped up. "It just pisses me off that they played me for a chump."

"Uh, Jack?"

"Yeah?"

"Your robe?"

Jack flushed and spun around when he realized that his robe had fallen open. It was his habit to sleep nude.

When he turned around again, he discovered Randi, with her hand over her mouth, struggling unsuccessfully to keep her composure.

The instant their eyes met, the dam burst. Jack, doubled over, had to hold on to the chair for support while Randi giggled uncontrollably on the bed. In those moments, the accumulated strain, from Simon's death to the discovery of the murder, spent itself in sidesplitting laughter.

When Jack finally caught his breath, he found that the release of tension had triggered an insight. "Of course! The odds are always with the house."

Wiping her tears on a sleeve, Randi asked,

"What do you mean, Tarzan? And by the way, pal, you could use a new loincloth."

After a second round of laughter left them completely wiped out, Randi, who was sprawled on the bed, rolled on her side and asked weakly, "What did you mean about the odds always being with the house?"

"Okay, but don't make me laugh anymore; I can't handle it." He took a deep breath, let it out, then retightened and knotted the belt on his robe. "When Pharaoh said that the programmed betting was spread evenly, I couldn't figure out why someone would go to all that trouble. Now you tell me that Keating says they can't lose, no matter whom they bet on. The key just hit me. The only people to make money, regardless of the bets, are the bankers—the house. That means Keating and his pals have part of the action."

"But, Jack, as successful as the competition has been, it's over tomorrow. And the bets are going to stop rolling in. There's no way that the take from this competition overshadows the oil economy, especially in this corner of the world."

"Yeah, that's true. But what if the competition is just the start of something bigger? A pump primer?"

"Have you heard of any new on-line betting events coming up?"

"No. But that doesn't mean there aren't any, or something else for that matter. You're right though, there's got to be another angle we're missing. And it has something to do with money making money because that is the only way I know that you can do it out of thin air."

"Is everyone in cahoots on this?"

"I don't know for sure who all the players are yet. But I'm willing to bet that the oil thing wasn't a fake. It was actually the council's agenda. In fact, I'm sure of it. What they didn't know, and neither did we, is that the king and our buddy, the prince, had something else up their sleeves."

"What are you going to do?"

"Right now, I'm going to crash. And so are you, young lady. I'll get up early and do some digging, but I'm useless without any sleep. So, if you don't mind, please get that little booty of yours off my rack and back where it belongs."

She stood and stretched languidly. "Well, that's the first time I've been kicked out of a man's bed, Mr. Warner."

He jumped onto the mattress and turned his back to her. Over his shoulder, he said, "Just don't let the door hit you on that cute little tushy on the way out."

Jack regretted his comment the instant he found himself airborne.

PART 6

EVENT FIVE

MASS DOGFIGHT

CHAPTER 34

Official Standings after Events One through Four
1. **Super Hornet**
2. **Raptor**
3. **Strike Flanker**
4. **EuroFighter**
5. **KFIR II**
6. **Lancer ***

* Did not finish

"Here they come!"

Even with the loss of nearly two hundred guests, the flight line was packed. Prince Salman had personally invited the workers to join the remaining guests and base personnel for the memorial flyby. For many, it was their first time above ground in a week. They found the morning air fresh and the sky dappled with high clouds heralding the upcoming change of season.

To the plaintive chords of a nameless dirge—piped expertly by Buckingham's Scottish crew chief—the seven aircraft approached in tight, V-shaped formation.

At the morning brief, the pilots elected Moshe Kohl to lead. The KFIR II was flanked on its right by an Omani Jaguar—flown by a Brit expatriate friend of Buckingham's known only as Smythe—and on the left by an Eagle flown by Major Jadin. To Smythe's right flew the Strike Flanker and the Super Hornet, with Randi at the controls. On the Eagle's left wing, Hiro had the EuroFighter tucked in, with the Raptor on his wing.

Jack climbed atop the hangar Kohl had briefed as the aim point. Below, he watched the prince energetically directing the camera crews. The man was a natural.

For the first time in six months, Jack Warner found himself without a deadline or crisis. His early-morning research had uncovered the missing element in the money equation. When the time was right, he would use it to set things straight, but there was no hurry. Arms clenched across his chest to still a shiver not warranted by the temperature, he took a deep breath and let the sound of the pipes and jet engines envelop him.

Despite the pilots' unfamiliarity in flying formation with each other, the vee was rock-solid.

"Jaguar: Detach."

With two mike clicks, Smythe plugged in the burners and pulled the Jaguar into the vertical, the wingtips leaving white wisps in their wake.

"Eagle: Detach."

Jadin matched the Jag's move. The thunder of the F–15 afterburners reverberated across the desert.

Mikhail and Whitefoot held their positions, the gaps in the formation left bare to honor the missing pilots. After the five remaining aircraft swept overhead in a furious crescendo, the two climbing fighters grew small, finally piercing the high clouds and disappearing from sight.

CHAPTER 35

Since there was an odd number of competitors with the Lancer gone, the pilots elected to change the rules. Instead of a series of one-versus-one fights, there would be a single one-versus-many dogfight.

After the flyby, the fighters were vectored to waiting tankers to top off. When they were done refueling, the controller would vector each to one of five points around the circumference of a circle fifty kilometers in diameter. The rules were simple: To encourage risk-taking, pilots could have heat-seeking missiles added to their arsenal by overflying the center point of the circle. Otherwise, they'd have to make do with cannon rounds. In any case, everyone was an enemy. The last one standing when the smoke cleared would win the event.

"If Squadron Leader Buckingham would have been the overall winner, then these pilots flying now, are they not fighting for second place?" asked the brewmeister.

"That's the way I see it." The sole customer held

out an ancient pewter stein for a refill. "You know, I promised I would repay you for letting me use this."

"That is not necessary, *Kapitan*."

"How much money do you have on you?"

"I have my entire check, fifty thousand United States dollars."

"See that kiosk over there?"

"Ja."

"Go bet a chunk on the Super Hornet. The odds are twenty-to-one."

"I thought you were not flying."

"Yes, but I taught that gal everything I know."

"This seat taken?"

The prince looked up from his chair in the half-empty dome and smiled. "No, of course not. Sit down, Jack. I was wondering where you were hiding. Is everything okay?"

"Yes, it is. As a matter of fact, things are excellent."

There was an edge in Jack's voice and demeanor that put the prince on alert. "Anything going on that you need to tell me about?"

Jack noted that the question's phrasing neatly and effectively asserted the prince's authority. "That's why I'm here."

"I'm all ears."

"Funny, somehow I thought you might say that." The prince looked at him strangely while Jack pressed on. "It seems that the oil dealings of the council were only one part of a more complex scheme. But the objective was the same."

"And that was?"

"To exploit the competition for money and power."

The prince sat back and crossed his legs, the picture of cool. To observers, the two men were just idly chatting. "Why don't you fill me in on this new theory of yours?"

"Certainly." Jack, too, leaned back and gazed into the dome's darkened ceiling. He spoke softly, with an easy cadence, as befit a bedtime story. "Once upon a time, key members of the royal family, in this case the king and his favorite heir, decided to do a little housecleaning and in the process found a way to make an incredible amount of money."

"Housecleaning?"

"Yes. There were some evil men who hatched a plot to overthrow the king by making a not-so-secret pact with another government."

"This is a good story. Go on."

"A festival was held. Teams of acrobats from all over were brought in to participate in a special competition and promised that the winner would receive fame and fortune. The richest and most powerful people in the world were invited to watch the acrobats perform their dangerous routines. These guests were indulged by their hosts and enjoyed the most luxurious surroundings imaginable. Everyone who came said it was a splendid affair."

"And the bad guys?"

"They cooked up a deal with one of the teams. In exchange for a guarantee to win the prize, the evil-doers would be allowed to share the world's last major oil supply. With that in hand, these conspirators would have the power to wrest control of the government from the king."

"But it didn't work, did it?"

"No. The king and his heir were too smart. They hatched a plan of their own. The first thing they did was to hire a famous court jester to entertain the guests and arranged it so that the plot was revealed in one of the jester's stories. The audience was suitably shocked, and the bad men were arrested, leaving the king and his heir with more power than ever."

"But these were good men. So everyone lives happily ever after, don't they?"

"That remains to be seen."

"Come again?"

"As the competition unfolded, it seems the king and his heir spotted the opportunity to make more money than even they dreamed possible. You see, pumping oil worked fine in the old days, but the costs of drilling, shipping, and refining, not to mention protecting all of that, are so high that the profits kept falling. What they needed was something that yielded a massive return on their investment."

"But isn't that everyone's goal?"

"For most it's a pipe dream, but not for these people. They came up with a scheme to make an incredible amount of money—almost all of it profit—with very little risk."

"Now, that sounds like a fairy tale, or perhaps just a scam."

"Believe it or not, that's exactly what they did."

"Are you going to sit there and tell me that these men invented a way to make money out of thin air?"

Jack turned to look at the prince. "Interesting choice of words."

"Why do you say that?"

"Because that's exactly the phrase one of the jester's sources used."

"A coincidence?"

"I think not. Be that as it may, please allow me to finish. It seems the jester, who as jesters are wont to do, kept poking his nose into places his employers wished he wouldn't. One bright morning, a lot like this one in fact, just when it looked like the plan was going to work without anyone being the wiser, he found something very interesting." Jack paused.

The prince said nothing.

"Don't you want to know what it was?"

"Go on." The smile was absent.

"The jester found news about a new and very exclusive investment opportunity. One that is quietly being circulated among the deep-pocketed blue bloods in the world's richest financial markets. In fact, it is so appealing that it's generating hundreds of millions of dollars from new investors, who are willing to pay great sums for the right to buy shares when the business goes public."

"What kind of business is it?"

"Actually, it is a virtual business. It really doesn't

exist, yet. But that's not important. These days, people pour money into businesses merely because of their potential. It's a phenomenon. They expect this one to become a worldwide news and entertainment network. But the irony is that it doesn't have to do anything, and these people will still make their money. All that matters is that people believe that it has *potential*. Because when it does go public, the price of the shares will skyrocket, since the demand, like everything else about the business, has been carefully orchestrated to appear unstoppable. In twenty-four hours, the investors who hold options fully expect to make their money back tenfold, while the original backers will make billions. And, of course, the king and his heir will make the most of all."

"What if it fizzles?"

"It can't. That's the beauty of it. The king and his heir have studied the market well and understand the secret to success."

"Which is?"

"That there are mountains of gold out there, and yet, most investors are lemmings. They follow the leader in hopes of picking up their crumbs. The king and his heir simply made sure that they packaged the deal to entice key, high-profile investors into becoming backers. When the markets see who is buying up shares, there will be a feeding frenzy as the speculators and then the institutional and fund managers grab their slice. By the time the lowly individuals in the public hear about it and add their fuel to the fire, the price of a share will have gone through the roof."

"From your tone, it would seem that you think this a bad thing."

"Maybe, maybe not. Except for some obscure and hard-to-enforce insider-trading laws that may or may not apply, they don't seem to be breaking any laws. Except . . ."

"Except for what?"

"There's that daemon the jester found running loose."

The prince was unable to contain his surprise. "What . . . what do you mean?"

"It was well concealed, almost impossible to detect, but the jester got lucky. To bolster the popularity of their business in the eyes of the investors, the king and his heir, or maybe just the heir, arranged for automatic betting to occur. This daemon spread their money across all the teams so as not to attract attention."

"But, as you say, that isn't illegal. Nobody was hurt."

"Possibly. One wonders what would happen to the confidence of the investors if word leaked out. But there's something even more disturbing than that."

"Go on."

"I have to ask myself: With so much money coming in, why didn't the king and his heir take care of the acrobats and others who risked their lives to make their business work?"

"That's an interesting question. And one with many implications and possible answers, I would imagine. For instance, if as you say, word leaked out about the investment too soon, the most important investors would not have time to get in position. There would also be the risk of blackmail, one that seems very serious all of a sudden. Tell me, what does the jester plan to do with his story?"

"He's in a dilemma. On one hand, he's in the employ of the king and answers to the heir, but on the other, he is, after all, a jester. A big part of his job is to point out flaws and pitfalls in royal behavior. If I had to guess, I'd say he planned to tell his story to the public, unless . . ."

"Unless what?"

"Unless he could be convinced that the little people are going to benefit."

"That sounds complicated and expensive. To be honest, it seems like the problem would go away if the jester was put in the dungeon and never heard from again."

"Perhaps. But jesters, at least those who live as long as this one, are wise to the whimsical moods of their employers. While the king and his heir slept, he took precautions to ensure that the story of the daemon would be published if he was to disappear."

"I see. Just for discussion, what kind of compensation would the jester see as fair for the, uh, little people."

"He made a list." Jack fished a piece of paper out of his shirt pocket. "Here, take a look. As you can see, there are substantial, but certainly reasonable amounts of stock for the acrobats as well as their teammates. And two stock funds will be set up in the names of acrobats who died during one of the events. Those funds will be used to take care of the acrobats' families and provide scholarships for young people in their countries. There's also an account to help people receive expert medical attention."

"These are quite substantial. Is it really necessary to make these acrobats millionaires? Perhaps . . ."

"The amounts are nonnegotiable. And you will note that the jester has left explicit instructions on how to distribute them."

"I see. It is indeed quite specific. Who is this Pharaoh character?"

"A young man with immense talent whose bravery almost got him killed by the heir's hired thugs."

"Men who were actually working for the evildoers I believe."

"Point taken."

"And what of the jester? I assume he'd expect something sizable for himself."

"He'll leave that to his employers to decide. Jesters trust that wise leaders value their willingness to point out when they are doing something wrong, because no one else will take the risk. And if they are serious about their new business, he has several ideas on how to make it successful."

"And if he doesn't get what he thinks is fair? Will he then tell his story to the world anyway?"

"As long as the conditions on that list are met, he will keep his mouth shut, regardless of whether he receives a single penny for his efforts."

"This has been a very interesting story. When does the jester need an answer?"

"Now."

"But, that's impossible! The king must be advised and given time to decide."

"The jester anticipated that. He says that it is time for the heir to assert himself. Kings may expect loyalty, but they respect power. This was, after all, the heir's plan. He should move quickly to consolidate his position before the king has time to neutralize his power."

"The jester makes a good point. Please thank him on behalf of the heir. And tell him he has a deal. As for how much he will be compensated, that will require some consideration."

"Very good. It appears that our story ends with everyone living happily ever after."

"Money has a way of helping that process, though I judge that it will be a rather painful chore for the heir to convince his king that this arrangement is to their mutual benefit."

"Think of it as an opportunity to master the fine art of diplomacy."

"Bite me, Warner."

"Touché. But, the fact remains that you have taken an important step on a path to use your wealth and power to lead this great country of yours into a new age. Don't screw it up." He tapped the prince on his chest. "Remember to lead with your heart as well as your head, *capisce*?"

"Point taken."

"Excellent. Now, my young friend, if my eyes do not deceive me, I believe that the last event in the competition is about to begin."

The fighters orbited at their stations, which were spread evenly around the edge of the dome. Some were flying high, some low. In a few seconds, their pilots would turn inbound; no quarter asked—none given. In point of fact, the competition had its winner, but the man was dead.

The time had come to crown a successor.

"Radio check."

"KFIR is ready to play."

"*Da!* Strike Flanker is armed and dangerous."

"EuroFighter . . . *Banzai!*"

"Raptor's on the prowl."

Randi smiled at their bravado. "Super Hornet's up and ready. Okay, boys; let's see what you've got."

"Range control copies. Good hunting."

"Three . . . two . . . one . . . Fight's on!"

"NORRIS PUTS YOU IN THE COCKPIT FOR A
   GRIPPING FLIGHT. . . . *Check Six!* is the best
flying story to come along in years."
                              —Stephen Coonts

CHECK SIX!
BOB NORRIS

"Bob Norris knows his air combat better than any other author
I've read. . . . *Check Six!* is a gripping, authentic, suspenseful
thriller. Norris not only takes you inside the dangerous world of
nuclear aircraft carrier flight ops, but masterfully takes you inside
the hearts and minds of the men ad women at the forefront of
today's military. It's a first-rate mystery and military techno-thriller
combined." —Dale Brown

"Norris takes you on a wild ride. The flight ops are authentic,
the story too real." —Richard Herman, Jr., author of
Power Curve and *Against All Enemies*

"In spite of a career in the Navy and five hundred carrier landings
in hot jets, Bob Norris was born to be a writer. . . . [He] put me
right up there in the sky and down there on the deck."
—Robert Campbell, Edgar Award-winning author of
The Junkyard Dog

Check out www.bobnorris.com

0-06-101353-6 • $5.99 ($7.99 Can.)

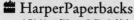